Praise For
Shirley Rousseau Murphy's
Award-Winning Cat Mysteries

"If Lilian Jackson Braun's Cat Who mysteries are just too starkly realistic for you, try the Joe Grey series. . . . It is entertaining to see cat behavior from the inside out."

Wilmington (NC) *Sunday Star-News*

"A delicious romp . . . of murder, revenge, and jealousy, interlaced with fantasy. This is excellent reading, whether you believe or not. Not to be missed!"

Armchair Detective

"Magical whimsy and deft writing."

Cats magazine

and *CAT IN THE DARK*

Shirley Rousseau Murphy

CAT to the DOGS

A JOE GREY MYSTERY

AVON BOOKS
An Imprint of HarperCollinsPublishers

AVON BOOKS
An Imprint of HarperCollins*Publishers*
10 East 53rd Street
New York, New York 10022-5299

Copyright © 2000 by Shirley Rousseau Murphy
Excerpt from *Cat Spitting Mad* copyright © 2001 by Shirley Rousseau Murphy
ISBN: 0-06-105988-9
www.avonbooks.com

First Avon Books paperback printing: October 2000
First HarperCollins hardcover printing: January 2000

Avon Trademark Reg. U.S. Pat. Off. and in Other Countries, Marca Registrada, Hecho en U.S.A.
HarperCollins ® is a trademark of HarperCollins Publishers Inc.

Printed in the U.S.A.

❖/10 9 8 7 6 5 4 3 2 1

*For every cat strange and different
and unusually wise about the world.
And for every human who wonders
at their cat's sly and secret wisdom.*

*For Lucy, ELT, and Toby,
and always, of course,
for my husband, Patrick J. Murphy*

A pretty little dear she was, but her wanted to know too much. There was fields down along as wasn't liked. No one cared much about working there. Y'see, 'twas all elder there, and there was a queer wind used to blow there most times, and sounded like someone talking it would.

From "Tibb's Cat and the Apple-Tree Man,"
Katherine M. Briggs and Ruth L. Tongue,
Folktales of England

1

FOG LAY so thick in Hellhag Canyon that Joe Grey couldn't see his paws, could barely see the dead wood rat he carried dangling from his sharp teeth. Moving steeply down the wall of the ravine, the tomcat was aware of a boulder or willow scrub only when his whiskers touched something foreign, sending an electrifying jolt through his sleek gray body. The predawn fog was so dense that a human would have barged straight into those obstacles—one more example, Joe Grey thought smugly, of feline senses far keener than human, of the superiority of cat over man.

The fog-shrouded canyon was silent, too, save for the muted hushing of the sea farther down and the occasional whisper from high above of wet tires along the twisting two-lane, where some early-morning driver crept blindly. Joe had no idea why humans drove in this stuff; swift cars and fog were bad news. As he searched for a soft bit of ground on which to enjoy his breakfast, another car approached, moving way too fast toward the wicked double curve, sending a jolt of alarm stabbing through Joe.

The scream of tires filled the canyon.

The skidding car hit the cliff so hard, Joe felt the earth shake. He dropped the wood rat and leaped clear as the car rolled thundering over the edge, its lights exploding against the fog, its bulk falling straight at him, as big as a hunk of the cliff, a mass of hurtling metal that sent him streaking up the canyon wall. It hurtled past, dropping into the ravine exactly where he'd been crouching.

The car lay upside down beneath a dozen young oak trees broken off and fallen across its spinning wheels. The roof and those tons of metal had likely flattened his wood rat into a bloody pancake—so much for his nice warm breakfast.

Where the careening car had disturbed the fog, and the rising wind swirled the mist, he could make out the gigantic form easing deeper into the detritus of the canyon, the car's metal parts groaning like a dying beast, its death-stink not of escaping body fluids, but the reek of leaking gasoline.

This baby's going to explode, he thought as he prepared to run. *Going to blow sky-high, roast me among these boulders like a rabbit in a stone oven.*

But when, after a long wait, no explosion occurred, when the vehicle continued only to creak and moan, he crept warily down the cliff again to have a look.

Hunched beneath the wreck's vast, dark body—its ticking, grease-stinking, hot-breathed body—he looked up at the huge black wheels spinning above him and listened to the bits of glass raining down from the broken windows that were half-hidden among the dry ferns, listened to the big metal carcass settle into its last sleep. He could hear, from within, no human utterance. No groan, no scream of pain or of terror, only the voice of the sea pounding against the cliffs.

Was no one alive in there? He studied the overturned car, listening for a desperate and anguished cry—and wondering what he was going to do about it. Wondering how a poor simple tomcat was going to render any kind of useful assistance.

He had been hunting Hellhag Canyon since midnight, first at the shore, dodging the rolling breakers, and then, when the fog thickened, moving on up the ravine. He had tracked the wood rat blindly, following only the sound of its scrabbling, had struck and killed it before the creature was ever aware of him. But all night he'd been edgy, too, still nervous from the quakes of the last week; the first instant the skidding car hit the hill and shook the earth he'd shivered as if another jolt were rocking the cliffs, rattling the central California coast.

The original temblor, two days earlier, at 5.2 on the Richter scale, had sent the more timid human residents of Molena Point fleeing from their cottages, to creep back hours later hauling out mattresses and camp stoves and setting up housekeeping in their gardens. All week, as the village of Molena Point experienced aftershocks, people were tense and excited, waiting for the big one, for the earth to crack open, for their homes to topple and giant seas to flood the land.

Well, it was only an earthquake, a natural, God-given part of life—a cat might be wary, but a cat didn't lose perspective. Humans, on the other hand, were hopelessly amusing. Facing a natural phenomenon, the poor, gullible bipeds invariably overreacted.

The earthquake had brought two reporters down from San Francisco, searching for anything sensational, seeking out the displaced and injured, running their cameras in a feeding frenzy, their hunger for alarming news as voracious as the hunger of seagulls attacking a handful of fish innards tossed from the Molena Point pier.

But the quake had disturbed the burrowing wild creatures, the mice and wood rats and voles, driving them from their holes, disorienting the little beasts so they were incredibly easy prey. All week, Joe Grey and Dulcie had gorged themselves.

Though Dulcie refused to hunt down Hellhag Canyon. She had lectured him on the dangers of high, rogue waves after an earthquake, and, when he laughed at her fears, she had turned away disgusted, growling and lashing her tabby-striped tail at what she called tomcat stupidity.

Still listening for a cry for help from within the overturned car, Joe could hear only the drip, drip of gasoline, or maybe radiator water; tensely, he circled the vehicle, ears low, body rigid, ready to spring away if the hulking wreck toppled or exploded.

The broken, fallen saplings that lay tangled across the wreck's greasy, exposed underside half covered the drive shaft and one bent wheel. He found the source of the dripping sound. It came from the left front wheel, where a viscous liquid, a substance as thick as maple syrup, dropped steadily into a pool among the crushed ferns. When he sniffed the little puddle, the stuff *smelled* a bit like syrup: the stink of pancake syrup laced with ether.

Backing away, he approached the upside-down windshield that rose from the bracken, the glass patterned like a spiderweb encased in crystal. And now, over the smell of gas, came the sharp scent of human blood.

Behind the glass he could see the driver, white and still, his contorted body wrapped around the steering wheel and impaled by a twisted strip of metal, his head jammed down into the concavity of the roof. There was no way this guy could be alive, not with his chest pierced through and the amount of blood pooling out. The passenger seat had come loose and lay across him. He hugged it firmly in a rictus of pain and death.

The victim's Levi's-clad backside was jammed against the shattered side window, an edge of broken glass pressed against the billfold that bulged in his hip pocket. The wallet had probably prevented a sharp cut across the buttocks, not that this fellow would have felt it.

There was no passenger. No one else in the car. The young man had died alone. He was maybe thirty, Joe thought. The victim's pale blue eyes stared at some entity that no one among the living would ever see.

His brown hair was neatly trimmed—a better haircut than Joe's housemate, Clyde, would ever spring for. The dead man's bloodstained shirt and torn, camel hair sport coat looked expensive. The scattered items that had fallen onto the inverted headliner included a suede leather cap, a California road map, a Styrofoam coffee cup spilling coffee across the fabric of the headliner, and bits of shattered safety glass decorating the bloody pools and clinging to the dead man's clothes like diamond-bright sparkles for some gory costume party.

The car was a '67 Corvette, a collector's car—you saw many antiques around Molena Point. It was pale blue and, until its mishap that morning, looked to have been in mint condition. The sticker on its license plate indicated that it had been purchased from Landrum Antique Cars in L.A. The wrecked windshield was marked by tape residue where a small piece of paper must have been affixed. He could see no tag ripped away or lying on the floor.

Carefully, Joe reached a paw though a hole in the crazed glass. Pushing out some of the rounded jewel-like bits, he squeezed his head through, then his muscled gray shoulders, and eased down onto the dead man's bent knee, his weight shifting the body and startling him; but then the victim settled again and was still.

Pressing his nose uneasily to the young man's nose, Joe sought some hint of breathing. But even as he crouched he could feel, through his paws, a faint drop in temperature as the body began to cool.

Grimacing at the smells that accompanied human death—very different from the smell of a dead rat—he backed away and crept out again, panting for gulps of fresh air. This stranger's death unleashed all manner of past associations for Joe Grey: visions of the police working a murder scene as he crouched watching from the roof above; of a dead man bathed in the green light from a computer terminal; of a man struck suddenly with a bright steel wrench, a memory so vivid that Joe heard again the crack of the victim's skull.

But those deaths had been murders. What he was viewing here was an accident, the result of careless driving on a fog-blind mountain road.

Except that something tickled at him, a puzzled unease, some detail of the crash—something he had heard before the car skidded and came thundering down into the ravine.

Frowning, the white strip down his gray face pinched into puzzled worry lines, the big tomcat padded along a fallen sapling between the upturned wheels.

What had he heard?

Dropping down on the far side of the wrecked car, his mind played back the crash in a quick rerun: the squeal of brakes, then the skid just about where Deadman's Curve began. Hellhag Hill was famous for that double twist. If a driver lost control on the first bend, he was hard put, when he hit the second one, to regain command. The too-sharp turn was on him, the canyon dropping straight down away from his front wheels. The locals took that road slowly. The warning signs were numerous and insistent—but in the fog a driver wouldn't see them. Even a local might not realize just where he was on the hairpin road.

Had he heard another sound before the squeal of brakes? Had he heard a horn farther away, muffled in the fog? The faint, quick stutter of a warning horn?

He squinched closed his eyes, trying to remember.

Yes. First a faint triple beep, then the skid and the crash and the car careening down at him—but had that earlier honking come from a second car, or had this driver honked at something looming out of the fog? Had there been one car or two, moving blindly along that narrow road?

He thought he remembered the hush of two sets of tires; but had they been coming from opposite directions? Then the faint stutter of the horn, then the scream of brakes and the heart-jolting thunder as the car came careening over.

The other car must have had gone on. Why hadn't it stopped? Hadn't the other driver heard the wreck?

Padding back across a sapling above the car's greasy innards, Joe studied the right front wheel with its thick discharge. The drip was abating now, only an occasional drop still falling, its viscous pool seeping down into the dead leaves. The same syrupy liquid coated the bent wheel. He crouched to look more closely.

The drip came from a short piece of black hose attached to the wheel and to a metal pipe that ran to the engine. The brake line. Padding back and forth along the sapling, studying each wheel with its corresponding hose, he found it interesting that only this one brake line was broken and leaking.

Living with Clyde Damen, his human housemate and a professional auto mechanic, Joe Grey had grown from kittenhood exposed to the insides of every possible motor-driven vehicle, subjected to endless photographs in automotive magazines and to countless boring articles on the intricacies of car engines; as he drowsed in Clyde's lap, he was treated to interminable, mind-numbing hours of Clyde's detailed dissertations on the subtleties of matters mechanical.

He had a clear picture of this car's master cylinder, empty now where the fluid had drained away.

No brakes when the guy hit that curve. Zilch. *Nada*.

He found it most interesting that the broken plastic tube was not ragged as if it had worn through naturally, but was separated by a knife-sharp incision, a cut slicing straight through the hose.

He was debating whether to climb the canyon wall and check the skid marks on the road, to try to get a picture of just what had happened up there, when a noise from above made him crouch.

Someone was descending the cliff, moving downward unseen but noisy, crashing through the fog-blurred tangles in a frenzy, rattling bushes and dislodging stones.

Maybe somebody had heard the crash; maybe the other driver was coming to render assistance after all.

Except, this didn't sound like a man descending. Even a man in a great hurry wouldn't break so many bushes; a man hurrying down that steep bank would be more collected so that he, himself, wouldn't fall. This sounded more like a wild creature running and sliding full out, though the sound was so distorted in the fog that he couldn't really be sure what he was hearing. One minute the approach was loud enough to be a bear, the next instant the noise faded to nothing.

A bear. Right, Joe thought, disgusted. There hadn't been bears on the California coast for a century. A bobcat? No bobcat would follow and approach a wrecked car; no wild beast would do that. Warily, he leaped onto a boulder, ready to fight or run like hell, whichever the situation suggested.

Straining to see above him through the disturbed patches of water-sodden air, he wondered if it could be a horse.

But a horse, escaped from one of the small local stables, wouldn't choose, on its own, to descend the rough and fog-bound canyon. A horse, breaking through his paddock fence, would prefer the slopes of Hellhag Hill above, where the grass was rich and nourishing.

He was considering that perhaps a local horseman had heard the wreck and saddled up to come and render help, when the beast charged out of the mist—not one creature, but two.

Two huge dogs plunged straight at him. Panting and

baying, they leaped up the boulder, scrabbling to reach him. Joe, hissing and snarling, prepared to bloody them both. Their eyes were wild, their white teeth flashing.

The boulder wasn't large. It protruded out of the cliff in such a way that if the dogs had thought about it, they'd have gone uphill again and jumped straight down on him. But they didn't think; they were all bark and gnashing teeth, fighting to reach him, their big mouths snapping so close that he could taste their doggy breath. He had raised his steel-tipped paw, ready to rake to ribbons those two invading noses, when he did a double take, studying their thin canine faces.

Joe dropped his armored paw and sat down, watching them, amused.

Puppies.

They were only puppies. Huge puppies, each as big as a full-grown retriever. Big-boned, big-footed pups. And thin. Two bags of canine bones held together by dry, buff-colored pelts, their black-and-white faces so fleshless they appeared skeletal, their whipping tails so skinny they looked like two snakes that had swallowed marbles.

Two oversized puppies, starving and harmless.

They had stopped barking. They grinned up at him, wagging and prancing spraddle-legged around the boulder, their skinny tails whipping enthusiastically.

They had no notion of eating him. Probably they were too young and stupid to imagine that a dog could kill and eat a cat; the idea would not have occurred to them. They simply wanted to be friendly, to be close to another animal. Now that they'd stopped barking, even their doggy smiles were incredibly downtrodden and sad.

They couldn't be more than four or five months old, but were so emaciated that even the weight of their floppy ears and floppy feet seemed to drag them down.

He wondered if they belonged to the dead driver, if somehow they had managed, as the car went over the cliff, to leap free?

But the crash happened in a split second; they would have had only an instant to escape. These clumsy mutts didn't look like they could get out of their own way in twenty seconds.

Maybe they'd been following the car, running along behind. Had the driver been running his dogs the way some country folk did, exercising them down the nearly empty highway? Joe sneezed with disgust. Any man who ran his dogs behind a car—to say nothing of starving them bone-thin—deserved a violent death.

He gave them a gentle growl to make them move back and dropped down from the boulder. They backed away two steps, fawning at him, bowing on their front legs and grinning in doggy obeisance. They seemed, actually, like rather nice young pups. Though only youngsters, they were already as big as Rube, Joe's aged Labrador retriever housemate. And though they were puppy-silly and disgustingly eager, with their stupid baby grins, Joe thought perhaps the expressions in their bright, dark eyes hinted at some possible future intelligence.

He thought they might be half Great Dane, and maybe half boxer. The smaller of the two had the happy-go-lucky grin of a young boxer. Actually, if they were fed properly and groomed, if their faces filled out a bit, and their ribs ceased to protrude, they might become quite handsome—as far as a dog could be handsome.

Too late Joe Grey saw where his thoughts had led

him. Saw that he had reacted with no more common sense than a mush-hearted human do-gooder, sucker for a pair of starving mutts—realized that he had actually been wondering where to find these beasts a meal.

Well, he'd been around Clyde too long; Clyde Damen was such a sucker for stray animals.

Not yours truly, Joe Grey thought. *I'm not playing animal rescue for these two bags of bones.*

The fact that he himself had been a rescued stray had no bearing on the present situation. This was entirely different. Turning his back on the gamboling pups, he studied the wrecked Corvette, wondering if anyone at all had heard the crash and called the cops. There were no houses near Hellhag Canyon, only the empty hills and, atop Hellhag Hill, to the north, the Moonwatch Trailer Park.

The instant he turned to look at the pups again, they were all over him, slobbering and whining, soaking him with dog spit.

"Stop it! Get off! Get back. Get off me!"

They ducked away, staring at him white-eyed with alarm.

Obviously they had never been spoken to in the English language by one of feline persuasion. Whining and backing, they watched him with such deep suspicion that he had to laugh.

His laugh frightened them further. The poor beasts looked so confused that he ended up reaching out a gentle paw, patting the smaller pup on his huge white foot, then lifting his own sleek gray face to sniff noses.

He knew he was acting stupid, that he was being suckered. Joe Grey, PI, taken in by a pair of flea-bitten, mange-ridden mongrels.

"Get on out of here! Go on back to the highway!"

They cowered away, crestfallen, and Joe turned his attention to the crash victim, peering in at the dead driver, thinking about the severed brake line.

The cops were needed here, the sooner the better.

He studied the twisted dashboard and the dark hole of the sprung-open glove compartment, but could not see a car phone. Where was the driver of the other car? How could he not have heard the crash? Was he clear down the coast by this time?

Behind Joe, the pups began a cacophony of heartrending whines. Joe ignored them. Whoever had cut the brake line must have known approximately how long it would take the brakes to fail. The car could not have skidded at a more dangerous spot. He pictured the driver hitting his brakes on the first curve, forcing out the last of the fluid, emptying the line, rendering the brake pedal useless when he hit the second twist.

He didn't know the dead driver, though he knew by sight nearly everyone in Molena Point. Peering in at the man's unsettling blue eyes, at his waxen face streaked with blood, he wondered where this guy had last stopped, maybe to get gas? Maybe the brake line had been cut then?

Letting his imagination go to work on the scene, he wondered if that other driver had been following the Corvette, waiting to startle the driver with sudden honking and make him hit his brakes at just the right moment, waiting to be sure the driver went out of control and careened over the cliff, before *he* went on his way.

That faint honking and the squeal of brakes formed, for Joe Grey, a frightening scenario.

Leaving the wreck, he bounded up the canyon wall, trying to ignore the whining pups, who clambered up beside him, stepping on his paws. If he'd had a tail—more than just a two-inch stub—the mutts would have stepped on it, too. He hadn't been troubled with that appendage since he was a gangling kit. The drunk who stepped on and broke his tail *had*, in that moment of careless cruelty, really done him a good turn. Life without a tail to get caught in doors and pulled by small children suited Joe Grey just fine.

Before the three animals reached the narrow road that wound precariously a hundred feet above the sea, Joe Grey knew, and the pups knew, that they were not alone. An unseen man stood silently somewhere on the opposite canyon wall—they could smell his heavily perfumed shaving lotion, and a whiff of shoe polish. Sniffing the scents that seeped through the mist, the pups cowered silently against Joe Grey; and Joe himself crouched low against the bushes, looking.

He waited for some time, but even though the fog was thinning above him along the road it was pea soup in the canyon. He could see nothing. The tiny sounds he heard from below, the small crackle of a twig or a dry leaf, could be a person moving around the wrecked car or it could be only a ground squirrel or another wood rat, venturing out to investigate the metal monster that had fallen into their canyon.

When nothing larger stirred, when he could detect in the mist no one climbing back up the cliff, he leaped impatiently up to the narrow two-lane to search the wet black macadam for tire marks.

2

IT'S GOING to be hard to dump these mutts, Joe Grey thought. They clung to him like road tar. When he tried to drive them back into the ravine they nearly smothered him with slurping kisses. Even his lancing claws no longer deterred them. They licked their noses where he'd slapped them and bounced around him like a pair of wind-up toys, fawning and trampling him, grinning with the delighted assumption that he was their dearest friend; they were so stupid and innocent that even if he could have ditched them and made his escape, something within Joe rebelled. He knew he couldn't abandon them; puppies and young dogs have no more notion of how to find food for themselves than does a human baby.

Well, he'd take them home to Clyde. Let Clyde deal with the problem. Clyde would love the stupid mutts. And maybe they'd cheer up old Rube. Rube had been mourning the death of Barney, their golden retriever who had succumbed to cancer, for far too long.

So, okay, he'd take them home. But did they have to make such a scene? By the time he reached the road above Hellhag Canyon his fur was sopping from their affection.

Atop the cliff, the sea breeze came stronger, lifting and thinning the mist. The narrow two-lane, clearing of fog, glistened wet and black. In the watery sunshine, the pups looked even more skeletal, every rib casting a curved shadow, their cheeks so deeply sunken that he could see each indentation of their canine skulls. Turning his back on them, he studied the slick black road.

Where the car had gone over the edge, the earthen shoulder was scarred raw, rocks tumbled, bushes broken and uprooted. Trotting along the verge watching for the man they had scented below, for a stranger to suddenly appear climbing out of the canyon, Joe could find no skid marks on the dark macadam. It looked, just as Joe had guessed, as if the driver, when his car hit the second curve, had no brakes at all.

Examining the wet paving, he found several splatters of brake fluid pooled like oil. He had to drive the pups away, cuffing and slapping them to keep them from licking the spills. He didn't know if brake fluid was poisonous like radiator coolant, but he didn't care to find out. It was not until he trotted around the second bend that he smelled burnt rubber.

Before him, S-shaped trails snaked across the asphalt, and a larger puddle of brake fluid gleamed. Joe imagined the driver stamping repeatedly on the pedal, trying to slow, the fluid spurting out until it was gone.

Pumping the pedal, jerking the wheel, he'd have hit that second curve like a missile, the car swerving back and forth, gaining speed on the downhill, hitting the shoulder to plow up half a ton of dirt and flip a double gainer straight into Hellhag Canyon.

He could find no sign of the second car, no trace of a second set of skid marks.

He wondered if the driver had braked suddenly to avoid not an oncoming car but the pups themselves looming in the fog.

Except, the horn had honked *before* the skid, not at the same moment, as one would expect if the driver were startled by the sudden appearance of animals in his headlights.

Crossing the road, Joe headed up Hellhag Hill through the tall, wet grass. He was halfway to the crest when he realized the pups had left him.

Rearing above the wild oats and barley, he saw them far below, creeping along the edge of the highway, staring up the hill white-eyed and quivering.

Joe didn't know what was wrong with them; something on the hill terrified them. He stood tall on his hind paws, observing them, smiling a sly cat grin.

Now would be the perfect time to ditch them. Take off across Hellhag Hill and leave them cowering down there.

A practical voice told him, *Lose them, Joe. Lose the silly mutts now, while they're distracted. You'd be stupid to take them home, they're sure to have mange, fleas, ringworm. They'll give it to the household cats and to poor Rube, and he's too old to fight a case of mange. Dump them. Dump them here. Now. Do it now.*

But a kinder voice whispered, *Come on, Joe. Have a heart. Clyde can take them to the pound, where they'll be fed and safe, not running along the highway. Even a dog deserves a little compassion.*

Ditch them. They'll learn to fend for themselves, live out of garbage cans. There's that trailer park up Hellhag Hill; some dumb human will feed them.

And above this internal argument, he kept wondering about the dead man, and about the unseen stranger in the canyon, wondering where he had come from, and why he didn't hike on into the village and report the wreck. Joe hadn't seen the guy come up out of the canyon.

He wondered how long before someone else would come along the road, notice the torn-up shoulder, take a look down into the canyon, and call 911. Get the cops and a wrecker down there. Meanwhile, below him on the road, the pups crept along shivering with fear. Poor dumb beasts.

Well, he'd take them home. Clyde would love them. They'd give him something to do: he'd feed them, get them in shape, have them vetted, walk them and bathe them, worm them, fawn over them. Find homes for them. He'd be so proud when they were sleek and had collars and homes of their own.

Right. And when did Clyde ever give away an animal? He won't find homes for them. He'll keep the beasts. You and Rube and the household cats will be sharing your nice peaceful pad with a pair of wild-mannered elephants. Think of poor Rube, he . . .

Sirens screamed from the village, and a rescue unit appeared around the farthest curve, moving fast and followed by a black-and-white. The pups stared around wildly and fled into the drainage ditch, but when a second police unit came scorching toward them, the pups chose the lesser of two evils and bolted up the hill to cower whimpering against Joe.

Joe couldn't see much with the pups milling around. He glimpsed four officers disappearing down the hill: he thought it was Wendell, Brennan, Davis, and Hendricks, following two paramedics with their stretchers and black bags. He could hear the officers' muffled voices mixed with the crackle of the police radio. The fog had broken into wispy scarves; now, beyond the cliff, the vast sweep of the Pacific Ocean gleamed up at him in the sun's first rays, the white surf crashing against the rocks. Off to the north, the red rooftops of the village caught the sun's light, too, and he could hear the distant, thin chime of the courthouse clock striking seven. The morning smelled of sea and iodine, and of coffee and frying sausages mixed, nearer at hand, with the pungent stink of wet dog. When, somewhere on the village streets, a little boy shouted, the pups cocked their floppy ears, whining and panting. Their eager innocence touched something tender in Joe Grey. "You poor, dumb puppies. So damn lonely."

They slobbered and drooled on him, so starved for affection that they made a cat barf. Gently he stroked their wet black noses with his velveted paw.

If Clyde takes them to the pound, they'll be locked in a cage.

They'll be fine in a cage; dogs have nothing like a cat's burning need for freedom, they'll thrive in a nice warm kennel. Dogs love structure. Look at police trackers, always on leash or on command.

But his other voice said, *Pound dogs are gassed, Joe. Euthanized. Sent west.*

Ignoring both voices, he moved swiftly toward home, the pups pressing so close that their legs were like a moving forest through which he had to navigate. He wondered, would the cops examine the wreck carefully enough to find the leaky brake line? Lieutenants Brennan and Wendell might very well miss that damning bit of evidence; Wendell had just recently made lieutenant, but he was better with street crime than with the subtleties of a possible murder scene.

But the new female officer, Davis, was thorough. Joe had watched these uniforms work a crime scene so often that he felt like part of the force.

The trouble was, they didn't know this was a crime scene. It looked like an accident that could too easily have happened in this early, foggy dawn.

Now, with the road quiet again, the pups left him, racing down the hill and glancing worriedly behind them.

"Get back up here, get off the road. The ambulance will be coming back. What's with you two? What are you afraid of?"

They stared up at him, whining.

"Come on, dummies. Get up here. There's nothing here to scare you, nothing but maybe a stray cat in the grass." Nothing but a few rats and ground squirrels, and the half dozen stray cats that had taken up residence some days before, following the quakes, appearing suddenly, a clowder of thin, wild beasts so fearful they would run from a bird shadow swooping overhead. No pup could be afraid of them. Dulcie said humans who abandoned cats ought to be stripped naked and dropped without food—without money and credit cards—in the icy wilds of Tierra del Fuego, and see how they liked being abandoned.

Joe thought those cats had probably come from the trailer park, a transient human community of the less-affluent snowbirds who trekked out to California in the winter to escape the blizzards of the Midwest. Usually those people, if they brought pets along, took care of their animals, but once in a while you got some lowlifes.

But Dulcie said these cats were too terrified of humans to have ever lived with people. She thought they were feral cats, the products of several generations of strays, gone as wild as foxes.

He wondered what Dulcie would say about his dragging home the pups.

He could just see her green eyes blazing with amazement. *Puppies, Joe? These aren't puppies, they're monsters.*

Dulcie was not afraid of dogs—she could intimidate any dog in Molena Point and often did—but after their recent encounter with the black voodoo cat, she'd had enough of involvement with any fellow creature. And just then, having appropriated Clyde's backyard for her own purposes, she'd take a dim view of two giant puppies plunging around barking and whining and getting in her way.

For two weeks she had spent every daylight hour—it seemed to Joe—and most of her evenings, crouched atop Clyde's back fence within a mass of concealing maple leaves, peering into the windows of the Greenlaw mansion, which stood on the big double lot behind Clyde's cottage. Clyde called Dulcie's preoccupation, *eavesdropping*; he told her she'd grown unspeakably nosy even for a cat. But Dulcie, staring in through Lucinda Greenlaw's lace curtains, was convinced that something in the old Victorian house wasn't right.

"Of course something isn't right," Clyde had snapped at her. "Lucinda's husband just died. Lucinda's suddenly a widow. Of course life isn't right—don't you think she's grieving! Cats can be so unfeeling!"

"Why would she grieve?" Dulcie had hissed, her ears tight to her head, her green eyes fiery. "Shamas Greenlaw was nothing but a womanizer. Going off for weeks, leaving Lucinda with practically no money while he took his expensive trips, and every time with a different bimbo. Why would she grieve! She's lucky to be rid of him."

Dulcie didn't hold with the shades-of-gray school of moral behavior. Shamas Greenlaw had been sampling the herd, and Dulcie called it like it was.

Shamas had been dead for two weeks, drowned in a boating accident off Seattle—leaving his current squeeze on the boat with Shamas's nephew, Newlon Greenlaw; Shamas's cousin, Samuel Fulman; and Winnie and George Chambers, an older Molena Point couple. Probably, Dulcie said, leaving the girlfriend deeply grieving as she contemplated an end to the money Shamas had lavished upon her.

"Anyway," she'd told Clyde, "Lucinda is doing more than grieving. Something else is the matter."

"And how did you arrive at this very perceptive conclusion?"

"You don't need to be sarcastic," the little cat had hissed. "And *I* don't need to listen! If you're not interested in my opinion, Clyde Damen, then stuff it. I don't need to come in here and be insulted. I have my own home, which is far nicer and more pleasant than this bachelor horror." And she had stormed out through Joe's cat door and up the street, her striped tail lashing.

Joe had looked after her, grinning. But Clyde had sat at the kitchen table cradling his cold coffee, scowling and hurt; looking, that early morning, like a particularly unfortunate example of homelessness, a soul in need of extensive assistance, his short, dark hair sticking up every which way, his ancient jogging shorts threadbare and wrinkled, his sweatshirt sporting three holes where it had gotten caught in the washer. His expression, as he stared after Dulcie, was one of deep puzzlement.

Clyde could mouth off at Joe, and get just what he gave, and that was okay. But he didn't know how to respond when sweet little Dulcie snapped back at him.

It had taken Dulcie a long time, after she and Joe found they could speak, before she would talk to Clyde. Then, there had been a far longer interval of mutual good manners between cat and human, before Dulcie had the chutzpah to return Clyde's smart-mouthed remarks in kind.

Now, leaving the jungle-tall grass of Hellhag Hill, Joe called the pups to him for the last time as he crossed a narrow residential street, heading back among humans. He would not raise his voice again to give them a command until he was sheltered within his own walls. The pups bolted up to him, wagging and panting, happy to leave the wild slope.

"Idiots," he muttered. But maybe he understood their fear; sometimes when he crossed Hellhag Hill, the fur along his own back stood up as rigid as a punk haircut.

Joe didn't know what caused his unease, but once when he was hunting high atop Hellhag Hill, he'd imagined he heard voices beneath the earth, and that same night he'd dreamed that Hellhag Hill vanished from under his paws, the earth falling away suddenly into a black and bottomless cavern.

He had awakened mewling with fear, as frightened as a helpless kitten.

Ahead of him, one of the puppies stopped, sat down

on the sidewalk, and began to scratch. The other pup copied him, nibbling at an itchy tail—causing Joe to itch all over, to imagine himself already flea-ridden, covered with hungry little freeloaders glad to move to fatter environs, parent and grandparent and baby fleas burrowing deep into his clean silver fur.

Hurrying through the village beside the pups, he saw the coroner's car heading out toward Highway One, and he wondered what the slim, bespectacled Dr. Bern would find. Around him, the village seemed very welcoming suddenly, very safe, the familiar little cottages tucked in among their old, twisted oaks and tall pines. Over the smell of sun-warmed geraniums came the lingering scents of bacon and pancakes and syrup.

Trotting past Molena Point's bright, tangled gardens and crowded shops, Joe was suddenly very thankful for this village. He would never admit that to Clyde, would never hint to Clyde how much he cherished Molena Point. Would never confess how glad he was to be away from the mean streets of San Francisco—an ignorant kitten trying to cadge a few bites of garbage, hiding from the bigger cats, always afraid, and cold, and mad at the world.

Suddenly, right now, Joe needed to be home. In his own safe, warm home.

Galloping eagerly in the direction of his cozy pad, he dodged the pups, who ran along grinning and panting as if their own salvation were surely near. Joe, racing up the sidewalk through blowing leaves and flashes of sunlight, wondered again: had those uniforms, up at Hellhag Canyon, seen the cut brake line?

Police Captain Max Harper needed to know about it, to know that that wreck had been no accident.

Turning down the little side street toward his and Clyde's white Cape Cod cottage, running beneath its sheltering oaks toward the ragged lawn that Clyde seldom mowed, and the gray shake roof that constantly needed fixing—repairs supplied by Clyde's girlfriend, Charlie Getz—Joe breathed in the comforting, warm smells of home.

But crossing the yard, eyeing Clyde's antique Chevy roadster still parked in the drive, knowing Clyde had not yet left for work, he began to wonder what Clyde *was* going to say about bringing the two puppies home.

And he wondered if, when he tried to get a message to Max Harper about the cut brake line, Clyde would respond in his usual supercritical manner—if Clyde would hide the telephone and give him another of his high-handed lectures about how cats should not get involved in police business. How he, Joe Grey, ought to mind his own simple affairs. How Max Harper needed to pursue his official police business unencumbered by inappropriate feline meddling.

3

TROTTING UP the three steps to his cat door, Joe could smell coffee and fried eggs mixed with the meaty scent of dog food. He slid inside fast, under the plastic flap. Behind him, the pups pushed their black noses through—two wet, disembodied snouts sniffing and shoving, forcing his cat door so hard he thought they'd rip out the metal frame.

The familiar room embraced him: the shabby, soft rugs; his own tattered, fur-covered armchair by the window; Clyde's new leather chair and ottoman, which were the latest additions to the room; the potted plants that Charlie had brought over to soften the stark bachelor quarters. And, best of all, Charlie's drawings of Joe and Dulcie, and of Rube and the household cats, handsomely framed and grouped on all four walls. These finer touches had turned the tatty room into a retreat with charm enough to please any human or feline. If Clyde ever married, Joe hoped tall, slim Charlie Getz, with her kinky red hair and freckles, would be the one. The fact that she could fix the roof and repair the plumbing, as well as decorate a house and cook a mean steak, was a definite plus.

Charlie had figured out on her own that Joe Grey and Dulcie were more than your average cats. But she had kept her mouth shut, and this was more than a plus. In Joe's book, Charlie Getz was already family.

Though so far there was no talk of a wedding. Charlie seemed happy in her own small studio apartment above the village shops, from which she ran her housecleaning-and-repair business.

"Joe? That you? What's going on out there? What's all the banging? You stuck in your cat door? I told you you're getting fat."

At the sound of a human voice, the pups went wild, pawing and whining.

"Shut up!" Joe hissed. "You want to get your heads stuck in that little square hole? Idiots!" He was rooting at his back to dislodge a flea—thanks to the strays—when Clyde strode out of the kitchen and stood looking at the two black noses pushing in through the cat door.

Joe concentrated on licking his shoulder.

"Now what've you brought home?"

"What do you mean, *now*? What have I ever brought home? I didn't bring *those* home." He regarded the noses as if he had never seen them before.

"You have brought home dead rats," Clyde began. "Dead birds. That live bird that plastered its feathers all over the kitchen. Live snakes. Not to mention a parade of randy and ill-mannered lady cats. Before you met Dulcie, of course."

"Dulcie is a lady."

"Don't twist my words."

"Are you implying that Dulcie is not a lady? Or that she is not welcome?"

"I am not talking about Dulcie. You have brought home enough trouble through that cat door to send me to the funny farm for life. There's never a week, Joe, that you don't get into some kind of new predicament and drag your problems home. Do you see these gray hairs?" he asked, pointing to his ragged, dark haircut.

"Debauchery," Joe told him. "That's what makes gray hair. Too many women and too much booze. That's where the gray hairs come from."

"I guess you should know about debauchery, every hair on your lecherous body is gray. Before Dulcie, you . . ."

"Can't you leave Dulcie out of this? What do you have against Dulcie?"

"I don't have anything against Dulcie. If you had half her decent manners—to say nothing of her morals and charm and half her finesse—life would . . ."

"Oh, can it, Clyde. Dulcie's a female. You want *me* to act all prissy, tippy-toe in here every morning smelling of kitty shampoo and primrose-scented flea powder?"

Clyde sighed and retrieved his coffee cup from atop the CD player. He was dressed for work in a pair of clean jeans, his new Rockports, and a red polo shirt beneath a white lab coat that, this early in the morning, was still unsullied by the grease from a variety of BMWs and Jaguars. His dark hair was damp from the shower, his cheeks still ruddy from shaving.

Clyde regarded the two large canine noses, then regarded Joe. "You'd better tell me what this is about.

But please, make it brief. Cut to the chase, Joe. It's too early for a long-winded dissertation."

Joe chomped the offending flea. The one-spot flea killer was okay, but it took the little beasts a while to die.

"Joe, where did you find the dogs? Why did you bring home two dogs? From the size of their noses, I assume they are rather large. From the sound of them and their behavior, I imagine that they are young. What are they, Great Danes? Are there more outside? What did you do, drag home a whole litter?

"*I did not bring them home!* There are only two. I think they're half Great Dane."

"They followed you by accident. You really didn't know they were there." Sighing, Clyde stepped to the front door.

The instant he turned the knob releasing the latch, the pair burst through, in their enthusiasm slamming the door against Clyde and slamming Clyde against the wall.

Dancing around the living room like two drunk buffalo in a phone booth, the pups leaped at Clyde, delighted to meet him, ripped his lab coat across his chest, and slurped dog spit across his face.

Joe, having fled to the top of the CD player, watched their happy display with interest.

"They're hungry, Joe. Look at them, they're all bones. They need food. Can't you see they're starving?" Clyde knelt to hug the monster puppies, his voice softening to a patter of pet words that sickened the tomcat.

"They can't be five months old." He looked up at Joe. "They're going to be huge. Where did they come from? Where did you find them? Well, you could at least have found some food for them—"

"Caught them a rabbit, I suppose?"

"Well, yes, you could have done that."

"And give them tularemia? Pierce their livers with rabbit bones?"

Clyde rose and headed for the kitchen, trampled by the fawning pups. "You don't have tularemia. Your liver seems okay."

"I'm a cat. Cats don't get tularemia. My liver can handle anything. They're here only because they followed me, because I couldn't ditch them. There was a wreck—"

"They're probably thirsty, too. Look at them. You could have led them to some water."

"I'm trying to tell you, there was a wreck. The cops are there now. If you would listen . . ."

Clyde lifted the loose skin on one pup's neck and let it go. It didn't snap back, but remained in a long wrinkle. "They're dehydrated, Joe."

He filled the dishpan with water and set it on the floor.

"Will you listen to me! There was a wreck. A car went into Hellhag Canyon," Joe shouted over the racket of the two pups slurping and splashing. "The guy lost his brakes—nice '67 Corvette—powder blue— totally trashed it."

"Really?" Clyde said with more interest. "A Corvette. I haven't seen a '67 Corvette around the village in a long time. Was the driver someone we know? How bad was he hurt? Are the police there?"

"They're there. But if they don't look at the brake line . . ."

Clyde turned to stare at him. "What?"

"The brake line. It was cut. If the cops—"

"Don't start, Joe."

"Start what?"

"You know what. Meddling. Don't start meddling. You always think—"

"If they don't look closely at the brake line," Joe said patiently, "they might not see it was cut."

Clyde sighed.

"Sharp slice. Near the right front wheel. The brake fluid—"

"Joe—"

"Brake fluid all over the road."

"*If* it was cut, Harper's men will find it. Don't you think they know their job? Can't you keep out of anything? You bring home two starving puppies, you don't bother to find water for them, and then you—"

"And you," Joe shouted, "you don't stop to wonder where they came from, you just bang open the front door and invite them right on in when they're probably full of ringworm and mange."

"*I* didn't bring them home."

"And now you won't listen when I try to tell you something important."

During this exchange, old Rube had risen from the kitchen linoleum and taken his aged black Labrador body into the laundry. Lying on the bottom bunk, he growled at the pups with a menace that drove them back into the adjoining kitchen.

The bottom half of the two-tiered bunk belonged to Rube, the top half to the cats. From there, the white cat peered down suspiciously. The other two household cats had fled out Rube's dog door to hide in the backyard; they were used to quiet dogs but didn't take happily to big boisterous puppies.

The pups, abandoning Rube and his uncertain temper, returned all their attention to Clyde, their forepaws on the kitchen table, barking in his face.

Clyde opened the lower cupboard and hauled out a fifty-pound bag of kibble.

"Don't feed them too much. You'll make them sick."

"They're starving, Joe."

"Feed them too much and they'll throw it all up."

"Don't be silly. They'll only eat what they need."

Joe headed for the bedroom, where he could find some privacy with the telephone. He had started to paw in the number of the police station when Clyde strode in and unplugged the cord.

Joe stared at him.

"Leave it, Joe. Those guys don't need your help to find a cut brake line."

"And if they miss it?"

"I'll find out from Harper."

Silence from the kitchen. The puppies had stopped chomping and smacking. Joe could hear them licking up the last crumbs, then heard them drinking again. Clyde said, "How many people in the car? Are you sure it was a '67 Corvette?"

"Of course I'm sure. I've been force-fed on your antique car trivia most of my natural life. I know a '67 Corvette as well as I know the back of my paw. There was just the driver. Dead on impact. Maybe from multiple contusions, maybe from a strip of metal stabbed through him, maybe a combination. A man I've never seen. Went over just at that double curve, driving south. Lost most of the fluid before the second curve. I was hunting down in the canyon, heard a skid, and that baby came over the bank like a bomb dumped from a B-27, fell right at me. If

I wasn't so lightning fast, it would have creamed me." He gave Clyde a yellow-eyed scowl. "That car could have killed a poor little cat, careening down into that gully, and what would you care?"

"You look all right to me. You shouldn't have been hunting in Hellhag Canyon. You know how the tides come up."

"That's typical. I'm nearly killed, and all you can do is find fault."

Two wrenching, gurgling heaves from the kitchen silenced them.

They returned to face two huge piles of doggy kibble steaming on the kitchen floor. The pups, having disgorged the contents of their stomachs, began to bark at the mess and then to lick it. Clyde shouted at them, swinging the kibble bag; the smaller pup, startled, yipped as though he'd been struck. Both pups raced around the kitchen barking. Clyde, trying to clean up the mess, yelled and swore to drive them out of his way. Joe, nearly trampled, leaped to the sink and let out a bloodcurdling yowl.

"Put leashes on them, Clyde. Take them out to the car. Take them to the pound—that's why I brought them home! So you could take them to the pound!"

This wasn't completely true, but he'd lost all patience. Couldn't Clyde handle two baby dogs? "Take them to the pound, Clyde."

"Don't be stupid! They'll kill them at the pound! Why would you bring them home and then . . ."

"*The pound will find homes for them!* I brought them home so you could drive them out there. You didn't expect me to walk way out there dragging those two? Expect me to jump up on the counter at the animal shelter and fill out the proper forms? Sometimes, Clyde, you don't show good sense even for a human!"

Clyde stared at him. The pups stopped barking and stared, too, their tails whipping and wagging.

Joe Grey, glaring at all three, leaped from the counter over the pups' heads and scorched out the dog door. He was crouched to bolt over the gate and go find a phone, when he saw Dulcie trotting swiftly along the back fence toward him, her green eyes wide with interest, her peach-tinted ears sharply forward, her whole being keen with curiosity.

4

CROUCHED ON the back fence, Dulcie had started at the sudden barking from Clyde's house behind her. Sounded like he had a kennel full of dogs in there—big, lively dogs, shouting with canine idiocy. Probably someone visiting had brought their mutts along, and Clyde was making a fuss over them, teasing and playing with them. He could be such a fool over an animal; that was what she loved best about him.

At first when she discovered her talent for human speech, she had been wary of Clyde, wouldn't talk to him. She'd left that to Joe, who had awakened from simple cathood into their amazing metamorphosis at about the same time. From the beginning, Joe had mouthed off to Clyde and argued with him, while she had hidden her new talents, too shy even to tell Wilma.

Oh, that morning when Wilma found out. When, sitting on Wilma's lap at the breakfast table secretly reading the newspaper right along with her, that instant when she laughed out loud at a really stupid book review, she thought Wilma was going to have a coronary.

Dulcie had been worrying about how to break her amazing news; she hadn't meant to blurt it out like that. But suddenly the cat was out of the bag, so to speak. And afterward, trying to explain to Wilma *how* it had happened, that she didn't *know* how it had happened, trying to explain how wonderful it was to understand human speech, oh, that had been some morning, the two of them trying to get it all sorted out, Wilma laughing, and crying a little, too, and hugging Dulcie.

Of course one couldn't sort out such a phenomenon; one doesn't dissect miracles. The closest she and Wilma could come—or that Wilma could—was to head for the library and dive into a tangle of research. Wilma and Clyde together had dug through tomes of history about cats, through Celtic and Egyptian history and myth. When they surfaced with their notes, the implications had swept Dulcie away.

Suddenly her head was filled with ancient folklore interlocked with human history, with the mysterious Tuatha folk who had slipped up from the netherworld into the green Celtic fields through doors carved into the ancient hills. There were doors with cat faces engraved on them, sometimes in a tomb, sometimes in a garden wall. Doors that implied feline powers and led deep into the earth, into another land.

Wilma's research had led Dulcie to Set and Bast, to Egyptian cat mummies and Egyptian tombs with small, cat-decorated doors deep within. From the instant she first realized that she could understand human language, could speak and read the morning paper, then realized there were books about cats like her and Joe, the entire world had opened up, her curiosity, her imagination, her very spirit expanded like a butterfly released from its cocoon.

But Joe Grey hadn't been so charmed; he didn't like those revelations of their own history, he didn't like thinking about their amazing lineage. It was enough for Joe that he was suddenly able to talk back to Clyde and express his own opinions, and could knock the phone from its cradle, to order takeout.

Nor was Joe thrilled to encounter others like themselves, rare creatures among the world of cats. He had certainly not been impressed with the black tom and his evil voodoo ways. That cat had caused more trouble than she cared to remember; she could have done without Azrael. She was glad he'd gone back to the jungles of Central America.

She had spent the early morning perched as usual on Clyde's back fence beneath the concealing branches of Clyde's maple tree, her dark stripes blending with the maple's leafy shadows as she watched Lucinda Greenlaw, alone in the parlor, enjoying her solitary breakfast. Looking in through the lace curtains of the old Victorian house, Dulcie felt a deep, sympathetic closeness to the thin, frail widow.

She thought it strange that Lucinda's tall old house was so shabby and neglected, its roof shingles curled, its gray paint peeling, when the Greenlaws were far from poor. At least when Shamas was alive, they'd had plenty of cash.

The interior was faded, too, the colors of the flowered wallpaper and the ornate furniture dulled by dust and time. But still the room was charming, furnished with delicate mahogany and cherry pieces upholstered in fine though faded tapestries. Each morning Lucinda took her breakfast alone there from a tray before a cheerful fire; her meager meal, of tea steeped in a thin porcelain pot and a plate of sugar cookies, seemed as pale and without substance as the old woman herself.

According to the pictures on the mantel of Lucinda and Shamas in their younger days, she had been a beauty, as tall and lovely and well turned out as any modern-day model; but now she was bone thin, shrunken, and as delicate as parchment.

Lucinda Greenlaw had had her own metamorphosis, Dulcie thought. From glamorous social creature when she was younger, into a neglected and lonely wife. From the vibrant, very alive person she had been, as Dulcie's friend Wilma had known her, to a faded and uncertain little person as colorless as the fog that drifted, that morning, in wisps around the parlor windows. Watching Lucinda Greenlaw, Dulcie was gripped with a painful sadness for her; Lucinda had a talent for distressing Dulcie, for stirring in her a desire to protect, almost to mother the old woman.

Dulcie's housemate responded to Lucinda in the same way. Wilma, too, felt the need to protect Lucinda, particularly now that Lucinda was newly widowed, and now that she had a houseful of her husband's noisy, rude relatives to bedevil her. A crowd of big, overbearing Greenlaws filled the five bedrooms awaiting Shamas's funeral, so many big men and women that they seemed to smother Lucinda with their loud arguing and careless manners.

Still, Lucinda knew how to find her own peace. She simply walked away, left the house. She might look frail, but Lucinda had been out as usual that morning before daylight for a solitary ramble of, very likely, several miles.

Earlier, as Dulcie leaped to the fence through the dark fog, she had seen Lucinda coming up the street returning home, her short white hair clinging in damp curls, her faded blue eyes bright and happy in the chill predawn.

Since Shamas's relatives began to arrive, these early-morning walks and her solitary breakfasts seemed the only moments Lucinda had to herself. Dulcie watched her often, sometimes late at night, too, from higher in the maple tree, watched Lucinda reading in bed from a stack of well-used volumes that stood on her night table; her books of European history and folklore were all Lucinda had to keep her company, alone in the big double bed. She seemed to have every volume of Sir Arthur Bryant, who was one of Wilma's favorite authors, too.

Lucinda's beautifully appointed bedchamber, with its high poster bed and long, gold-framed mirrors, was faded like the rest of the house, the velvets as colorless as Lucinda herself, the once luxurious love chamber deteriorated as if love itself was forgotten, and only sadness remained.

Wilma said Lucinda had been a late bride, that she had met Shamas Greenlaw when she was working in Seattle as a doctor's receptionist. They had married there, where Shamas owned a machine-tool company. Soon after the wedding he sold his Seattle apartment and they moved to Molena Point, to his old family home. Wilma said the handsome, charming couple had launched immediately into a busy social life, that for nearly five years they had circled brightly among Molena Point's parties and social gatherings, its gallery openings and benefits and small concerts. But then Shamas grew restless; the limited society of the small village began to bore him.

He bought a yacht, a sixty-foot catamaran in which they could take their friends on interesting junkets. Money seemed in ample supply—both Lucinda and Shamas had new cars every year. Surely the clothes in the photographs on the mantel looked expensive. The yacht parties, Dulcie thought, must have been happy times—until Shamas's shipboard affairs became apparent.

Lucinda shared her uncomfortable memories with few people, but she trusted Wilma. Dulcie's housemate and Lucinda saw a good deal of each other, particularly since Shamas's death. The last two weeks Wilma had made every effort to be supportive, to help Lucinda through this hard time. During their quiet meals together, Lucinda had opened up to Wilma, expressing her pain at the unhappy marriage, describing how, on the yacht, Shamas would slip out of their cabin in the small hours, returning just before dawn, imagining that she slept.

Lucinda had never confronted Shamas, had never protested his affairs. She simply quit going with him, choosing to stay home alone.

"Giving up," Dulcie told Wilma. Wilma agreed. That was what made Dulcie sad. "Why didn't she fight back? Why didn't she leave him, change her life, make a new life?" Dulcie had hissed. "She just gave in—to exactly what Shamas handed her."

Dulcie didn't understand why Shamas hadn't loved

Lucinda, had treated her so shabbily when she had been so beautiful, when she had such a gentle warmth. Lucinda was still beautiful to Dulcie, like an aged porcelain doll, so frail one would not want to press a paw hard against the old lady's cheek for fear of tearing her fine, powdery skin, so delicate that Dulcie would hesitate to leap hard into Lucinda's lap, for fear she might fracture a bone.

Yet Lucinda was not too frail to walk miles along the shore each morning or to climb the steep slope of Hellhag Hill. Sometimes Dulcie followed her on those lonely predawn jaunts, trotting well behind her, staying, for some reason she could not explain, warily out of sight.

Lucinda must have been miserable all those years while Shamas played fast and loose. She told Wilma she had almost left him a year ago, when he first turned down a rich offer on the old house. But she hadn't left, hadn't found the courage.

Brock, Lavell & Hicks, a local developer, had begun buying up the property on the Greenlaws' block. By the time they approached Shamas, they had purchased all the houses across the street, planning a small, exclusive shopping paseo. Eager to acquire the Greenlaws' two lots, they made Shamas a generous offer. Lucinda had wanted badly to sell, to go into an easily maintained condo, but Shamas refused, perhaps out of family sentiment, perhaps simply to thwart Lucinda. He reminded her frequently that the old house was his family home, though before they moved to Molena Point from Seattle he had rented it out for many years; there was no family nearby to use it—Shamas's cousins had long ago moved across the country to North Carolina.

The relatives were all returning now, flocking to Molena Point to quarrel over Shamas's leavings—while Shamas himself waited, dead and cold, tucked into a vault at the Gardener Funeral Home, for his family to bid him a last farewell. A few more arrived each day, strident, demanding, all alike in their brashness.

But they had charm, too. Loads of charm, Dulcie thought, amused. Big, cheerful Irishmen and women: loud laughing, loud arguing, never able to simply be quiet. Ruddy-faced, sandy-haired folk, ill-mannered, noisy, irritating, and endearing.

Dulcie was certain that none of them had really cared about Shamas, that they had come only to lick up the leavings. So far, more than a dozen cousins and nephews and nieces had descended, the first arrivals moving into the Greenlaws' unoccupied bedrooms. The remainder of Shamas's kin were living in their campers and trailers, in which they had driven out from the East Coast, taking over the Moonwatch Trailer Park south of the village, on the crest of Hellhag Hill. Shamas's funeral would be scheduled when all relatives were present.

Well, the Greenlaws hadn't let Shamas's body cool before they'd begun harassing Lucinda about his estate, pressuring her not to sell the house. Dirken Greenlaw was the worst: Shamas's twenty-year-old nephew had been the first to arrive, moving into the largest guest room. Dirken was louder and more brash than his cousin Newlon.

It was Newlon Greenlaw who had tried to rescue Shamas when he fell overboard in the storm. Newlon had remained on board with their cousin Sam Fulman and two other passengers, to bring the *Green Lady* back to Molena Point harbor. They had docked first in

Seattle for two days, where they were questioned by Seattle police, then sent on their way. Newlon, thinner and slighter than most of the Greenlaw clan, was somewhat quieter, too, and perhaps kinder; surely he was gentler with his uncle's widow than was Dirken.

And speak of the devil, here came Dirken down the stairs, stamping and yawning, his red hair curled over his collar, his teal green polo shirt straining tight over sleek muscles. Settling into a chair beside the fire, treating Lucinda to his charming Irish grin, Dirken was all Gaelic magnetism: testosterone and guile. For Dulcie, Dirken Greenlaw's appeal grew less each day, with each successive argument.

"Any coffee, Aunt Lucinda?"

"In the kitchen, Dirken. It's freshly brewed."

He didn't move, but eyed her, waiting. She smiled back at him, but didn't rise, and Dulcie wanted to cheer—Lucinda was no longer leaping up to fetch Dirken's morning brew.

Immediately after Shamas's death, Lucinda, in an uncharacteristically decisive move, had begun arrangements to sell the house; the papers had been drawn by the time Dirken arrived.

Dirken had put a stop to the sale. Dulcie had watched him pace the parlor alternately cajoling and intimidating Lucinda, playing on her uncertainty, telling her she would throw away hundreds of thousands of dollars if she didn't keep the house and let it increase in value as all real estate was increasing along the California coast.

The house was in a living trust, with Lucinda as her own trustee. If she sold it, the proceeds would go into the trust, and she could spend them as she liked.

Apparently Dirken thought that Lucinda, in some bizarre change of character, would throw away the money in wild debauchery, leaving no cash for the clan—for Dirken, himself, to squander.

Of course Lucinda could revoke any part of the trust; but she was not often so quick to take action as she had been to try to sell the house; generally, the old lady had a hesitant nature. Maybe, Dulcie thought, Dirken was banking on that, hoping Lucinda would die before she changed anything about the trust. He argued, he harassed, and if Newlon was not around to stand up for her, Lucinda would grow very quiet, then soon slip away alone—sometimes these human complications were enough to give a cat fits.

Get some spine, Dulcie would think, feeling her claws stiffen. *Don't let Dirken bully you! Send him packing, send the whole tribe packing. Oh*, she wanted to shout, *get a life, Lucinda. Don't just roll over for them! Sell the house, do something wild and extravagant with the money! Go to Europe. Spend it on diamonds. Don't leave a cent to that clan!* Lucinda was so docile that Dulcie wanted to snatch her up and shake some sense into her; if their roles had been reversed, if Dulcie were bigger than Lucinda, she'd have done it, too.

"You're up mighty early, Aunt Lucinda."

"I'm always up early, my dear. And what brings you down at this hour?" Lucinda poured fresh tea for herself and sat cradling her cup, looking quietly into the fire as if attempting to hold close around her the tranquillity of her early-morning solitude.

"About an hour ago," Dirken said, "I thought I heard noises outside. I went out, tramped around. Did you hear anything?"

"Not a thing, my dear. What kind of noise?"

"You must have been dead to the world. When I came in, I knocked at your bedroom door, but I guess you didn't hear me. Why do you lock your bedroom, Aunt Lucinda?"

Lucinda's eyes widened. "Why would you try my bedroom door, Dirken? I lock it because I don't want someone barging in unannounced, certainly not before daylight."

"A bedroom lock with a key," Dirken said. "So you can go out and lock it behind you." He hadn't the decency to apologize for his snooping, or even to look embarrassed; he simply turned his face away, scowling with anger.

"I expect you'll be working on the house again this morning, Dirken?"

The young man rose, heading for the kitchen and his coffee. In the doorway he turned, watching Lucinda, the firelight catching at his red hair. "I must work on it, Aunt Lucinda. The house needs so much repair. So much to do, if we're to save this old place—save your inheritance."

His tone implied that if he didn't undertake such refurbishing, the house would collapse within weeks, its remains sinking tiredly into the weedy yard, and Lucinda would be out on the street.

Lucinda, Dulcie thought, *must not know much about houses.* Dirken's repair and replacement of some of the lap siding had been grossly shoddy work. And Dulcie had observed with considerable interest his curious method of patching the concrete foundation. It did not appear to her that that little project had anything to do with strengthening the decrepit structure.

She had learned, from watching Clyde and Charlie fix up Clyde's recently purchased apartment building, a good deal about such repairs—though Clyde limited his work mostly to tear-out. But Dulcie had seen how siding should be applied, and how a crumbling foundation looked; she had spent hours lying on the sunny brick patio beside Joe waiting for mice to be dislodged by the workers and observing just such reconstruction operations.

And how arrogant Dirken was about the supposed repairs. His attitude had been, ever since he arrived, not one of tenderness toward his newly widowed aunt, but of confrontation. Not the behavior of a nurturing young relative caring for his uncle's frail old widow, but of a selfish young man out for his own gain.

Nor did the rest of the Greenlaw clan spend any time comforting Lucinda; they were either harassing her or prowling the village on endless sightseeing excursions, rudely fingering the wares in Molena Point's expensive shops, leaving grease stains and torn wrappings, their loud complaints seeming to echo long after they had departed. And in the evenings, in Lucinda's parlor, they were no more pleasant, quibbling about the sale of the house, turning the prefuneral gathering into a bad-tempered brawl.

Send them packing, Dulcie would think, crouching on the fence, her ears back, her tail lashing. She'd hardly been in the public library in two weeks, where usually she spent several hours a day greeting the patrons and playing with the children. She meant to do better; she was, after all, the official library cat, but she couldn't stop racing across the village to Lucinda's, to watch the drama unfolding there. Some force was building, she thought. A confluence of emotions and events that was just the beginning of a larger drama, she was certain of it. And she didn't want to miss a minute. Whatever lay in Lucinda's immediate future, Dulcie wanted to know about it.

But the most puzzling twist of all was that, while the Greenlaws were so prickly and unpleasant to Lucinda, on the rare evenings that they settled in for a round of Irish storytelling, filling Lucinda's parlor nearly to bursting, something strange happened: their attitudes were totally different. Suddenly the frail parlor seemed no longer in danger of collapse under their fierce emoting. On storytelling nights a kind of magic sprang alive among the Greenlaws. They seemed gentler, easier with one another, nurturing, and warm.

And Lucinda was easier, too. The old woman seemed drawn to the family, clasping her hands at their tales, weeping or laughing with them. They *seemed* a family, then, this obstreperous clan, and Lucinda no longer an outsider against whom they were solidly ranked.

Wilma said it was the old family stories and family history, which Shamas had told so well, that had first drawn Lucinda to him, that Shamas's commitment to the old ways was perhaps the only real thing about him, that surely this had been the strongest tie between the mismatched couple. Every marriage, Wilma said, must have a fabric of shared philosophy to tie it together. Wilma truly believed that. For Shamas and Lucinda, that richness had come from the old myths that had been handed down for generations through the Greenlaw family.

And oh, those tales drew Dulcie. On warm evenings when the parlor windows were open and she could hear the stories, she would slip across the yard and up a half-rotten rose trellis to cling beside the screen, listening.

She could have pushed right on inside beneath the loose screen. Who would wonder at a little cat coming in? But she didn't fancy wandering among those big-booted men and bad-mannered kids with too many hands to snatch at her. The Greenlaws might charm her with their stories, but she didn't trust a one of them.

But how lovely were their Irish tales, filling her with a longing for worlds vanished, worlds peopled with shapeshifters and her own kind of cat. To hear those stories whispered, hear their wild parts belted out, to hear their wonders dramatized as only an Irishman could tell a tale, those were purr-filled hours. Afterward, she would trot away to join Joe, hunting high on the hills, filled with a deep and complete satisfaction.

These were her stories that the Greenlaws told, she had read and reread them, alone at nighttime in the library, when she had the books to herself; this was her history, hers and Joe's. The Greenlaws didn't know that, and they never noticed a little cat crouched at the window.

Strangely, even the taleteller's language was different on those evenings, the loud Irishmen abandoning the clan's rough speech for the old, soft phrases and ancient words. And there was one old, wrinkled man among them who had such a beguiling way with a story.

"Semper Will," old Pedric would begin, "he were a packman, and there wadn't no carts their way, 't tracks was all mixey-mirey and yew did need a good pack-donk to get a load safe droo they moors."

Pedric, unlike his strapping relatives, was thin and bony and wizened; Pedric looked, himself, like an over-grown elven man or perhaps a skinny wizard.

"Will's track was all amuck, then, with gurt reeds

a-growing up and deep holes for tha donk to fall in, yes all a-brim with muck . . ."

Oh, Dulcie knew that tale of the high banks full of burrows that the donkey would pass, and the strange little cats that would appear there, peering out of their small caves.

"All sandy-colored tha little cats was, and wi' green, green eyes." She knew how those burrows led down and down through dark caverns to other lands, to subterranean mountains and meadows lit by a clear green sky. And Pedric told how the cats were not always in cat form but how, down in that emerald world, a cat might change to a beautiful woman dressed in a silken gown. Oh yes, Dulcie knew those stories, and, just as she knew that at least one part of them was true, the Irishmen believed fully in their wealth of tales. They believed just as surely as they believed that the earth was round and the moon and stars shone in the heavens. The Celtic tales were a part of the Greenlaws' lives, to be loved as music is loved but to be put aside in their everyday dealings, as a song might be put aside.

Lucinda finished her tea and cookies and rose to carry her tray to the kitchen, seeming hardly aware of the loud barking through the open windows, though Clyde's house seemed to explode with human shouting and canine bawling.

Looking through the leaves, watching Clyde's empty yard, Dulcie heard Joe yowl with rage. Half-alarmed, half-amused, she slipped out from the maple tree and hurried along the fence.

"Take them to . . ." Joe shouted. "Take them to the pound . . . That's why I brought them."

"Don't be stupid! . . . kill them . . ." Clyde yelled.

And Joe came bolting out the dog door, his ears flat, his yellow eyes slitted with rage. As he crouched to leap the gate, he turned and saw her.

He said nothing. He stood glowering, his ears back, the white strip down his gray face narrowed by anger. Dulcie, ignoring him, flicked her ears, leaped down into the yard, and trotted past him to see for herself. She hurried up Clyde's back steps, her ears ringing with Clyde's shouting and the wild baying.

Nearly deafened, Dulcie poked her head through the dog door.

The room was filled with giant dog legs, huge paws scrabbling, two giant tails whipping against the cabinets. Clyde was racing around the kitchen trying to put collars on two huge dogs, and such shouting and swearing over a little thing like a collar made her yowl with laughter, then yowl louder to get his attention.

He turned to stare at her.

"If you don't shut up, Clyde, and make those dogs shut up, every neighbor on the street is going to be down here!" And of course the moment she spoke, the two dogs leaped at her. She hauled back a paw to slash them.

They backed off, whimpering.

She paused, and did a double take. She had scared them silly; they cowered against Clyde's legs, rolling their eyes at her.

Why, they were puppies. Just two big, frightened pups—two whining pups the size of small ponies and as thin and pitiful as skinned sparrows.

She slipped in through the dog door and sat down on the linoleum.

They seemed to decide she wouldn't hurt them.

They crept to her. Two wet black noses pushed at her, two wet tongues drenched her with dog spit; they were all over her, licking and whining. Oh, what pitiful, lovable big babies. Gently, Dulcie lifted a soft paw and patted their sweet puppy faces.

5

JOE FOLLOWED Dulcie through the dog door, watching half with disgust, half with amusement, as she preened and wove around the pups' legs. She was purring like a coffee grinder. Any other cat, confronted by the two monster dogs—even puppies—would have headed for the tallest tree.

Not Dulcie, of course. She wasn't afraid of dogs. But he hadn't counted on that silly maternal grin, either.

He'd expected her to be disgusted with the rowdy young animals, as most adult cats, or dogs, would be. How ridiculous to see a lovely lady cat, self-contained and sometimes even dignified, certainly of superior intelligence, succumb to this ingratiating canine display. He watched with disgust as the pups licked her face and ears. Not until she was sopping wet did she move away from them, shake her whiskers, and leap to the kitchen table; and still her green eyes blazed with pleasure.

"Puppies, Joe! Clyde, where did you get the huge puppies?" Her peach-tinted paw lifted in a soft maternal gesture. "They're darling! Such cute, pretty pups!"

"They're not darling," Joe snapped. "They're monsters. Flea-bitten bags of bones. Clyde's taking them to the pound."

She widened her eyes, twin emeralds, shocked and indignant.

"They are not," Clyde said evenly, "going to the pound." He sat down at the kitchen table. "So what's with you? What's the attraction, Dulcie? You're known all over the village as a dog baiter. What . . ."

"Dog baiter?"

"Of course. No resident dog will confront you. And the tourists' dogs try only once." Clyde looked hard at her. "You think I don't know about your little games? I know what you do when life gets boring; I've seen you sauntering down Ocean early in the morning when the tourists are walking their pets; I've seen you waltz past those leashed canines waving your tail until some showoff lunges at you.

"I've seen you bloody them, send some poor mutt bolting away screaming. I've seen you smile and trot off licking your whiskers." Clyde looked intently at the smug little tabby. "So what gives?"

"They're only babies," Dulcie said haughtily. "Why would I want to hurt babies? Really, Clyde, you can be so unfeeling." She leaped down to where the pups lay sprawled, panting, on the linoleum. Turning her back on Clyde, she licked a black nose. She couldn't help the maternal warmth that spread over her as she began to wash the two big babies.

Clyde shook his head and stepped past her toward the door, carrying a bucket of trash. Joe, scowling at the silly grin on Dulcie's little, triangular face, muttered something rude into his whiskers and left the scene, pushing out behind Clyde. Let Dulcie play "mama" if that was what pleased her. He was out of there.

Scaling the back fence, he galloped across the village, dodging tourists and cars, heading for Dulcie and Wilma's house, where he could find some peace and quiet without that zoo, and where Wilma's phone was accessible. If the cops missed that cut line, if they didn't look for it before the wreck was lifted from the canyon and hauled away, the evidence might be lost for good.

Wilma didn't like him and Dulcie meddling in police business any more than Clyde did, but she had better manners. She wouldn't stop him from using the phone.

Trotting past early joggers and a few shopkeepers out watering the flowers that graced their storefront gardens, sniffing the smell of damp greenery and of breakfast cooking in a dozen little cafés, Joe kept thinking of the dead man lying in the wrecked Corvette. A fairly young, apparently well-to-do stranger, and very likely an antique car buff—a man, one would think, who would be closely attuned to the mechanical condition of his vehicle.

Did the guy have some connection in the village, maybe visiting someone? Seemed strange that, just passing through, he would meet his doom at that particular and precarious location.

Whoever cut the brake line had to have known about that double curve. Joe didn't believe in coincidence, any more than did Captain Max Harper.

The question was, who in the village might have wanted this guy dead?

Hurrying beneath the twisted oaks, past shop windows filled with handmade and costly wares or with fresh-baked bread and bottles of local wines, he passed Jolly's Deli and the arresting scent of smoked salmon.

But Joe didn't pause, not for an instant. Galloping on up the street to Wilma's gray stone cottage, he made three leaps across her bright garden and slid in through Dulcie's cat door.

Wilma's blue-and-white kitchen was immaculate. The smell of waffles and bacon lingered. He leaped to the counter, where breakfast dishes stood neatly rinsed in the drain. The coffeepot was empty and unplugged. The house sounded hollow.

Heading for the living room and Wilma's desk, he was glad he'd left Dulcie occupied with the pups. She hadn't been in the best of moods lately—though the pups had evidently cheered her. He didn't like to admit that something might be wrong between them, had been wrong for weeks, ever since the earthquake. Ever since that three A.M. jolt when he raced down the street to see if Dulcie was all right, only to meet her pelting toward him wild with worry for him, then wild with joy that he was unhurt. After the quake and the ensuing confusion when people wandered the streets sniffing the air for gas leaks, he and Dulcie had clung together purring, taking absolute comfort in each other; he telling her how he'd heard the bookshelves fall in the spare bedroom as he felt the house rock; she telling him how Wilma had leaped out of bed only to be knocked down like a rag toy. It hadn't been a giant quake—not the Big One—a few shingles fallen, a few windows broken, one or two gas lines burst, people frightened. But at the first tremble, Joe had run out— Rube barking and barking behind him and Clyde shouting for him to come back—had sped away frantic to find Dulcie.

But then a few days later, a kind of crossness took

hold of Dulcie, a private, sour mood. She wouldn't tell him what was wrong. She left him out, went off alone, silent and glum. All the clichés he'd ever heard assailed him: familiarity breeds contempt; as sour as old marrieds. He didn't know what was wrong with her. He didn't know what he'd done. When he tried to talk to her, she cut him short.

But that morning, distracted by the idiot puppies, she'd smiled and waved her tail and purred extravagantly.

Mark one down for the two bone bags. Maybe they were of some use.

Now, settling on Wilma's clean blotter atop the polished cherry desk, he could smell the lingering aroma of coffee where, evidently, Wilma had sat this morning, perhaps to pay bills. A neat stack of bill stubs lay beneath the small jade carving of a cat. He could imagine Wilma coming to her desk very early, catching up on her household chores. Beyond the open shutters, the neighborhood street was empty, the gardens bright with flowers; he could never remember the names of flowers as Dulcie did. Sliding the receiver off, he punched in the number for the police.

He got through the dispatcher to Lieutenant Brennan, but Captain Harper was out. He didn't like passing on this kind of information to another officer—not that Harper's men weren't reliable. It simply made Joe uncomfortable to talk with anyone but Harper.

Besides, he enjoyed hearing Harper's irritable hesitation when he recognized the voice of this one particular snitch. He enjoyed imagining the tall, leathered, tough-looking captain at the other end of the line squirming with nerves.

Max Harper reacted the same way to Dulcie's occasional phone tips. The minute he heard either of them he got as cross as a fox with thorns in its paw.

"Captain Harper won't be back until this afternoon," Lieutenant Brennan said.

"That wreck in Hellhag Canyon," Joe said reluctantly. "I'm sure the officers found that the brake line was cut. Sliced halfway through in a sharp, even line."

Brennan did not reply. Joe could hear him chewing on something. He heard papers rattle. He hoped Brennan was paying attention—Brennan had been one of the officers at the scene. Maybe they hadn't found the cut brake line, maybe that was why he was uncommunicative.

"There was a billfold, too," Joe told him. "In the dead driver's hip pocket. Leather. A bulging leather wallet. Did you find that? An old wallet, misshapen from so much stuff crammed in, the leather dark, sort of oily. Stained. A large splinter of broken glass was pressing against it."

He repeated the information but refused to give Brennan his name. He hung up before Brennan could trace the call; a trace took three or four minutes. He didn't dare involve Wilma's phone in this. She and Harper were friends. Joe wasn't going to throw suspicion on her—and thus, by inference, cast it back on himself and Dulcie.

Pawing the phone into its cradle and pushing out again through Dulcie's plastic door, he headed toward the hills, trotting up through cottage gardens and across the little park that covered the Highway One tunnel. Gaining the high, grassy slopes, he sat in the warm wind, feeling lonely without Dulcie.

She was so busy these days, spying uselessly on Lucinda Greenlaw. Maybe that was all that was wrong

with her, watching Lucinda too much, feeling sad for
the old woman; maybe it was her preoccupation with
the Greenlaw family that had turned her so moody.

All day Joe hunted alone, puzzling over Dulcie. At dusk
he hurried home, thinking he would find Dulcie there
because Clyde had invited Wilma to dinner, along with
Charlie, and Max Harper.

He saw Wilma's car parked in front of the cottage,
but couldn't detect Dulcie's scent. Not around the car,
or on the front porch, or on his cat door. Heading
through the house for the kitchen, he sniffed deeply the
aroma of clam sauce and twitched his nose at the sharp
hint of white wine. Pushing into the kitchen, he looked
around for Dulcie.

Clyde and Charlie stood at the stove stirring the
clam sauce and tasting it. Charlie's red hair was tied
back with a blue scarf rather than the usual rubber band
or piece of cord. Her oversized, blue batik shirt was
tucked into tight blue jeans. She had on sleek new san-
dals, not her old, worn jogging shoes.

Wilma was tossing the salad, her long white hair,
tied back with a turquoise clip, bright in the overhead
lights. The table was set for four. Two more places,
with small plates and no silverware, were arranged on
the counter beside the sink, on a yellow place mat. That
would be Charlie's doing; Clyde never served so fancy.
The sounds of bubbling pasta competed with an Ella
Fitzgerald record, both happy noises overridden by the
loud and insistent scratching of what sounded like a
troop of attack dogs assaulting the closed doggy door.

He wondered how long the plywood barrier would last before those two shredded it.

"I just fed them," Clyde said defensively. "Two cans each. Big, economy cans."

Joe made no comment. He did not want to speak in front of Charlie.

Charlie knew about him and Dulcie—she had known ever since, some months ago, she saw them racing across the rooftops at midnight and heard Dulcie laughing. That was when she began to suspect—or maybe before that, he thought, wondering.

Well, so that one night leaping among the village roofs, they'd been careless.

Charlie was one of the few people who could put such impossible facts together and come up with the impossible truth. And it wasn't as if Charlie was only a casual acquaintance; she and Clyde had been going together seriously for nearly a year. Joe liked her. She treated him with more respect than Clyde ever did, and she was, after all, Wilma's niece. But still he couldn't help feeling shy about actually speaking in front of her, not even to ask where Dulcie was.

"She's on the back fence," Wilma said, seeing him fidgeting. "Where else? Gawking into Lucinda's parlor." Wilma shook the salad dressing with a violence that threatened Clyde's clean kitchen walls.

Joe, pretending he didn't care where Dulcie was, leaped to the kitchen counter and stared at his empty plate, implying he didn't need Dulcie, that he'd eat enough pasta for both.

"I talked with Harper," Clyde said. "About an hour ago. I want you to behave yourself tonight."

Joe widened his eyes, a gaze of innocence he had

practiced for many hours while standing on the bathroom sink.

"Harper says he had another of those snitch calls this morning. Guy wouldn't give his name. Left the message with Brennan—something about a cut brake line." He gave Joe a long, steady stare.

Joe kept his expression blank.

"He says this one was a dud. Totally off track. Said that after the call, two officers went back down Hellhag Canyon for another look."

Joe licked his right front paw.

"The officers said the brake line wasn't cut. Said the line burst, that it was ragged and worn. That there was no smooth cut as Harper's informant described. They said they could see the thin place, the weak spot in the plastic where it gave way.

"Nor was there a billfold," Clyde said. "The officers didn't find a scrap of ID on the body, or in the car, or in the surround, as the snitch had said."

Joe could feel his anger rising. Which uniforms had Harper sent down there? Those two new rookies he'd just hired?

Or had the cut line been removed?

Had the man he scented in the ravine that morning replaced the cut, black plastic tube with an old, broken one, and lifted the driver's wallet?

Those two pups knew the guy was there. He remembered how silent they had grown, how watchful, creeping along sniffing the man's scent.

"So this time," Clyde said, "Harper's snitch was all wet."

So this time, Joe Grey thought crossly, *Harper's men didn't have the whole story—and Max Harper needs to know that.*

Staring at the dog door, then out the kitchen window, Joe managed a sigh. He looked at the two plates set side by side on the kitchen counter, then back to the window, his nose against the glass. He continued in this vein until Wilma said, "For heaven's sakes, go over there and get her. Quit mooning around. She doesn't need to spend all night watching Lucinda."

He gave Wilma a grateful look and began to paw at the plywood, seeking a grip to slide it out of its track.

"Not the dog door!" Clyde shouted. "They'll be all over the place."

Joe widened his eyes at Clyde, shrugged, and headed for the living room. Clyde said nothing. But Joe could feel him staring. The man had absolutely no trust.

He went on out his cat door, making sure the plastic slapped loudly against its frame.

But as he dropped off the front porch he heard Clyde at the living-room window, heard the curtain swish as Clyde pulled it back to peer out.

Not an ounce of trust.

Not until he heard Clyde go back in the kitchen did he beat it around to the backyard and up onto the back fence where he could see into the kitchen. And not until Clyde was occupied, draining the spaghetti, did he slip around to the front and in through his cat door again, stopping the plastic with his nose to keep it quiet.

Heading for the bedroom, he punched in the number. Quickly he explained the urgency of his message. He got a sensible dispatcher, who patched him through to Harper in his car. Probably Harper was already headed in their direction, on his way for clam pasta.

Joe told Harper that he had *seen* the cut brake line, that there were three little slice marks just above the cut. He said he'd heard someone else in the canyon, but couldn't see him in the fog. Said he had *seen* the billfold in the guy's back pocket, with a piece of the broken glass pressing into it.

He reminded Harper where the captain had gotten the information that nailed Winthrop Jergen's killer. Reminded him where he got the computer code word that opened up Jergen's files. He jogged Harper's memory about who identified the retirement-home killer months earlier, to say nothing of finding the arsonist who killed the artist Janet Jeannot. He said if Harper remembered who laid out the facts in the Samuel Beckwhite murder case, then Harper should take another look down Hellhag Canyon, before the wreckers hauled away the blue Corvette.

The upshot was that, five minutes after Joe nosed the phone back into its cradle and returned innocently to the kitchen, Harper called Clyde to say not to wait dinner, that he'd be late, that he needed to run down the highway for a few minutes.

Clyde hung up the kitchen phone and turned to stare at Joe, anger starting deep in his brown eyes, a slow, steaming rage that struck Joe with sudden, shocked guilt.

What had he done?

He had acted without thinking.

Max Harper was headed out there alone, to scale down Hellhag Canyon in the dark. With perhaps the killer still lurking, maybe waiting for the car to be safely hauled away? Harper without a backup.

Cops can be hurt, too, Joe thought. *Cops can be shot.* He was so upset, he dared not look back at Clyde. What had he done? What had he done to Max Harper?

He wanted to call the station again, tell them to

send a backup. But when he leaped down to head for the bedroom, Clyde unbelievably reached up and removed the kitchen phone from its hook.

Joe wanted to shout at Clyde, to explain to him that he *needed* to call, but Wilma started talking about Lucinda Greenlaw, and Clyde turned his back on Joe. He couldn't believe this was happening. Didn't Clyde understand? Didn't Clyde care about Harper?

The phone stayed off the hook as Charlie dished up the plates. Wilma looked around at Joe, where she stood tossing the salad. "Where's Dulcie?"

"She didn't want to come," he lied—he had to talk in Charlie's presence sometime. And to Charlie's credit, she didn't flinch, didn't turn to look, not a glance.

"We stopped by Jolly's alley earlier," Joe said. "Dulcie's full of smoked salmon, and too fascinated with the Greenlaws to tear herself away."

Wilma gave him a puzzled look, but she said nothing. When Wilma and Clyde and Charlie were seated over steaming plates of linguini, Wilma said, "Lucinda and I had lunch today. She was pretty upset. Shamas's lover is in town. She's been to visit Lucinda."

Charlie laid down her fork, her eyes widening. "Cara Ray Crisp, that bimbo who was on the boat when he died? That hussy? What colossal nerve. What did she want?"

"Apparently," Wilma said, "Cara Ray had hardly checked into the Oak Breeze before she was there on Lucinda's doorstep, playing nice. Lucinda really didn't know what she wanted."

"I hope Lucinda sent her packing," Charlie said. "My God. That woman was the last one to see him alive. The last one to—"

"She told Lucinda she came to offer condolences."

Charlie choked. Clyde laughed.

That midnight on the yacht, when Shamas drowned, Cara Ray told Seattle police, she'd been asleep in their stateroom, she'd awakened to shouting, and saw that Shamas was gone from the bed. She ran out into the storm, to find Shamas's cousin, Sam, frantically manning lines, and his nephew, Newlon, down in the sea trying to pull Shamas out. They got lines around Shamas and pulled him up on deck, but could not revive him. Weeping, Cara Ray told the police that when the storm subsided they had turned toward the nearest port, at Seattle. George and Winnie Chambers, the only other passengers, had not awakened; Cara Ray said they had not come on deck until the next morning, when the *Green Lady* put in at Seattle.

According to the account in the *Gazette*, the storm had come up suddenly; evidently Shamas had heard the wind change and gotten up to help Newlon furl the main sail. On the slick deck, he must have caught his foot in a line, though this was an unseaman-like accident. As the boat lurched, Sam and Newlon heard Shamas shout; they looked around, and he was gone. Newlon had grabbed a life jacket, tied a line on himself, and gone overboard.

He told police that he got Shamas untangled, got him hooked onto a line to bring him up. When they got him on board, they saw that he had a deep gash through his forehead, where he must have hit something as he fell. Seattle police had gone over the catamaran, had thoroughly investigated the scene. They did not find where Shamas had struck his head. The rain had sloughed every surface clean. They found no evidence that Shamas's death had been other than an accident. According to Seattle detectives, Cara Ray had been so upset, weeping so profusely, that no one could get much sense from her. She had given the police her address and flown directly home to San Francisco, leaving Newlon and Shamas's cousin Sam and the Chamberses to sail the *Green Lady* back to Molena Point.

And now Cara Ray was in Molena Point, making a social call on Shamas's widow.

"Poor Lucinda," Charlie said. "Mobbed by his relatives hustling and prodding her. And now his paramour descends."

Wilma nodded. "Apparently Cara Ray is as crude and bad mannered as the Greenlaws."

"They are a strange lot," Clyde said.

Wilma pushed a strand of her white hair into its clip and sipped her wine. "Every time I see a Greenlaw in the village, my hackles go up."

Clyde grinned. "Retired parole officer. Worse than a cop."

"Maybe I'm just irritable, maybe it's this temporary job at Beckwhite's. It's no picnic, working for Sheril Beckwhite. I wouldn't have taken the job except to help Max."

At Max Harper's urging, Wilma had been running background checks on loan applicants for the foreign-car agency. Beckwhite's had had a sudden run of buyers applying for car financing with sophisticated bogus IDs and fake bank references. They had lost over three million dollars before Harper convinced Sheril of Wilma's investigative prowess.

"Other than her visit from this Cara Ray Crisp person," Charlie said, "how's Lucinda getting along?"

"She'll do a lot better," Wilma said, "when Shamas's relatives go home."

"Seems to me," Charlie said, "that being Shamas Greenlaw's widow would be much nicer than being his wife."

Wilma laughed.

"She's certainly a very quiet person," Charlie offered. "She seems . . . I don't know, the few times I've talked with her, she's seemed . . . so close to herself. Secretive."

"I don't think—" Wilma began when, in the backyard, the pups roared and bayed, their barks so deafening that no one heard the front door open; no one heard Max Harper until he loomed in the kitchen doorway.

"What the hell is this? The county pound?" He glared at Clyde. "What did you do, get more dogs? Sounds like a pack of wolfhounds."

Clyde rose to open a beer for Harper and dish up his plate, liberally heaping on the pasta and clam sauce. Skinny as Harper was, he ate like a field hand. Clyde had known him since boyhood; they had gone through school together, had ridden broncs and bulls in the local rodeos around Sacramento and Salinas.

Dropping down from the kitchen counter, Joe took a good sniff of Harper. The captain's faded jeans and old boots bore traces of dirt and of bits of leaves and grass, and carried the distinct combination of scents one would encounter in Hellhag Canyon.

"So what's with the cat killers?" Harper said, glancing toward the back door.

"Stray pups. Followed my car," Clyde lied. "Up along Hellhag Hill."

The police captain looked at Clyde narrowly for a moment, perhaps sensing a twisting of the truth. He sat down in his usual chair, facing the sink and kitchen window, his back comfortably to the wall. For an instant, his gaze turned to Joe Grey, who had returned to the counter and was busily licking clam sauce off his whiskers.

"How sanitary can it be, Damen, to let your cat sit on the kitchen sink?" Harper scowled. "Is that a little place mat? Did he have his dinner up there?"

"That's Charlie's doing. And you know I don't lay food on the counter," Clyde said testily. "You know I use that plastic breadboard and that it goes in the dishwasher after every meal." He looked hard at Harper. "So what's with you? Bad night picking up hustlers? Ladies of the night make you late to dinner?"

Harper brushed the dry grass and leaves from his jeans. "Took a swing down Hellhag Canyon."

Clyde stiffened; Joe saw his jaw clench. He did not look in Joe's direction.

"The brake line was burst, not cut," Harper said.

Clyde cast a look of rage at Joe Grey.

"I took some photographs of the surround, though. Infrared light and that new film. Shot some footprints that my men may have missed—the few they didn't step on," Harper said uneasily.

"What are you talking about?" Clyde said.

Harper shrugged. "Maybe someone messed with the car. Maybe someone switched brake lines. If so, it would be nice to have some evidence, wouldn't you say? I have a crew down there now, working it over."

Clyde closed his eyes.

It must be hard, Joe thought, working a crime scene when the uniforms had already been over it, under the impression it was an accident. And, washing his paw, he hid a huge feline grin. At his word, Harper had not only gone down Hellhag Canyon, he had called in the detectives.

Harper's detectives were good; they'd probably remove the jagged shards of the driver's window, see if the lab could find cloth or leather fragments along the broken edges, probably try for fingerprints around the brake line.

Harper's confidence in the phantom snitch pleased Joe Grey so much that he almost leaped on the table to give Harper a purr and a face rub. But he quickly thought better of that little gesture.

He could see, beneath the table, Clyde's toe tapping with irritation; choking back a laugh, he turned his back and washed harder.

"Good linguini," Harper said. "Reminds me of that Italian place in Stockton, down from the rodeo grounds. So tell me about these dogs, Damen. Pups, you said? The way they're banging on the door, I'd say a couple of big bull calves lunging at the gate. Strays, you said? You plan to keep them?"

"If he keeps them," Charlie said, pushing back her wild red hair, "he's—we're taking them to obedience school."

Clyde did a double take. "We're what?"

She stuck out her arm, exhibiting a dozen long red scratches where the pups, in their excitement at having new and wonderful friends, had leaped up joyfully raking her.

"Obedience school," she said. "You can work with the happy, silly one. I'll take the solemn pup; I like his attitude."

Joe looked at Charlie, incredulous. There was no way she was going to get Clyde involved in dog-training classes. She'd as easily get him into a tutu and teach him to pirouette.

Well, she'd learn.

And Joe Grey sat grinning and washing his whiskers, highly amused by Charlie, and immensely pleased at his rise in stature with Max Harper. Harper had moved fast and decisively on Joe's phone tip, had beat it down Hellhag Canyon posthaste, and that made the tomcat feel pretty good. Made him feel good, too, that Harper was back from the canyon in one piece.

Though he would never let Harper know he cared. Stretching out on the cold tile, he gave the captain his usual sour scowl.

Harper returned his frown in spades. The two of them got along just fine with an occasional hiss from Joe, and Harper grousing about cat germs; anything less would spoil the relationship.

6

TWO NIGHTS later, as Clyde fetched the cards and poker chips and began to lay out a cholesterol-rich array of party food, Joe was all set for an evening of imbibing the fatty diet necessary to his psychological well-being and picking up interesting bits of intelligence courtesy of the Molena Point PD, when Clyde dropped the bombshell.

"You are not invited, Joe. You are not wanted in this house when my friends are here playing poker. No more snooping. You're done listening to private police business."

"You have to be kidding."

"Not kidding. No cats on or near the poker table. No cats in the house tonight."

"You're making crab-and-olive sandwiches, you know that's my all-time favorite. And I'm not invited to the party?"

"You can take a sandwich with you. Brown-bag it."

Joe looked at Clyde intently. "You're serious. You are turning me out of my own home."

"Very serious. No more eavesdropping." Turning his back, Clyde resumed spreading crab and green olives.

"I see what's wrong. You have your nose out of joint because I was right about that wreck in Hellhag Canyon."

"Don't be silly. And even if there *was* something strange about that wreck, whatever Max Harper might, in the presence of his officers and closest friend, find fit to discuss in this house, will be restricted to those human listeners, and to no other. No tomcats. No lady cats. No snooping. *Comprende?*"

Joe drew himself up to his full, bold, muscular height, his growl rumbling, his yellow eyes blazing. "For your information, if that wreck turns out to be a murder, I'm the one who put Harper onto it. Me. The tomcat you're booting out of his own home for no conscionable reason. Without yours truly, without the information that I tipped to Max Harper, the killer would go scot-free."

Clyde turned from the counter to glare at him. "You don't have much respect for the abilities of our local law enforcement. You don't seem to think that Harper is capable of—"

"I think Harper is very capable. Why should I expect one of your limited reasoning to understand that if the brake line *was* switched, and the billfold *was* removed *before* the police got to the scene of the accident that morning, and if the wreck looked in every other way like an accident, and Harper had no information to the contrary, he would have no reason to search for evidence.

"That is a dangerous curve," Joe explained patiently.

"There has been more than one wreck there. The morning was foggy. Thick as canned cream. Without my help, Harper would have no reason to think the wreck was any more than an accident."

"I've had enough, Joe. I don't intend to argue with you. You are out of the house. Don't come home until Harper leaves. Go now. Go hunt. Go hang out on Lucinda's fence with Dulcie. Get out of here."

Joe leaped down, so incensed that, stalking through the living room, he paused long enough to deliberately, maliciously rake his claws down the arm of Clyde's new leather chair, leaving long, deep indentations just short of actual tears.

And, shouldering out through his cat door in a mood black and hateful, within three minutes—never reentering Clyde Damen's pokey little cottage—he was set up to listen to every smallest whisper from Clyde's sacrosanct poker game.

He, Joe Grey, would miss nothing.

Dulcie discovered Joe's hideaway when she came along the fence from Lucinda's. The night had turned chill, and Dirken had closed the windows. Annoyed at being shut out, she had left the Greenlaws, galloping along the fence top to see if Joe wanted to hunt.

Clyde's kitchen lights were all burning. She smelled cigarette smoke and heard Max Harper laugh. She was about to go on, knowing Joe wouldn't budge on poker night and miss some juicy bit of police gossip, when she saw the two pups behaving so strangely that she stopped to watch them.

Instead of pawing at the back door to get inside and join the party, the pups were down in the dirt beside the back porch, teasing at a vent hole, a little rectangular opening in the foundation that should have had a screen over it but was yawning, the screen cover pushed aside.

Both pups were crouched, heads down, their back-sides high in the air, their tails wagging madly as they tried to push in through the small space. Dulcie, leaping down and racing across the lawn, slipped in between their noses—and caught Joe's scent, over the reek of damp earth.

Peering into the musty blackness, she saw a flash of white—two white paws and white chest, where Joe Grey crouched atop a furnace duct, just below the kitchen floor.

A blanket of fiberglass insulation hung down, as if Joe had clawed and torn it away to bare the floor joists. Atop the heat duct, he stared up toward the kitchen, his ears cocked, his expression sly and triumphant. The voices came clearly to Dulcie.

"I'll call," Harper said. They heard the clink of poker chips dropped on the table.

Lieutenant Brennan said, "I'll raise you two." Dulcie could imagine Brennan sitting back a little from the poker table to accommodate his ample stomach. A woman's voice said, "No way, Brennan. I fold." That would be Detective Kathleen Ray, the dark-haired young detective who had worked the Winthrop Jergen case.

Not all men liked to play poker with women. Not many male cops liked women on the force. Well, these guys were okay. But just for eveners, Dulcie hoped

Kathleen Ray went home a huge winner—cleaned them out, even if they were only playing penny ante.

A loud groan announced a pot won. Clyde laughed, and they heard chips being raked in.

"Why are you down here?" Dulcie whispered. "Did you and Clyde have a fight?"

Joe cut her a scowl as sour as yesterday's cat food. "Clyde shut me out."

"He what? You can't be serious. Out of the house? But why?"

"Said he didn't want me spying on Harper."

Dulcie stared at him. "What's the matter with Clyde?"

"The minute I left, he went right out to the living room and slid the plywood cover into my cat door. Talk about cheap . . . I could claw the plywood off, go on in the living room, and listen, but I'm not giving him the satisfaction."

"I can't believe he did that. Maybe he isn't feeling well," Dulcie said softly.

"He feels just fine. His usual bad-tempered self. Earlier, when I first got down here, Harper said something about fingerprints. Clyde interrupted him—just in case I was listening." Joe gave her a narrow-eyed leer. "Well, Clyde can stuff it. I'm hanging in here until I know what Harper's found."

Dulcie snuggled next to Joe on the warm, softly insulated heat duct, settling down to listen to endless rounds of poker talk punctuated with scattered gems of police intelligence. Only when the pizza delivery guy arrived, to augment the crab sandwiches, did the ringing doorbell trigger a round of frantic barking from the backyard, and some of the conversation was lost. But then, soon, Harper's dry, slow voice seeped down through the kitchen floor again, along with the scent of pepperoni pizza.

Besides the infrared photos that Harper had taken the night he went down Hellhag Canyon, and some casts of partial footprints that Detective Ray had made, the department had one fingerprint, which Detective Ray had lifted from the engine near the brake line.

The department, contacting Landrum Antique Cars in L.A., had learned that the Corvette had been purchased only a few days before, a cash sale to a Raul Torres. "Torres," Harper said, "gave them a Portland, Oregon, address that turned out to be a vacant lot. Very likely the name is just as fake. We're waiting for the fingerprint ID. State lab's weeks behind as usual, even for a possible murder investigation."

The information should have cheered Joe; he remained dour and silent.

Clyde's poker games had been one of his best sources of information. Four or five cops playing stud poker could do a lot of talking. Clyde was the only civilian, but Harper trusted him like another cop. Maybe, Joe thought, that was why Clyde felt embarrassed to let him sit in. If Joe was lying on the poker table nibbling at the chips and dip, Clyde could hardly halt the conversation, could hardly tell Harper and his officers not to talk in front of the cat.

"So what the hell," Joe said softly but angrily, as the poker game resumed. "All I've ever done is help Harper. Without the evidence you and I turned up, several of those no-goodniks sitting in state prison right now would be out on the street, to say nothing of Troy Hoke cooling his heels for murder in the federal pen."

Dulcie curled closer to Joe and licked his ear. She had never seen him and Clyde at such odds.

But it was when Harper mentioned Lucinda Greenlaw that Dulcie's own temper flared.

"Your neighbor," Harper said. "In the old Victorian house behind you. You know her very well?"

"Lucinda? Not really," Clyde said. "Wilma sees her pretty often."

"She's an early-morning walker," Harper said.

"I don't really know. What's the interest?"

"Houseful of relatives right now gathered for Shamas's funeral. Pretty loud bunch, I'm told."

"They don't bother me. I don't hear them."

"Had a talk with Lucinda yesterday," Harper said. "Asked her to come down to the station, give me a few minutes away from the family." There was a pause. The cats could smell cigarette smoke.

"She walks on Hellhag Hill a lot. I asked her if she'd happened to be up there the morning that Corvette went over into Hellhag Canyon."

"And?" Clyde said shortly.

"Said she hadn't been, that she'd stayed home that day. You . . . didn't happen to notice her that morning? Happen to see her go out?"

"What the hell, Max? No, I didn't happen to notice. What is this? What time are you talking about?"

"Around six-thirty. The 911 call came in, from someone in the trailer park, about that time."

"At six-thirty I'm in the shower," Clyde said testily. "Or just getting out of bed. Not staring out my back window at the neighbors."

Harper said no more. The talk from that point was limited to poker. The game ended early. The cats, dropping down from the heat duct, slipped out through the vent, forcing the pups aside, and headed for the open hills.

They hunted most of the night, until the first gray of dawn streaked the sky. Joe's mood brightened once they'd killed a big buck rabbit and shared it. Settling back to wash blood and rabbit fur from his paws, he said, "Do you think she might have seen something that morning? Maybe saw one of Shamas's relatives down there, around the canyon, and didn't want to tell Harper?"

Dulcie shrugged. "I don't think she cares enough about any of Shamas's relatives to protect them—well, maybe she cares about Pedric and Newlon. But would she lie for them?"

Joe looked at her intently.

"What are you thinking? That's stretching it, Joe, to look for a connection between the Greenlaws and that wreck."

"Why *does* she walk so early?"

Her green eyes widened. "You're as bad as Harper. She likes to be alone. You're a cat, you should understand that kind of need." She rose. "Fog's blowing in. She'll walk this morning. Come see for yourself." And she spun away at a dead run across the hills, perhaps running from a nudge of unease, from the faint discomfort that Joe's questions stirred.

Down two valleys and across open hills they ran, through a little orchard and a pasture and up Hellhag Hill—to find Lucinda already there. They paused when they saw her, and went on quietly through the tall, concealing grass, watching Lucinda climb through the drifting fog to the outcropping of boulders where she liked to sit.

Dropping her small blanket and her jacket, she moved on beyond the rocks some twenty feet to a stand of broom bushes. There, producing a package from her canvas tote, she arranged its contents on an aluminum pie plate; the cats caught the scent of roast beef, probably leftovers from last night's supper. Setting the plate among the bushes, she pushed it deep enough in so it was sheltered, but she would be able to see it.

"The wild cats," Dulcie whispered. "They'll come through the bushes from deeper in."

Among the boulders, Lucinda made herself comfortable on her folded blanket. Quietly turning, she looked up behind her in the direction of the trailer park. The cats didn't think she could see the trailers from that angle, nor could the occupants see her. There was no one else on the hill, yet she scanned the empty slopes expectantly, looking across the grassy rises and down toward the sea.

"She's watching for the wild cats," Dulcie whispered—but she wasn't sure. Lucinda seemed unusually tense, to be watching only for the cats she fed.

"Why do you follow her, Dulcie?"

"I don't know. Sometimes . . . sometimes when she's here on the hills, she seems almost to be listening." She glanced at Joe. "Almost as if she hears some sound, something—"

"What kind of sound?" he said irritably.

"Some . . . something . . . stirring within the hill."

Joe scowled and flattened his ears; he didn't like that

kind of talk. She said no more, not mentioning that one day she had seen Lucinda lie down in the grass and press her ear to the earth.

Maybe Lucinda had only been feeling the beat of the sea throbbing through the hill? Could Lucinda feel that vibration, as a cat could? Or had she simply been resting, comforted by the earth's solid warmth?

It had seemed a very personal moment. Dulcie had felt embarrassed watching her.

"Maybe she thinks she hears the ghost," Joe said.

"Maybe." The local yarns that had given Hellhag Hill its name described a crazy old man, living a hundred years ago in a shanty atop Hellhag Hill, who spent his time throwing clods at trespassers, and who had been stoned, in turn, by a band of village boys; two days later he had died from the wounds to his head and chest. The story said that his spirit had entered inside the hill, and, even to the present day, he haunted the cave that yawned higher up Hellhag Hill—an angry and possessive ghost drawing the winds to him and screaming out at strangers; sometimes you could hear his shouts and curses.

Early-morning joggers claimed to have seen the ghost, but in the coastal fog one could imagine seeing anything. Tourists came to look for the hag, and spun wonderful stories to take home.

Lucinda waited patiently, they supposed for any small sign of the stray cats approaching the food she had left. The shy animals didn't show themselves. Only when she rose at last and headed back, the hill now bright with sun, did the strays come out.

They appeared swiftly behind her, thin, wary, dark-faced cats crowding around the pie plate, snatching up the old lady's offerings. Dulcie and Joe remained very still, watching them. The fog had blown away, the ragged cliffs below emerging dark and wild, the sea black and heaving, the narrow ribbon of highway glistening wet— only the crest of the hill seemed to be warmed by the rising sun. A scream startled Joe and Dulcie. They leaped for shelter. The strays vanished. Lucinda, halfway across the hill, stopped and turned, looking below her.

The yelp came again: It was a dog, one of the pups. The cats knew that voice. A pup yowling with pain and fear. They reared up in the grass to see.

There was no car on the highway to have hurt a puppy. Stretching taller, they saw Clyde and Charlie standing at the edge of the road staring back toward the village. Charlie held the bigger pup on a leash—that was the pup she had named Hestig. The pup fought his lead, lunging and trying to bolt away, his feet sliding on the asphalt as he tried to join his brother, who raced madly toward the village, yipping and screaming.

Clinging to Selig's back was a small animal, a dark little creature yowling and clawing, its fluffy tail lashing with rage. When Selig swerved from the road, the little animal rode him like a bronc-buster; they vanished among the houses.

Joe stared after them, torn between amazement and a huge belly laugh. "So that was what the pups were afraid of—a mangy little cat. That's why they didn't want to come up Hellhag Hill."

Below them, down the hill, Clyde stood on the road, staring at where the pup had vanished. "What *was* that thing? What kind of wild—"

"Cat," Charlie said, doubled over laughing, and trying to hold the plunging Hestig.

"No, not a cat. It was some kind of wild animal. No cat would . . . My God. A cat?"

"A very small cat," Charlie said. "And very, very mad." She knelt and pulled Hestig close to her, stroking him and speaking softly until he became quiet. "A cat, Clyde. A tiny, angry little cat." She watched Clyde take off jogging, hoping to round up Selig. "They never," she told Hestig, "cats never cease to surprise me."

"I hope," Dulcie whispered, "that little cat finds her way back." She imagined the little stray leaping off Selig's back in the middle of the village, confused among so many cars and people, not knowing where to run.

"Those cats might be wild and shy," Joe said, "but they haven't survived without being clever. She'll be okay. Why was Clyde walking the dogs here? The highway's no place for those two."

"Do you think he came to follow Lucinda, after Harper's questions about her?"

"After he ragged *me* for being nosy? That would be more than low."

They watched Lucinda, across the hill, hurrying down to join Charlie; Charlie had slowed, waiting for her. Lucinda fell into step, smiling as if she had enjoyed the spectacle of runaway Selig, as if she had liked seeing one of the wild, shy felines show some unexpected spunk.

Lucinda and Charlie had known each other only casually, through Wilma, until Shamas's death drew Wilma, herself, to see Lucinda more often. Then Charlie, with her usual warmth, had taken a deeper interest in the old woman. Gently, Charlie put her arm around Lucinda, gave her a hug. "Did you see poor Selig? Was that one of the little cats you've been feeding?"

"I believe it was," Lucinda said, laughing. "Wild is the word for that one."

"How many cats are there, Lucinda? Are they all that wild? Where did they come from?"

"I think there are six or seven. They appeared a few days after the quake. I only get glimpses of them, usually one at a time. Only that dark little cat—the one that just rode away on the back of Clyde's dog—only that one has had the nerve to approach me."

"Cat the color of charred wood," Charlie said with interest. "Black and brown swirled together on the palette."

"Tortoiseshell," Lucinda said.

"They must be glad of the food you bring. Though surely they are hunters."

"I'm sure they are. They're most likely feral cats, they're far too shy to be simply strays."

The old woman was silent a moment. Joe and Dulcie slipped quickly through the grass, following close behind the two women. "Maybe," Lucinda said, "Pedric would have some knowledge about feral cats. Pedric is Shamas's first cousin. He seems to have some interesting theories about—feral animals." She hesitated. "Strange theories, maybe. But these cats strike one as rather strange."

"Is Pedric the thin old man? The one of slighter build?"

"Yes, that's Pedric." She glanced at Charlie. "He's . . . very kind. He's one of Shamas's relatives that I . . . feel comfortable with. He and Newlon Greenlaw. Newlon . . . tried to save Shamas, you know."

Charlie nodded.

"Pedric is . . . perhaps not as harsh as the others. Perhaps he has more of the old-country ways," Lucinda said shyly. "Pedric Greenlaw might have stepped right out of his own myths, out of the same dark and shadowed worlds that shape his folktales."

"He sounds interesting," Charlie said, pushing back her windblown red hair. "I've always loved storytellers. It's a wonderful art: the skill to draw you in, make you see and live a tale as if you were there, to truly wrap you in the story."

"Pedric . . . I think he looks at life through the lens of his stories . . . through the lens of dead ages. He clings to the old myths just as Shamas did, to the Irish beliefs and folklore woven through their family. That history was very important to Shamas."

"I didn't know that about your husband."

Lucinda smiled. "All the Greenlaws live to some extent a strange double existence. I think that in many ways they truly believe the old tales—believe in the old-world magic."

She glanced at Charlie. "And yet another part of them—except perhaps Pedric and Newlon—is as cold and selfish as it is possible to be. That . . . that is the way Shamas was."

Charlie turned to look at her.

"Well, I'm not grieving for Shamas," Lucinda said softly. "If I am grieving, it is only . . . for myself, for what I have . . . missed."

And, Dulcie thought, *grieving for a life wasted*. She thought about what Lucinda had told Wilma, in a moment like this when Lucinda seemed to feel the need to talk, perhaps to bare a bit of her soul.

Lucinda had come to have tea with Wilma; Dulcie had been lying in her favorite spot on the blue velvet couch pretending to nap. Lucinda told Wilma that when the police came to her door that morning to tell her that Shamas was dead, she'd felt a drop of emotion straight down into panic, and then, almost at once, she'd been swept by a surge of relief so powerful that she'd tried to hide it from the officers, such a sense of freedom, of elation that the painful burden had gone from her life, that Shamas's lies and cheating were ended. That she could, at last, know some peace. Her words had seemed to spring from such a strong need to unburden herself; and when Wilma put her arm around her, Lucinda wept helplessly.

She told Wilma that she should have walked away from Shamas years before, should have taken the responsibility to change her life, but that she'd never been brave enough. Had never had the courage to walk out on Shamas Greenlaw.

But Charlie was saying, "Wherever those wild cats came from, the little creatures are lucky to have you, Lucinda." Gently, Charlie shortened Hestig's leash, to make him walk by her heel.

"Maybe with time," Lucinda said, "they'll grow tame, and I can find homes for them. The strange thing is," she said, glancing at Charlie, "how powerfully those wild cats draw me. I don't usually think about stray animals; the world is full of strays, and I can't change the world. But these cats . . ." Lucinda shrugged. "Maybe they're something to hold on to, just now. Something outside myself, to love and care about."

Charlie smiled at her, and nodded.

"Perhaps," Lucinda said, "it's their freedom, too, that

draws me—and the mystery of why they appeared so suddenly on Hellhag Hill, where, in all my years of walking there, I've seldom seen any creature."

The two women turned down Ocean onto the grassy median, Hestig walking sedately at Charlie's side, watching his manners now, as if the spectacle of a cat attacking his brother had made a lasting impression. If the pup was aware of Joe and Dulcie slipping through the shadows behind him beneath the eucalyptus trees, he gave no sign other than to twitch an ear back, once, and wag casually. And soon Lucinda turned away, not toward her own street as she usually did, but in the opposite direction, into the heart of the village, leaving Charlie and Hestig to cross to Charlie's apartment above the shops on Ocean.

None of the shops was yet open, but the little cafés were busy. The cats followed Lucinda, padding along behind, dodging joggers and dog walkers. The old lady was just passing the post office, watching a yardman across the street watering the planter beds in front of Cannady's, that nice Western shop that Dulcie loved, which had such beautiful embroidered denim and leathers. Cannady's front garden was brilliant with impatiens and lilies, behind its low wrought-iron fence. Lucinda had stopped to admire the garden when Dirken and Newlon Greenlaw came around the corner—and immediately Lucinda drew back into the shadows, stood very still, watching them.

The two men were walking slowly just at the curb, so close to the line of parked cars that the cats heard Newlon's jacket brush against a rearview mirror. Both men walked hunched, their heads bent as if looking into the car windows.

It took only a second. The two were quick; they paused, the cats heard a little click as if a car door had opened, another click as it closed again, and the men moved on, Newlon shoving something into his jacket pocket, some small item he had snatched from the seat of the car. A camera? A purse? Perhaps a cell phone.

Lucinda stood staring, a look of shock and anger on her face—a look as if she had been personally affronted.

Then she turned away and hurried into the Swiss House, taking refuge in the first empty booth, busying herself with the menu. The cats, leaping up onto the window box among the flowers, watched her ordering, watched her settle back sipping her coffee. Lucinda was more than usually pale, and her thin old hands were shaking.

7

Dino's HAD the best fish and chips in the village.
Max Harper, having picked up an order of takeout, sat
in his king cab pickup eating his dinner and watching,
through the lighted motel window across the street,
Cara Ray Crisp skinning out of her sweatshirt. Cara Ray
hadn't bothered to pull the blinds. She was only a slip of
a thing, tiny and thin, but well endowed, the kind of delicate creature who would have appealed exactly to
Shamas Greenlaw.

Harper had backed his truck into a narrow drive
between Harren's Gallery and Molena Point Drugs, a
lane so overgrown with jasmine that the vines trailed
across the truck's roof and down the side windows. For
some time Cara Ray had talked on the phone, lying
nude on the bed, propped against the pillows, sipping
on a canned drink; and now she was tying on a bikini
top. As he watched her roll her long blond hair into a
knot and secure it, and pull on the bottom half of her

bathing suit, Harper had no notion that he, in turn, was watched, from the backseat of the king cab.

Sitting on the cab floor behind Harper, peering up between the bucket seats, Joe Grey could see through the windshield the little pantomime in Cara Ray's lighted motel room, and he had to smile. Max Harper, spying on Cara Ray's strip act like some cheap voyeur, would be enjoying every rousing minute—free entertainment served up with his takeout dinner, all in the line of duty.

The fish and chips smelled so good that Joe was tempted to slash out with a quick paw and snag a nice warm chunk of fried cod. Maybe Harper wouldn't miss just one piece. Why was it that, so often when he did a bit of surveillance, the watchee enjoyed a nice meal, while the watcher ended up faint with hunger?

As Cara Ray stepped to the window, Harper drew back behind a lifted newspaper. She stood looking down at the street, then turned away again, a towel over her shoulder as if she were headed for the pool: a little break between her callous and bad-mannered visits to Lucinda Greenlaw. She'd been to see the old woman three times in three days, the last encounter stretching into dinner and on to midnight—Dulcie said the sleek little blonde had made herself very much at home among the male Greenlaws, drawing the cousins and nephews to her like flies to honey, despite the fact that the Greenlaw clan didn't take quickly to strangers. She said Newlon and Dirken had been all over Cara Ray. "No queen in heat, with a dozen toms raking around her, has any more nerve than that one."

Cara Ray had pulled up at Lucinda's that first day in a gleaming new Jaguar, wearing a fur wrap against the chill of Molena Point's ocean breeze. The mink and the car, Dulcie said, were very likely gifts from Shamas. Lucinda had answered the door wearing a voluminous apron and wiping flour from her hands.

"I'm Shamas's friend, Mrs. Greenlaw. From the boat. I was there the night Shamas died."

Talk about brass. And Lucinda too polite to send her packing. The older woman had asked Cara Ray in and even made tea for her. Dulcie had watched, disgusted, as they settled down before the fire. But the day was chill, and through the closed windows, she couldn't hear a word; it wasn't necessary, though. From their expressions and Cara Ray's body language, even a dunce could see that the little blonde was buttering up Lucinda shamefully.

The moment Lucinda rose to make fresh tea, Cara Ray had gone into action.

She was swift and thorough, riffling through Lucinda's desk and through her checkbook. She had begun on the books that lined the fireplace, reaching behind the lower rows to feel along the walls, when she heard Lucinda return.

Lucinda entered the room to see Cara Ray sitting innocently cuddled in her chair beside the hearth.

Of course Dulcie couldn't leave that little episode alone; since Cara Ray's arrival, Dulcie had hung on the fence every waking moment. If Molena Point Library had a resident cat, she was not currently in residence; she hardly went home for meals. Cara Ray returned the next day and the next, and Dulcie was there. Again on the third day Cara Ray stayed until midnight.

Now, with Joe and Dulcie's "meddling," as Clyde would put it, with Dulcie's anonymous suggestion to

Harper, the captain was—pardon the pun—taking a good look at Cara Ray. It had begun earlier that afternoon, when Harper had stopped by Clyde's and mentioned he had a make on Raul Torres, and Joe and Dulcie decided to take a ride.

It was Saturday, and at Harper's suggestion, Clyde planned to take Selig up to Harper's pasture to work on the pup's obedience training in a large, open area. The two pups were impossible together; Charlie had taken Hestig home to her apartment. She and Clyde couldn't even attend the same obedience class; the pups did nothing but taunt each other, play on each other's foolishness. Joe had been shocked out of his claws when Clyde actually signed up for the class at the community center.

Surprisingly, both pups had learned to *Sit*, to *Come* on command, and, sometimes, to take the sitting position at *Heel*—except when they were together. Then they were oblivious, had never before heard those words, had no notion what they meant.

So that afternoon Harper, still in uniform, had taken a few hours off, left his unit parked in front of Clyde's, and he and Clyde had headed up the hills in Clyde's '34 Chevy, the convertible top folded down, Selig securely tethered in the rumble seat—and Joe and Dulcie concealed on the little shelf behind the seats, beneath the folded leather top.

It was hot as sin in there, but, crouched just behind the men's heads, they could hear every word.

"You started to tell me about this accident victim," Clyde said, turning up Ocean. "Torres, you said?" He seemed far more willing to talk with Harper about the case when he thought Joe wasn't around.

"Raul Torres. He did give the antique car agency his right name. Torres was a PI working out of Seattle. I don't know why he used the fake address. Maybe he used that routinely, for security reasons." Even Max Harper, Joe thought with interest, seemed more comfortable relating information in a supposedly cat-free environment.

"I called Torres's office a dozen times before I got his secretary. She was closemouthed until I identified myself. Said she'd call me back. While I waited, she called the station, checked me out. Called me back to say Torres was on vacation, that she didn't expect to hear from him for maybe another week. She'd gone in to do the billing.

"I told her Torres was dead. Took her a few minutes to take that in. When she felt like talking again, she said she'd made reservations for Torres at the Oak Breeze, in Molena Point, beginning last Saturday. That he'd gone down to L.A. on a case, had planned to leave there Saturday, was meeting someone in Molena Point Saturday night, a woman—girlfriend, she said."

"You find a motel registration?" Clyde asked as he turned up the long dirt road leading to Harper's acreage.

"Nothing under Torres, not in Molena Point. But the fact he was a PI keeps me digging."

"So he was a PI," Clyde said. "That doesn't mean he was murdered."

"Of course not," Harper said, amused. "But it does make me wonder."

The house at the end of the lane was white clapboard, with a four-stall barn behind and an open, roofed hay shed. The stable yard was shaded by three huge live oak trees, the garden weedy and neglected since Harper's wife died. They pulled up beside the barn, and while the two men were occupied tying a long, thin line to Selig's choke chain, the cats, panting from the heat, slipped out from under the folded leather top and beat it for the hay shed.

Scorching up the stacked bales to crouch high beneath the shadowed roof, they watched Harper head for the house and return carrying two cans of Coke. The slam of the screen door started Selig barking, and Clyde couldn't shut him up.

One word from Harper, and the pup was silent.

Clyde scowled at Harper and led Selig out into the pasture; the puppy pressed his nose immediately to the ground, jerking on the lead, ignoring Clyde, snuffling deeply at the delicious scent of horse manure.

Dulcie made herself comfortable on the baled hay, raking her claws deep. "Torres died Sunday morning," she said softly.

Joe rolled over, slapping at straws, and turned to look at her.

"If Torres drove up from L.A. Saturday," she said, "and if he was with a woman in the village on Saturday night, as his secretary told Harper, then what was he doing driving south again, before dawn on Sunday?

"And who was the woman?" Her green eyes narrowed. "Cara Ray told Lucinda she arrived Saturday. Don't you think it strange that Torres and Cara Ray would come to Molena Point on exactly the same day?"

"Dulcie . . ."

"Torres worked in Seattle. Shamas still had a business there."

"So?"

"Lucinda told Wilma that when Shamas went up to Seattle she was sure he took a woman with him, not someone from Molena Point but someone he'd meet at the San Francisco airport—Lucinda did keep an eye on his phone bills."

Dulcie smiled smugly. "Cara Ray lives in San Francisco, not too far from the airport. Shamas flew to Seattle, out of that airport, about once a month.

"So?" Joe said.

"Cara Ray was Shamas's lover. But was she Torres's lover, too? Did she see Torres, as well, when she was in Seattle? She must have been busy."

Joe rolled over again, scratching his back against the rough straw; he looked at her upside down. "Say you're right, Torres was in Molena Point to meet Cara Ray. What was he doing on the highway, Sunday morning?"

"Maybe they had a fight. Maybe he drove off mad, and that's why he skidded."

"What about the other car—the second car I heard, just before the crash?"

"Could someone else have known he was here? Cut his brake line, then—maybe phoned him, brought him out on some wild-goose chase, maybe something to do with the case he was working on in L.A.? That might explain why he was headed south again. Then they followed him, in the heavy fog, and honked to confuse him?"

"That's really reaching for it, Dulcie."

"Whatever the truth, there's a connection. Cara Ray and this Torres didn't just happen to arrive in the same town, on the same day. And why was Cara Ray snooping through Lucinda's papers?"

Joe sighed at the monumental tangles that female logic could weave. "Even if there was a connection, we can't pass on that kind of shaky guesswork to Harper."

"Maybe no one's mentioned Cara Ray to him. Maybe he has no reason to be interested in her. If he doesn't know about the Seattle connection . . ."

"Dulcie . . ."

"We'd only be telling him the name of the woman Torres may have met. What harm in that?"

"Maybe. But we can't call Harper from here."

"Why not? There's a phone on his belt."

"Do you see a phone in this hay shed?"

She gave him a sweet, green-eyed smile. "There in the dinette, you can see it through the bay window; the phone's right there on the table."

Joe sighed.

"Go up on the shed roof, Joe. Where I can see you from the house. Signal me if he heads that way." She leaped down the baled hay and was gone, streaking for the screen door.

Joe rose and shook the hay off. Sometimes Dulcie was impossible. He swarmed up a post to the roof of the shed. Impossible, clever, and enchanting.

Clyde thought that he, Joe Grey, got rabid over a robbery or suspicious death. But Dulcie set her teeth into a murder case as if she were fighting rattlesnakes.

Keeping low, out of the men's view, and trying not to let his claws scritch on the galvanized roof, Joe slipped to the edge, where he could see the house.

Behind the bay window, a small shape moved, padding across the table.

Watching her paw at the phone, he remembered the night they'd memorized Harper's various phone numbers from Clyde's phone file. Clyde had pitched a fit because they'd left a few tooth marks in the cards; he could be so picky. It was a huge stroke of luck that Pacific Bell had recently offered free blocking for that insidious caller ID service that so many phones had subscribed to—including Molena Point PD.

Harper had caller ID blocking for his own phones, and with a little encouragement Clyde had come around—it was free, wasn't it?

Wilma, always sensible, had subscribed at once. Wilma told Clyde there was no way he could stop Joe using the phone. She said if Clyde wanted to save himself acute embarrassment, he'd better go along with the blocking.

Out in the field, Clyde stood fifty feet away from Selig, his arm raised in an exaggerated signal, shouting "Sit! Sit, stay."

Selig grinned at him and bounced around, playing with the nylon line that was supposed to control him.

Max Harper stood looking on, trying not to laugh. Faintly, Joe heard Harper's phone buzz.

Harper picked up, and listened. An irritated look spread across his lean face. His replies were brief. But he didn't hang up.

Harper might not like these anonymous phone calls, might not like the unsettling and impossible suppositions that they stirred, but he didn't ignore them.

Behind Harper, Clyde walked across the field to Selig. With a lot of pushing, he made the pup sit. Then backing away, holding the line, Clyde didn't take his eyes from the pup. The object was to get maybe fifty feet from Selig, making sure he remained sitting, to wait for a little while, then call him. The trainee was supposed to sit still until summoned by the trainer, then run directly to him and sit again, facing the tall human god.

What actually occurred was that the pup kept moving his butt around, only barely remaining in the sitting position, wild to lunge and run, and when Clyde did finally call him, Selig ran around Clyde, circling until Clyde's legs were wrapped in the line. Harper, scowling into the phone, couldn't help a lopsided grin as the pup hog-tied Clyde like a roped calf.

So far Clyde had made five attempts at this maneuver. During the first four lessons, Selig, when he was called, had run in the opposite direction, his nose to the ground.

Harper still had the phone to his ear, his expression sour but thoughtful. Dulcie would be telling him that Raul Torres arrived in Molena Point the same day as Cara Ray Crisp. That Cara Ray was staying at the Oak Breeze Motel. Dulcie wouldn't elaborate on that point. She'd probably say something like, *I know it's not really police business. Yet. Unless, of course, Shamas Greenlaw didn't die naturally.* Joe could almost hear her whispering into the phone, *Don't you wonder, Captain Harper, why a PI from Seattle—where Shamas used to live, where Shamas still had a business—would plan to meet Shamas's lover in Molena Point just two weeks after Shamas was drowned?*

Joe watched Harper tuck the phone into his belt and cross the field to Clyde. If Harper had paid attention to that phone call, and if he meant to head back to the village to check on Cara Ray, he'd have to take either Clyde's car or his own pickup; he'd left his police unit parked in front of Clyde's place. Harper hadn't made a call after Dulcie hung up, as if to send one of his officers to check on Cara Ray.

Harper and Clyde stood talking, then Harper headed toward the house. Joe, flattening himself against the metal roof, was about to signal Dulcie when Harper turned toward the stable, where his pickup was parked.

Joe beat him there. As Harper stepped into the cab, Joe had slid behind him into the back section of the king cab—avoiding the slamming door by a split second. There'd been no time to get Dulcie, she was still in the house.

He'd hoped she wasn't snooping around Harper's place, prying into the police captain's personal life. She was so nosy. Oh, that would be too low.

Joe had liked the feel of the big truck careening down the hills, had listened to Harper calling the motel office, asking the location of Cara Ray Crisp's room and if she had anyone with her. Not until Harper had stopped for takeout did Joe realize how hungry he was. The aroma of fish and chips had been almost more than he could stand. Then Harper was backing into the alley, Joe drooling for a bite of fried cod.

But now the cod was gone. And Cara Ray Crisp had turned out her light and left her room. Joe listened to Harper wad up the sack and napkins and stuff them in the trash bin. Wind swirled into the cab as Harper opened the door.

And Joe was alone, shut into Harper's pickup, the door slammed practically in his face.

Leaping to the back of the front seat, he watched Harper cross the street into the patio of the Oak Breeze and move on past the pool toward the manager's office, never glancing toward Cara Ray as she descended the stairs and chose a chaise by the pool. Dropping her towel across it, she stretched out.

Cara Ray was not the only sunbather. Half a dozen other greased bodies reclined like oiled sardines laid out on grids to dry. The sun was low, but the evening was still warm, the pool as blue as the eyes of a rutting Siamese.

The police captain, moving on into the office, would quickly find out when Cara Ray had checked in, what name and credit card she had used, if she had arrived in a car, if Raul Torres had been registered, if Cara Ray had registered for a single or double, if she had been seen with anyone.

But, Joe wondered, if she had come here to meet Torres, and Torres came up missing, why hadn't Cara Ray gone directly to the police? Why wasn't she looking for the guy?

With questions buzzing in his head as thick as flies on stale cat food, he watched a young man come around the corner from the direction of the parking lot, wearing loose swim trunks, flip-flops, and an open shirt, heading for the pool. Choosing a chaise near Cara Ray but facing the opposite direction, he adjusted the back to a moderate recline, made himself comfortable, and opened a newspaper.

Behind the paper, he spoke; he didn't look around at Cara Ray. He was a big-boned, wide-shouldered guy. Square jaw, sandy hair, and freckles—*If this guy isn't a Greenlaw*, Joe thought, *yours truly is a ring-tailed gorilla*.

And was he staying at the Oak Breeze? Or had he parked in the visitors' lot behind the motel? As far as Joe knew, none of the Greenlaws was staying in a motel; they were all too tight with their cash. Had this guy met Cara Ray at Lucinda's and made a date with her? Or were they old friends? And why the secrecy?

Dropping down onto the front seat of the king cab, Joe fought the door handle, pawing and pulling at it—but even his considerable tomcat strength was almost no match for General Motors. He got the door open at last, bruising his paws. Within seconds Joe was across the street crouching in the geraniums that bordered the wide tile patio, looking out at Cara Ray reclining on her chaise beside the long, blue pool.

8

T HE GERANIUM thicket was dense and tall enough
to conceal a dozen tomcats, but the long stretch of tiled
paving beyond it, between Joe Grey and his quarry,
offered no cover. Away across the open patio, Cara Ray
and the man behind the newspaper were speaking quietly. Cara Ray, stretched out on her chaise on her stomach, had untied her bikini bra to avoid strap marks, her
well-oiled body highlighting a golden tan. Joe, watching her lips moving, tried to tell what she was saying,
but he wasn't any good at lipreading. He supposed, like
most things in life, that skill took some effort to master.
Near him under the geranium leaves, a sparrow was
hopping, picking up seeds, forcing Joe to exercise every
ounce of self-control not to snatch the dumb little
morsel and chomp him.

The flowers were so pungent and spicy that his fur
would smell like geraniums for the next week. Beneath

his paws, the earth was damp; as he sauntered out onto the patio he left a trail across the tiles of dark, wet paw-prints.

Cara Ray had her eyes closed. Joe lay down beneath her chaise, behind her visitor, stretching out on the warm tile paving. His view up through the webbing was of Cara Ray's cheek and a lot of her anatomy. She smelled like coconut oil. He couldn't see her companion's face, only the breadth of his shoulders, and his legs and feet, which were indecently hairy, for a human. Dark, curly hair, though the hair on his head was light. His body had the kind of tan that, once it has peaked, begins to look dull and flaking. Compared with Cara Ray's blond radiance, he looked like a dust-covered mannequin that someone had dragged from an attic and posed on the chaise with an open newspaper.

"Are you sure you didn't find anything, Cara Ray? Where were you looking?"

"Sam, you'd know if I did. It's only been three days. Sitting in that old woman's stuffy parlor drinking tea until I think I'll throw up—and at night, listening to their boring stories. Grown men and women, telling fairy tales." She raised her head to look at him. "*You* made yourself scarce enough." Glancing down, she saw Joe under her chaise, and caught her breath. Snatching up her towel, she flapped it at him. "Shoo. Shoo."

Joe rose and moved away, out of her line of sight.

"Wha'd you want me to do, Cara Ray, jump up and throw my arms around you? Anyway, who'd have the chance, with Cousin Dirken all over you?"

Cara Ray laughed. "Farting around repairing that house. What a joke." She glared under the chaise, didn't see Joe.

Sam sniggered. "Pulling off the siding, chopping holes in that old cement and filling 'em up again." He fished a pack of cigarettes from his shirt pocket, carefully selected one from the center, where it presumably wasn't crushed, and lit up. "Dirken tags me around every minute I'm at the house, won't let me out of his sight. Nearly has palsy if I head out into the yard."

She half rose, holding the bra. "If he watches you so close, then how do you think *I* can do any better? He tags me, too—as bad as Newlon."

"When Dirken watches you, Cara Ray, his mind isn't on what you're looking for. More likely on what he's *wanting* to look for."

She bellowed out a laugh, an alarming bray for such a sleek, petite lady.

"And the old woman?" he said. "She suspect anything?"

"Not a clue. Dim as a blind deacon passing the collection plate." She rolled over on her back, clutching her untied bra to herself, revealing more white skin than tan. "What about Torres?"

He lowered the paper and raised up, looking around at the other sunbathers. "Torres died in an accident, Cara Ray. His brakes failed." He half turned, his face in profile behind the raised newspaper. "It's time you got some results out of that old woman."

She sat up, straddling the chaise, tying on her bra. "I'm working on it. You think I can just waltz in there and make nice to his *widow*, right away we're bosom buddies? You think that dry old biddy is going to trust me? Share all her girlie secrets, right down to what Shamas was like in bed—if she can remember that far back. You think she's going to cozy up to me the way she does to Pedric? And we don't need that buddy-buddy stuff, either, between those two. I think . . ."

"Well, *I* have to be careful, Cara Ray. You know my old parole officer lives in this burg."

"Not likely you'll run into him. Why would you? If you stay out of jail."

"It's a her. And I damn sure might run into her. She and Lucinda are thicker than cats in a bowl of cream. All I need is for that bitch to get on my case. She sent me back twice, always hassling me. Sent me right damn back to federal prison."

"So? You're clean now. You told me you were clean."

He glanced back at her and smiled.

She laughed. "If you . . ." She stopped speaking, rolled over suddenly onto her belly, hiding her face.

Joe, stretching up to see what had startled her, backed deeper under the chaise as the uniformed captain swung out of the motel office. Harper didn't seem to notice Cara Ray, not a blink as he headed across the patio toward the street. Joe kept his head down, hiding the white strip on his face and his white paws, muttering a little cat prayer that Harper, watching Cara Ray out of the corner of his eye, wouldn't notice one small, gray, immobile hunk of cat fur crouching in the shadow under the chaise.

Leaving the patio, Harper walked right on past his king cab, never glancing at it. Probably he'd leave the truck parked between the buildings under the jasmine vine until Cara Ray and her friend had left the pool area. It was just after Harper left that the conversation turned even more murky. Sam, turning the newspaper page as if he were reading, said, "I need to move on, Cara Ray. Before the funeral. I've details to tend to."

"You leave before the funeral," she snapped, "don't you think someone will wonder? The funeral's what you came for. And as to the machine sales, that little adventure was your idea, not mine."

"One road leads to the other, Cara Ray."

"What about the boat? The cops been back on it?"

"Why would they? They got no reason. And what would they find? There's nothing *to* find." He snapped the newspaper irritably. "It was an accident, Cara Ray."

"One road leads to the other, Sam, only if you make a track between them." Cara Ray rose; her look was as brittle as broken glass. Heading for the stairs, her blue eyes and delicate features shone as cold as an arctic ice field.

9

T HE TEA tray, on the coffee table before the fire, was set with Wilma's hand-thrown ceramic cups and saucers and arranged with an assortment of lemon bars, scones, and fruit-filled custards. The blazing fire cast bright reflections across Wilma's deep-toned oriental rug and across the blue velvet couch and love seat. Above the mantel, a rich Jeannot painting of the Molena Point hills lent further richness to the cozy room. Behind Wilma's cherry desk, the white shutters were open to the stormy afternoon, framing the old oak trees that twisted across her tangled flower garden. Wilma had put on a CD of Pete Fountain, the bright clarinet jazz filling the house with its happy sound. Dulcie sat on Wilma's desk, her green eyes deeply amused. They were waiting for Lucinda.

"It was a cat," Dulcie was telling Wilma. "A tiny little cat, riding that big pup. You should have seen Selig racing away with the littlest, scruffiest kitten you can imagine raking his backside. Kitten the color of charred wood, and fierce—angry as a tiger."

It seemed to Dulcie that all her world suddenly was filled with young animals, both exasperating and lovable. She had spent the morning sitting on Clyde's back fence beside Joe, watching as Clyde tried to train Selig. Selig had accepted the command, *Sit*. He knew what it meant, and he obeyed when the mood struck him. But *Down* seemed a position with which he was not conversant. Clyde might be a fine auto mechanic, but as a dog trainer he was about as effective as a declawed cat in a room full of Rottweilers.

Wilma adjusted the quilted tea cozy and glanced across at Dulcie. "Where do you suppose those cats came from? You always told me the hill wasn't inviting to cats, that the village cats didn't like to go there."

"Sometimes it does seem a frightening place," Dulcie said. "But that young cat doesn't seem to mind; she acts as if the whole hill belongs to her."

Dulcie licked a bit of scone and custard that Wilma had put on a small flowered plate for her. "I saw those cats, the first time, a week after the earthquake, slipping across the hill like shadows. I couldn't get close, I could hardly see them except the little dark one. She stopped and looked back at me, stood for a long time, staring, before she raced away. I thought she wanted to come nearer, but then she'd glance behind her almost as if the others didn't want her to get friendly."

Dulcie smiled. "She's a terrible little morsel, with that dirty blackish-and-brown fur all matted and sticking out every which way. No more than skin over bones, and she can't be four months old."

"Do you suppose they lost their home in the earth-quake?" Wilma asked.

"Maybe," Dulcie said. "Maybe they're a small feral colony that fled up the coast when the quake hit." The epicenter of the earthquake had been some eighty miles to the south of Molena Point. "Maybe they're from one of those managed colonies that you read about."

Occasionally, Dulcie's favorite cat magazines would do a story about feral-cat colonies that were fed by groups of volunteers, people who trapped the cats to treat them for illnesses or injuries and give them their shots, then turned them loose again, to live free.

"Little feral kittens," she said softly.

Wilma stopped fussing with the tea tray and gave her a long look; but something in Dulcie's tone kept her from pursuing the subject.

That little feral kitten, Dulcie thought. *So bold and wild.* She ate a bit more scone, lapped up her custard, and watched through the window as Lucinda Greenlaw's New Yorker drew to the curb. Wilma's purpose in asking Lucinda over for tea, that day, was not simply social, but to find out about Cara Ray Crisp, a favor for Max Harper. Harper didn't often ask his friends for this sort of snooping.

Of the five people on the boat when Shamas drowned, Newlon had come directly from docking the *Green Lady* at Molena Point harbor, to be with Lucinda. Winnie and George Chambers had made their condolence call a few days later; Winnie Chambers had been sympathetic and gentle, but her husband George had seemed stiff. Dulcie had watched him fidget, definitely ill at ease—as if tenderness and excessive emotion were not in his nature. Sam Fulman had come sauntering in two days after Newlon arrived, saying he'd had to run up to the city on business. *I'll just bet*, Dulcie had thought. Lucinda had not, of course, expected to see Shamas's mistress at her door at any time, come to make condolences.

The six members of the sailing party had all performed the duties of crew on the three-cabin vessel, though Dulcie had her doubts about how much work Cara Ray undertook. More likely her contribution was in bed.

In Seattle, where the *Green Lady* had gone into port after Shamas drowned, the police had put the death down as a drinking accident; Shamas's blood alcohol had been high enough to easily account, under the midnight-storm conditions, for a fatal error of judgment and balance.

With Dulcie's phone tip, Captain Harper had become increasingly curious. He had no real grounds, however, to question Cara Ray—hence Wilma's conversation with Lucinda.

Dulcie, curling down on the desk as Lucinda settled comfortably before the fire, watched Wilma pour out the tea and serve the little plates and listened through the small talk about Wilma's garden and the weather, as Wilma gently moved the conversation toward Cara Ray's visits.

"I suppose Cara Ray drove down to Molena Point alone?"

"Oh, I'm sure she's here alone. Well, at least she hasn't mentioned anyone else. She doesn't drive over, except that first time. She walks the few blocks from her motel. The second time she came, Dirken drove her home. The next night, too, because it was late, nearly midnight." Lucinda raised an eyebrow. "I expect Newlon and his cousins would all have liked the opportunity."

"She didn't mention anyone she might have driven down from the city with? Or perhaps someone she knew here in Molena Point?"

"No, she didn't. The woman is not that free with information about herself. What is it, Wilma? Why the questions?"

"Nothing," Wilma said. "Simple curiosity. If she is such a beauty, as you say, I thought perhaps ... one would wonder if there's a ... gentleman friend."

Lucinda went silent, drawing into herself. "You mean another gentleman friend, since Shamas." She looked at Wilma helplessly.

This was not, Dulcie thought, easy for either of them.

"She spent a lot of time with you," Wilma said. "I suppose she talked about the accident."

Lucinda nodded stiffly. "She did. On her first visit. But she said nothing that the Seattle police didn't tell me, if that's what you're after."

"She seems," Wilma said smoothly, "to have made herself very much at home."

Lucinda flushed. "She ... made no bones that she was Shamas's 'good friend,' as she put it."

Lucinda sipped her tea nervously. "She has no shame. She told me how she had loved to sit on shipboard in the evenings listening to Shamas tell his wonderful tales."

"That first visit—what else did she talk about?"

"What is this, Wilma? What are these questions? Why are you doing this?"

"I'm trying to understand," Wilma said quietly. She did not mention Max Harper, nor would she. What she was doing for Harper, Dulcie knew, put Wilma almost in the category of a police snitch. And a snitch didn't reveal her role; that did not make for good law enforcement.

"I'm trying," Wilma said, "to understand why Cara Ray came here. And why you've allowed her in, Lucinda. Not once, but three times. What could she possibly . . ."

"It was the Greenlaws," Lucinda said crossly. "Dirken, Newlon—they made her very welcome; that first day, they asked her to stay the evening."

"Did you . . . show her around the house?"

Lucinda flushed. "She said . . . that Shamas had bragged so about it."

Dulcie felt her tail lashing. She couldn't believe that even Lucinda would be so spineless. She could just imagine Lucinda taking that woman on a nice little guided tour of Shamas's home, pointing out all the valuable antiques.

Was that what Cara Ray was looking for? Small items she might steal, valuable pieces that perhaps Shamas had mentioned? His old and valuable chess sets, for instance, which had been written up once in the *Gazette*. Or the authentic scrimshaw and carved-ivory collection that Shamas had liked to show visitors. Had Lucinda showed them all to Cara Ray? What was it in human nature that made people so trusting?

"Why do you allow it?" Wilma said gently. "Why don't you send her packing?"

"I truly don't know. Partly, I suppose, a false sense of good manners. It's hard to break habits instilled in you so severely as a child. The same hidebound manners," Lucinda said with uncharacteristic boldness, "that keep me from sending the whole Greenlaw tribe packing.

"Well," she said, smiling, "at least the Greenlaw women have begun to do the cooking. Not that I like their heavy meals, or like them in my kitchen. But I don't have to cook for that tribe."

I bet you still have to buy the groceries, Dulcie thought with a catty little smirk.

"The rest of the clan will arrive in a few more days," Lucinda said. "Then the funeral, and they'll be gone again, and Cara Ray, too.

"Oh, I dread the funeral, Wilma. His family is going to turn it into a regular dirge of moaning and weeping and showmanship. I don't think they cared a fig about Shamas, but they're planning all manner of things for the wake, weepy poetry readings, flowery speeches—I'd rather have *no* ceremony."

"Certainly," Wilma said, "this Cara Ray won't have the nerve to show her face."

"She has bought a new dress for the occasion. 'A little black dress,' she told me."

Wilma's eyes widened. "She wouldn't actually . . ."

Lucinda's face flushed. "She intends to be there. She's a whore, Wilma. Nothing but a common whore."

Dulcie stared—she had never heard Lucinda speak so plainly. Maybe there was more grit to Lucinda Greenlaw than she had ever guessed.

"Lucinda, send that woman packing," Wilma said. "Back to San Francisco. Don't let her take advantage of you."

"I . . . have a feeling about her, Wilma. That . . . that she knows things about Shamas I should be privy to."

"What sort of things?"

"Something important. Something . . . I don't know. Not personal things, but something to do with the estate, with his businesses. I want . . . to keep her around for a while.

"She's buttering up Shamas's nephews shamefully, but—well, they were all on shipboard together. I just . . . don't want to send her away, yet, Wilma."

Dulcie washed her paws, puzzling over Lucinda. All the pieces she knew about Lucinda Greenlaw never seemed quite to fit together. Lucinda seemed so shy and docile, yet sometimes she was surprisingly bold.

Dulcie was still wondering about the old lady that evening, as she and Joe peered through the lighted window into the crowded parlor—as they watched Cara Ray make nice with the younger Greenlaw men, the little blonde flirting and preening, drawing cold looks from Lucinda.

 10

SEATED ON the Victorian couch between Dirken and Newlon, Cara Ray looked like a porcelain doll, her short pink skirt revealing a long expanse of slim, tanned leg as she dished out the giggles and charm.

If I were a human person, Dulcie thought jealously, *I'd have legs even nicer. And I wouldn't be a cheap hussy.* From the fence, the cats enjoyed front-row seats to Cara Ray's brazen display—she was the center of attention. They watched, fascinated, as she drew the Greenlaw men in like ants to syrup. Only Sam, Cara Ray's friend from the Oak Breeze Motel, sat across the room as if he didn't much care for her company.

The half dozen big-boned Greenlaw women watched Cara Ray's performance with quiet anger. The dozen Greenlaw children who hunkered on the floor between the chairs of their elders watched their mothers, watched Cara Ray, and smirked behind their hands. The children, Dulcie thought, were amazingly obedient and quiet tonight, nothing like the way the little brats shouted and pushed and broke things in the village shops. Near the hearth, beside old Pedric, Lucinda sat quietly, too. The cats couldn't read her expression.

Of those on board ship when Shamas drowned, only Winnie and George Chambers were not present. Harper had told Clyde he talked with them twice. Their answers to his questions were the same as they had given Seattle police, that they had not awakened that night, that they were heavy sleepers, had slept through the storm, did not know that Shamas had drowned until the next morning.

But tonight was story night and the cats forgot questions and police business as Dirken rose to tell his tale, standing quietly before the fire waiting for silence to touch the crowded room. But outdoors, around the cats, the breeze quickened. Wind whipped the parlor curtains and a gray-haired Greenlaw woman rose to shut the windows.

A series of slams, the windows were down, and the cats could hear nothing; Dirken's voice was lost.

"Come on," Dulcie hissed, "before they shut the back door, too. Maybe the screen's unlatched."

"And get shut in with that bunch?"

But he dropped from the fence and was across the weedy grass ahead of Dulcie and in through the screen, leading the way through the kitchen behind two stout Greenlaw women who stood at the sink rinsing dishes.

In the shadows of the dining room beneath the walnut buffet, they gained a fine view of table and chair legs, of human legs and a child here and there tucked among their elders' feet. Neither Joe nor Dulcie liked the assault of so many human smells and so much loud talk and louder laughter; but who knew what the evening might offer?

Before the fire, Dirken looked smug and full of himself. His red hair hung over his collar in a shaggy ruff; his blue shirt fit tight over muscles that indicated he worked out regularly—prompting Dulcie to wonder if he had installed, in his travel trailer, some sort of gym equipment, to keep in shape while he took his little jaunts.

All the clan lived in new and luxurious trailers or RVs when they were on the road, which, Dulcie gathered from Lucinda's remarks, was more than half the year. What these people did for a living wasn't clear. If they traveled on business, what kind of business? Some kind of sales, Lucinda had told Wilma. But that was all she told her.

When the Greenlaw clan first arrived at the Moonwatch Trailer Park, the dozen nearly new travel vehicles checking in as a group, the proprietor had spoken to Max Harper, and Harper had checked them out. Since then, Dulcie had seen the police cruising that area on several occasions. She didn't know what such a large traveling group might add up to, to alert Max Harper, but she didn't laugh at him.

Standing before the hearth, Dirken waited. The parlor was hushed. The family, usually so violent and loud, so rude, was quiet now, and gentle—as if the tradition of story time touched powerful emotions, drawing them together.

"What shall it be?" Dirken said. "What will you hear? 'Paddy's Bride'? 'The Open Grave'?"

"Tell 'Drugen Jakey,'" Lucinda said softly. "Tell 'Drugen Jakey' again?"

"Yes," said old Pedric, laying his hand on hers. "'Drugen Jakey' fits these hills."

Dirken looked at them with annoyance.

But then he masked his frown, whatever the cause. His voice softened, his manner and stance gentled, his voice embracing the old-country speech. "That tale be told twice before," he told Pedric.

"Tell it," a young nephew spoke up. "That tale belongs well to these coastal hills."

"Ah," Dirken said. "The green, green hills. Do they draw you, those rocky hills?" His laugh was evil. No one else laughed. Lucinda looked startled. Pedric watched quietly, clasping his wrinkled hands together, his lined face a study in speculation.

"All right, then," Dirken said, "'Drugen Jakey' it will be. Well, see, there was a passel of ghosts down the village coomb, and worse than ghosts . . ."

Standing tall before the fire, his red hair catching the flame's glow, his booted feet planted solidly, Dirken seemed to draw all light to himself.

"No man could graze his beasts down there for fear of th' underworld beings. Th' spirits, if they rose there and touched his wee cattle, wo'd send them flop over dead. Dead as th' stones in th' field. Devil ghosts, hell's ghost, all manner of hell's critters . . ."

In the silent room, cousins and aunts and nephews cleaved to Dirken's words, as rapt as if they had never before heard the ancient myth.

"Oh yes, all was elder there . . ." Dirken said, and this was not a comfortable tale; Dirken's story led his listeners straight down into a world of black and falling caverns that, though they excited Dulcie, made her shiver, too. Joe Grey didn't want to hear this story; it made him flatten his ears and bare his teeth, made him want to scorch across the room and bolt out the nearest window.

But as the tale rolled over them all, painting the deep netherworld, Lucinda looked increasingly excited. Soon she seemed hardly able to be still, drinking in the nephew's words as he led his listeners down and down among lost mountains and ragged clefts and enchanted fields that had never seen the sun, never known stars or moon.

Speaking the old words, Dirken seemed caught, himself, in the story, though he might have told it perhaps a hundred times—his broad Irish face gleaming as he painted for them a Selkie prince who, taking the form of a ramping stallion, charmed three human girls and led them down from this world through a clear, cold lake to waters that had never reflected earth's sky. He spoke of griffons, of harpies, of a lamia rising from the flames of hell; he described so convincingly the hellbeasts that soon Dulcie, too, wanted to escape. Dirken spoke of upper-world fields and hills quaking and opening to that cavernous land. The stories made Joe Grey swallow back a snarl, made Dulcie back deeper beneath the buffet, hunched and tense.

It's only a story, she told herself. *Even if it were true, this place and this time are safe. Those stories, those times are ancient, they are gone. Whatever might once have lain beneath these hills, that was olden times, that isn't now. Whatever strange tie that Joe and I might have to such a place, it can't touch us here in this modern day, can't reach us now.*

And that knowledge both reassured and saddened her. Crouched in the shadows beneath Lucinda's buffet, she felt a sense of mourning for her own empty past.

She had no certain history such as the Greenlaws knew. No real, sure knowledge of the generations that had come before her. The stories she had adopted as her own, from the Celts and Egyptians, were tales she had taken from books. She could not be certain they were hers, not the same as if the mother she had never known had given them to her.

If you don't know the stories of your own past, Dulcie thought sadly, *what can you cling to, when you feel alone? If you don't have a family history to tell you who you are, everything flies apart.*

It was when the storytelling had ended and trays of sandwiches were brought out from the kitchen with pots of tea and coffee, and everyone was milling about, that the cats saw Cara Ray rise and move away through the crowd, through the kitchen, and out to the backyard. They followed her, winding between chair legs and under the kitchen table and swiftly out through the screen door.

Crouched beside the back porch, they watched Newlon come out, too, furtively looking about. He saw Cara Ray, a dark shadow standing by the far fence, and approached her through the weedy yard. Cara Ray turned away stiffly, not as if she were waiting for Newlon, but as if she didn't want him there. When he moved close to her, she pushed him aside so hard he lost his balance and half fell against the fence.

"Leave me alone, Newlon. Stay away from me."

"What did I do, Cara Ray? You were all sweetness, there in the parlor."

"Only in front of the others, so they wouldn't . . . Stay away, Newlon. And stay away from Lucinda. You didn't need to come here."

"Of course I needed to come. On the boat, you . . . Shamas is dead, Cara Ray. Now we can . . ."

"I told you, Newlon, leave me alone. I don't want to see you. Do you want me to go to the police?" she said, glancing toward the house. "Do you want me to tell them how Shamas died?"

"What would you tell them, Cara Ray?"

"You might be surprised."

The cats, crouched in a tangle of dead weeds, listened with interest but drew back when the back door opened again and Dirken stepped out, moving through the dark yard as if he knew exactly where Cara Ray would be standing.

"Go on, Newlon. Dirken won't like to find you here."

"But I . . . But Cara Ray . . ."

"Go on, Newlon." And, watching Newlon slip obediently away, Cara Ray smiled as lethally as a pit viper coiled to strike.

 **11**

"**I** DON'T like to give you advice," Joe told Clyde from atop the back fence, "but dogs really don't respond very well to . . ."

Clyde looked up from the ragged lawn where he was trying to make Selig sit at heel. "Of course you like to give me advice. When have you ever been shy about laying your biased feline opinions on me?" Selig, in response to Clyde's command, lay on his back, waving his paws in the air.

"So do it your way," Joe said, amused.

Clyde turned his back, giving the pup his full attention. "Up-Sit," he told Selig.

Selig wriggled and whined.

Clyde jerked the lead. Selig flipped over onto his feet and danced in a circle around Clyde, leaping to slurp his tongue across Clyde's nose.

Silently Joe watched the little display of superior human intelligence.

Clyde turned to glower at him. "Shut up, Joe, and go away."

"I didn't say a word. But I can see that you're right. You don't need my advice. Anyone can tell you're doing wonders with that puppy. I'd say you have absolutely no peer as a dog trainer. In fact—"

"Can it, Joe. The truth is, he's just too young to train. He's still a baby. In a few months when he's older, he'll—"

"In a few months when he's older, if he keeps on playing with you and ignoring your commands, he'll be a hundred times harder to deal with."

Clyde sighed.

"For one thing, he'll be twice as heavy, twice as hard to lift when he pulls that stuff. What you ought to do, is—"

"You're going to hand out advice whether I want it or not. You can never keep your opinions—"

"You're losing him, Clyde. You're losing him before you have a good beginning. You can't train a puppy like this—you're going to make him untrainable."

"And how do you know so much? What makes a mangy tomcat an authority on dog training?"

"I'm an animal. I know how an animal's mind works. Cat or dog. You're not thinking like a puppy. You just—"

Clyde stepped closer to the fence, fixing Joe with an enraged stare. "You are an expert in every facet of life. You not only read the editorial page and treat me to your learned interpretations, you are now a dog-training expert. To say nothing of your unmitigated conceit in furnishing the law-enforcement officers of this community with your invaluable consultation."

"Can't you move on past that incident? You've been chewing on it for days." Joe glanced around at the neighbors' houses. All the windows were blank, the yards empty; but he kept his voice low. "What was I supposed to do? The guy's lying dead in his car, brake fluid dripping all over the place from a brake line that was cut as straight as if it had been sliced with a meat cleaver, and I'm supposed to walk away and say nothing?

"I hear a second car on the highway, hear it honk its horn just before the skid, and there are no other witnesses that I know of, and just because I'm a cat, I'm supposed to withhold that information from the law.

"Well, thank you very much, Clyde, but I don't think so. And as to the dog training, if you're so stiff-necked you can't accept a little friendly advice when it's offered in a kindly manner, then screw it. Go ahead and ruin a good dog!"

Selig, driven to madness by the lack of attention and his need to play, reared up against the fence, drawing his claws down the wood in long gouges—knowing that if he kept at Clyde long enough, Clyde's ridiculous attempt at lessons would end and they'd have a nice roughhouse, rolling in the grass. Leaping at Clyde, raking at his arm and cheek, Selig left four long red welts down the side of Clyde's face, narrowly missing Clyde's eye, all the time barking with excitement into Clyde's left ear. Joe imagined Clyde's eardrum throbbing and thickening from the onslaught of those powerful sound waves. Clyde whacked the pup across the nose with the folded leash, his face red with pain, anger, and embarrassment, and his cheek bleeding.

Joe said no word.

"All right," Clyde shouted, tossing the leash at the

tomcat. "If you're so damned smart, you train him!" And he spun around and slammed into the house.

Joe stared down at the leash lying in the grass. Selig began happily to chew it, working the good leather into his back incisors and gnawing with relish, his brown eyes rolling up to Joe, filled with deep satisfaction.

Joe considered taking the leash away from the pup and settling him down to a lying position with a sharp command and a few claws.

But he'd only make Clyde more angry, and more out of control.

And what good, for Clyde, if *he*, Joe Grey, trained the pup? What would Clyde learn?

A cat had to balance his willingness to help humankind with the knowledge that people must learn to do things for themselves.

After all, Clyde *had* bought a highly recommended dog-training book, and had actually read it. He had registered for, and attended two sessions of the dog-training class that Charlie insisted on—though so far, nothing seemed to have sunk in.

All Clyde did was baby the pups, laugh when they acted silly, and get mad when they didn't mind him. The trouble with Clyde was, he was a pushover. He wanted the puppies to love him, he wanted to play with them and have fun.

If he'd just figure out how to make learning the best game of all, he could teach them anything. If he could make those babies love their obedience routines, he wouldn't have a problem.

Trotting along the top of the fence to the maple tree that had become Dulcie's second home, Joe stuck his nose in among the leaves.

Dulcie, curled up atop the fence, was glued to the scene at the Greenlaw house like ticks to a hound's ear. The sporadic hammering he'd been hearing all afternoon came from a second-story dormer, where Dirken, perched on a tall ladder, was replacing some siding, nailing on the boards none too evenly. Joe nudged her. "You want to hunt? It's getting cool. The rabbits . . ."

She shook her head, watching Dirken. "He ripped the siding off and looked all around inside with a flashlight. There's a dead space in there, I think it goes under the attic. Those boards he took off, they're maybe a little bit soft, but not really rotted. I had a look—until he chased me away." Dulcie smiled. "I don't think Dirken likes cats.

"Anyway, that siding's no worse than the rest of the house."

She glanced at Joe, saw his expression, and her eyes widened. "Okay, so I'm hanging out here too much. So come on," she said softly. "Let's hunt. Whatever he's looking for, I guess he didn't find it." She gave him a sweet, green-eyed smile. "Come on, Joe. Let's go catch a rabbit." And she fled along the fence, dropped down into the next yard, and led Joe a chase through the village and up the tree-shaded median of Ocean, slowing at the cross streets, racing across the park above the Highway One tunnel and up into the hills.

There, among the tall, dense grasses, they killed and feasted, reveling in warm blood—for a few hours, indulging their wild, pure natures, forgetting the tedious intricacies of civilization and the trials of the human lives that touched them. Racing across the hills, madly, deliciously dodging and leaping, they came to ground at dusk in the ruins of an old barn and curled up together for a nap, daring any fox or raccoon to approach them.

But just before dawn they shrugged on again the cares of civilized life. Trotting home, they indulged in a detour up the roof of the Blankenship house and heard, through the open window, Mama talking to black-and-white Chappie, whom Dulcie had brought to her when he was a kitten. Chappie was grown now and handsome. Mama talked, but Chappie didn't reply; nor could he, except with soft, questioning mews. *A good thing*, Dulcie thought, *that he's just an everyday cat. If he* could *talk, Mama wouldn't let him get in a word.* Leaving the Blankenship house, they fled through the village to Jolly's alley—a lovely example of civilization, the brick paving regularly scrubbed, the stained-glass windows of the little shops all polished, the jasmine vine neatly trimmed and sweet-scented, and the gourmet offerings always fresh, set out for village cats.

There they breakfasted on Jolly's cold prime rib, leftover shrimp cocktail, and a dab of Beluga caviar; and it was not until the next night that Joe's opinion about dog training was vindicated, that Max Harper gave Clyde exactly the same advice, word for word, that Joe Grey had given him.

Joe was sauntering up the back steps to the dog door when he heard dog claws scrabbling inside, on the linoleum, and Harper's angry voice. "Get down! Stop that!" There was a *yip*, and puppy claws skidded across the kitchen floor.

Pushing inside to the heady smell of broiling hamburgers, Joe paused in the laundry, where old Rube and the three cats were taking refuge.

The kitchen was alive with the two gamboling pups

rearing and bouncing like wild mustangs crazy on loco weed. Max Harper sat at the kitchen table, his long legs tucked out of the way, observing the enthusiastic youngsters in much the same way he might watch a gang of hophead street kids tearing up his jail.

Harper did not hate dogs. Harper loved dogs. When his wife, Millie, was alive they always had several German shepherds around their small ranch.

But Harper's dogs, like his horses, were well mannered, carefully and patiently trained. As Joe stepped into the kitchen, Harper was saying, "I don't mean to tell you your business, Damen. But these young dogs need a bit of work."

Joe turned away, hiding a grin.

"They're growing pretty fast," Harper said. "The bigger they get, the harder they're going to be, to—"

Clyde turned from the stove. His expression stopped Max.

"You don't want my opinion?"

Clyde said nothing.

"Well, of course you're right. They're your pups, you don't need to be told how to handle them." He gave Clyde a long, droll stare. "I'm sure you'll work it out—find homes for them before they tear down the walls."

"They're only puppies, Max. Don't be so critical. You sound just like—like *Charlie*," Clyde said hastily, glancing down at Joe. "Charlie says that stuff." He took a long swallow of beer. "They're just puppies. The vet says they're only four or five months old. Give them time, they'll settle down."

"You're saying they're too young to train."

"They're just babies!" Clyde repeated.

"And already as big as full-grown pointers. If you

don't do something now, before they get any larger, they'll be completely out of hand. If you don't mind my saying, what you ought to do is . . ."

Clyde banged a plate of sliced onions onto the table, slammed down bottles of catsup and mustard, and dropped two split buns into the toaster.

Joe dared not make a sound. Laughter stuck in his throat like a giant hair ball. He watched Hestig rear up to smell the grilling hamburgers, watched Clyde drag the pups out to the backyard and shove the plywood barrier across the dog door. Clyde turned to look at Harper.

"Wilma says you were asking her some questions about Shamas Greenlaw's relatives. What are you working on?"

"Simple curiosity," Harper said shortly.

Clyde raised an eyebrow.

"For the last week or so, we've had a rash of shoplifting. Petty stuff."

"The past week," Clyde said.

"About the same length of time that Shamas's relatives have been camped up at the Moonwatch. I'm just a bit curious."

"Same kind of curiosity that took you sliding down Hellhag Canyon the other night."

"What's this, some kind of cross-examination?"

Clyde just looked at him.

"That trip down the canyon was well worth the trouble," Harper said.

Clyde said nothing.

"I got a phone tip. Okay?"

Clyde's gaze flickered.

The toaster popped the buns up. Clyde snatched them out and began busily to butter them.

Harper sipped his beer, watching Clyde. "Maybe I didn't give you all the details. The night I went down the canyon, I get down to the wreck, my torchlight picks out a couple of scrape marks in the earth, where my men hadn't stepped."

Clyde dished up the burgers and put them on the table. Harper reached for the mustard. "There were pawprints on top of the scrapes. Big pawprints. And a small set of prints, like maybe a . . . squirrel."

"You saw animal prints," Clyde said.

"On top the animal prints was the clear print of a jogging shoe."

"So someone went down the canyon. People go down there to hike. Naturally a hiker would be curious, seeing a wrecked car, particularly a vintage Corvette. Pity, to wreck a nice car like that."

"To say nothing of getting dead in the process," Harper said dryly.

"So you found a shoe print," Clyde said with less rancor. "And . . . ?"

"Portions of the same print leading to the brake line, and two going away from it. Fragments, but enough to show a grid."

Clyde put down his hamburger and paid attention.

"Several of the prints had been stepped on by the diamond pattern of my men's boots—both those men wear the same brand of boots. Someone besides my men was down there," Harper said, "just after the wreck. First, some kind of animals came prowling, directly after the wreck. Then a man wearing jogging shoes—those sets of prints were laid down before my men arrived—and my men were on the scene not ten minutes after the accident."

"I don't understand what you're saying."

Harper looked hard at Clyde. "I'm saying that the brake line could have been switched after the wreck. That there's evidence it may have been switched. Why are you so defensive?"

"Why would I be defensive?"

Harper shrugged and sipped his beer. "Maybe those two pups belonged to the dead man. That would explain why they were roaming around Hellhag Hill where you said you found them. Or maybe they belonged to the guy in the jogging shoes, maybe they followed him down the hill, were milling around while he switched the brake line."

"That's a lot of conjecture. I've never heard you—"

"All conjecture, so far. All bits and pieces. I'm simply playing with the possibilities. Say the pups wouldn't follow him back up the canyon, say they got silly and ran off the way pups will, and later wandered up Hellhag Hill, where you found them."

"So what does that prove? What does that have to do with the brake line?" Clyde looked hard at Harper. "For that matter, what about the dead man? What have you got on him?"

"I thought I told you. Raul Torres was a PI working out of Seattle."

"That's all you told me."

"Hotshot PI. Irritated the hell out of Seattle PD."

"Hotshot in what way?" Clyde asked, popping another beer.

"In the way he ran his investigations. Always mouthing off, Seattle tells me. Making people mad."

Clyde shrugged.

"Seattle's interested in what Torres might have been

working on, down here. Torres's secretary said he was meeting a girlfriend, but Seattle thinks he was on a case."

"You have a line on the girlfriend?"

"A Seattle girl, living in San Francisco. Had a connection in Molena Point, a friend down here."

Joe watched Harper, puzzled. Was Harper not telling Clyde everything? And what, exactly, did that mean?

"Seattle says she's something of a high roller. Particularly likes yacht cruises."

"Cara Ray Crisp?" Clyde asked.

Joe relaxed. Harper was just stringing it out.

Harper nodded, and busied himself arranging sliced onions on his burger.

Clyde rose, fetched a jar of horseradish from the refrigerator, and behind Harper's back cast a scowl at Joe that was deep with meaning, that said, *Get out of here. Now. Go out to the backyard, Joe, and catch a mouse.*

Joe leaped to the counter and settled down, glaring.

Clyde looked as if he might wring a little cat throat. But he turned back to Harper. "Do you suppose Cara Ray was seeing Torres while Shamas was alive? What kind of case was Torres working?"

"We think it's possible he was running an investigation on Shamas."

Clyde couldn't help but glance at Joe. "What kind of investigation? Women? You mean Lucinda actually—"

"No, Lucinda didn't hire him. He had apparently been checking into a Seattle machine-tool manufacturer, for some company that got stung on their products. It's possible Shamas was involved. The secretary wasn't too sure what it was all about, she said she only does a few letters and the billing. She thought it was some kind of lawsuit." Harper busied himself with his second burger.

Clyde was quiet.

Joe Grey sat very still, pretending to look out the window into the dark backyard. But beneath his sleek silver fur, every muscle twitched. Max Harper's words had fired every predatory cell; he was as wired as if Harper had waved a flapping pigeon in his face.

 12

T HE NIGHT was fading. A thin moon hung low over the sea, and a sharp wind whipped across Hellhag Hill, pushing at the scrawny, half-grown kitten, flattening the grass around her where she crouched sucking up a meager meal, licking up bits of kibble mixed with dirt, a thin scattering left from the previous day after the bigger cats had fed. A woman had brought the food.

Always she wanted to approach the woman, but the other cats would never let her; they hazed her away, wanting nothing to do with humans except to take their food—and they took it all. Hunkering down, belly to the earth, she gulped the last crumbs, shivering.

The kit was fierce enough when she was alone; certainly she had no fear of dogs. Many days earlier, when the two huge puppies had jumped and barked at her, she had attacked one of them as wildly as a bobcat— had been greatly amused to ride it right among the village streets. Oh, that had been a wild race, all her claws digging in.

But she feared her feline peers; she feared the vehemence of the clowder leaders, their fierce circling and hissing and striking out. She wouldn't challenge that hierarchy of big, mean cats. Not many cats ran in a clowder like a pack of dogs, but feral cats often lived together in such a clan—the pack leader had told her that—for strength within their own territory and for protection. He said her own group ran in a clowder because of who they were, because they were not like other ferals.

The dog had found that out. Found out that she was not simply another frightened kitty.

The woman had been on the hill when she rode that dog; the woman must have laughed. The clowder cats didn't like the woman, but the kit liked to slip close to her, unseen. She liked to see the woman take pleasure in the fog and in the dawn. The woman loved the hill and loved the sky and the sea, and so did the kit love those things. Nor did she think it strange to have such thoughts, any more than it was strange to be always hungry. Her thoughts were part of her, her hunger was part of her—hunger was a beast's natural condition. What else was there but this wary and hungry existence—and then her private thoughts to warm her?

Yet there *was* something else. There *was* more in life than hunger and fear and cold—more, even, than her own excited musings. But what that something was, she hadn't worked out. She knew only that somewhere food was plentiful and delicious and that one could be warm and there were soft beds to sleep on—the kind of sleep where a cat needn't doze with one eye open, jerked awake by the slightest sound.

Finishing the crumbs, and finding no homely wisdom scattered among them through the dirt, she crept out of the grass into the gusting wind and leaped atop a boulder, stood up bold in the blow, surveying the hill that tossed and rippled around her. Grass lashed and ran in silver waves, and beyond it the sea crashed and surged like a gigantic and sensuous animal spitting its foam white against the sky.

With her mottled black-and-brown coloring, her blazing yellow eyes, and the long hair sticking out of her ears in two amazing tufts, the young cat resembled a small bobcat more than a domestic feline. Her thin body seemed too long for a normal cat, and she was far more swift and agile.

She hadn't a bobcat's tail, though, but a long, fluffy plume, an appendage of amazing length lashing as importantly as a flag of national significance; and though her coat was dense and short, she had long-haired pantaloons like furry chaps, her fluffy parts so bushy that one had to wonder if God, in some tempo-rary absentmindedness, had fashioned this cat from leftover and mismatched parts.

Perhaps God had been in a joking mood when he made her? He seemed, as well, to have filled her with more imaginings than any proper cat could contain. The very look in her round yellow eyes and the set of her little thin face implied teeming and impatient dreams, wild and untamable visions.

This cat had no name. She had made for herself a dozen names as ephemeral as the wildflowers that came and went across the hillside. But if she had a real, for-ever, and secret name that belonged to her like her own paws and tail, she didn't know what it was.

Standing in the wind atop the boulder, she speculated

about the mice that burrowed beneath the stone, that she could never catch, and about the songs the wind whispered and the habits of the cottontail rabbits she had scented in the grass (*I'm faster than any rabbit. Why can't I catch them?*), and about the nature of the gulls that wheeled and screamed above her. And, filled to bursting with questions, in her fierce small presence shone a power far bigger than she, a power that glowed from her yellow eyes, and of which she had little understanding.

But now, far below her along the highway, another cat came trotting, leaped into the grass at the foot of the hill, and started up toward her. This cat was not one of her clowder.

But it was not a stranger, either. She had seen this one before, this brown tabby with the peach-tinted nose and ears. The cat disappeared suddenly, into the whipping tangles. She waited for it to appear again, her yellow eyes wide, her pink mouth open in a soft panting.

The cat poked her head out, looking up toward the boulders, her gaze so intent that the tortoiseshell kit took a step back. The two remained frozen in a staring match not of confrontation but of curiosity. Intense, wary, excited. Diffidently, the scrawny kit waited for the older cat's lead—but suddenly the adult cat backed away again and vanished into the grass as if uncertain in her own mind.

The stray fascinated Dulcie but filled her with a peculiar fear. Even at this distance, she could see in the kit's eyes a difference, a bright wildness.

How thin the kit was, all frail little bones, but with

that balloon tail and those huge pantaloons. When Dulcie drew back out of sight, the kit, shifting nervously from paw to paw, opened her pink little mouth.

She yowled.

Three shrill, demanding yowls, amazingly loud and authoritative for such a small morsel, an imperative command. Fascinated, Dulcie was about to show herself again and approach closer when the kit crouched, staring away past Dulcie, wide-eyed, and suddenly she spun and fled like a feather sucked away in a whirlwind.

She was gone. The hill was empty. Dulcie reared up to look behind her and saw Lucinda Greenlaw coming up the hill, and with her, stumbling along at a hurried and uneven gait, came Pedric.

But perhaps it was not Lucinda who had startled the kit, nor even Pedric, because at the humans' approach, a half dozen cats reared up in the grass staring at Lucinda and Pedric, then leaped away like terrified birds exploding in every direction, vanishing wild and afraid. These were surely a part of the kit's clowder, surely she had run at their cue.

Dulcie thought it strange that Lucinda would bring Pedric on her solitary walk, that she would bring anyone—though she did seem to trust the old man; she seemed to have a closeness to Pedric as she had with Newlon.

Her friendship with Pedric was new and tentative. She had not met Pedric or most of the Greenlaw family until they arrived for the funeral, while she had known Newlon longer, Wilma said; and it seemed to Dulcie that Lucinda had some sort of quiet understanding with Newlon.

When Pedric and Lucinda headed in her direction,

Dulcie slipped beneath a tangle of dense-growing broom bushes. How very much at home old Pedric looked as he climbed Hellhag Hill, almost as if he belonged there. Watching the two approach, she glimpsed the tortoiseshell kit again creeping down the hill toward the two humans, her yellow eyes bright with curiosity.

"Such a peaceful hill," Pedric said, sitting down with his back to a boulder, very close to where Dulcie sat unseen.

Lucinda made herself comfortable on the little folded blanket she always carried. "I've come here for years. I like its solitude."

Pedric looked at Lucinda strangely. "Solitude. That puts a kinder shape to loneliness."

She looked at him quietly.

"The loneliness of living with Shamas."

"Perhaps," she said.

Pedric's lean old body cleaved easily to the lines of the hill. "It is a fine hill, Lucinda."

"Do you sense its strangeness?"

He inclined his head, but didn't answer.

"I come here for its strangeness, too."

They were silent awhile; then he turned, looking hard at her, his thin, wrinkled profile fallen into lines of distress. "Why didn't you ever leave him? Why, Lucinda? Why did you stay with him?"

"Cowardice. Lack of nerve. When he began with the women, I wanted to leave. I tried to think where to go, what to do with my life. I have no family, no relatives."

She picked a long blade of grass, began to slit it lengthwise with her thumbnail. "I was afraid. Afraid of what Shamas might do—such a lame excuse."

She looked at him bleakly. "How many women have wasted their lives, out of fear?

"I never really believed that I could sue Shamas for divorce and get any kind of community property— there was so much about his various ventures that seemed peculiar. I did snoop enough to know he did business in a dozen different names, and I . . . it was all so strange to me, and frightening.

"Shamas said that much of the income was from bonds, stocks, investments that would bore me. I thought, if I left him, there would be a terrible legal muddle trying to sort it all out."

She looked down, then looked up at him almost pleadingly. "I was afraid of Shamas. Because he controlled the money, and . . . that he might harm me. He was so . . . demanding. Autocratic. He would not tolerate being crossed."

"Not an easy man to live with."

"Not at all. So instead of leaving, I went off by myself for a few hours at a time—returned to care for the house and make the meals."

Pedric shook his head.

"It helped to get away alone, take long walks and lick my wounds."

"And now that he is dead?"

"Now I'm free," she said softly.

Pedric nodded.

"With Shamas gone, slowly I am healing. The stress and anger are easing. One day, they will be gone."

Lucinda sat up straighter. "I mean to take charge

now, where I never did before. It may seem mercenary, Pedric, but I'm going to think, now, about my own survival.

"There's more than enough money for my simple tastes. Money can't make me young and pretty again, but it can bring me some small pleasures. I have retained a financial advisor. There's so much I don't know, records I haven't found."

Dulcie watched Lucinda, puzzled. She sounded as if she had planned for a long time what she would do if she outlived Shamas.

"The trust was the one thing Shamas did that . . . has been of benefit. He did it not for me, but simply to avoid probate taxes. Shamas hated any kind of taxes."

Lucinda looked at Pedric intently. "The things I don't know about how Shamas made the money—I really didn't want to know. I could have snooped more efficiently, found out more. I . . . didn't want to get involved in knowing, in deciding what to do if Shamas's ventures were . . . illegal.

"Cowardice," she said softly, and her face colored. "I just . . . I just wanted out."

"You were married late in life," Pedric said gently. "Shamas grew into certain ways long before you met him. Ways that were not always respectable." A wariness crossed Pedric's face. "Family ways," he said, "that I cannot condone, that I have tried to remain free of, though I have lived all my life near the family. Tell me— what did you know about Shamas, when you married?"

"He let me know that he was well established in his Seattle enterprises, but he was vague about what they were. He said he wanted our time together to be filled with delight, not with mundane business affairs."

"And you never questioned that."

"Not in the beginning. The longer I waited to press him for answers, the more difficult that was. He took care of the banking and gave me a household allowance. He didn't offer any information. That rankled. But I didn't do anything about it.

"There was plenty of money for trips, for new cars every year—until I said I didn't want a new car, that I liked the one I had." She looked at Pedric. "I was afraid to ask him the important questions. I grew afraid of where the money came from. The longer we were married, the more secretive he was. I knew he spent a lot on his own. At first on clothes, and on business lunches, he told me. Then, later, it was obvious that he was with other women.

"Yet as miserable as I was, I was too cowardly to change my life."

"So you escaped into your long, lonely rambles."

"They never seemed lonely—only soothing. From where we're sitting you can't see the village, not a single rooftop, and in the wind, you can't hear the occasional car. I would sit up here imagining there was not another soul for hundreds of miles, that this little piece of the world was all my own."

"Yes," Pedric said, "I understand that."

She looked at him quietly. "I have continued to come here for that kind of aloneness, so very different from being lonely *with* someone."

She smiled. "The hills are so green, the sea so wild. It is easy to imagine that I am in the old world, somewhere on the sea cliffs of Ireland."

Pedric turned to look above them. From where Lucinda had chosen to sit that day, they could see the trailers lined up, each in its own little patio. The wind had overturned deck chairs and whipped the laundry on a clothesline. A trailer door, left on the latch, banged and slammed. Above the trailers and RVs, the eucalyptus trees that shaded the park crackled in the wind as loud as the snapping of bonfires.

Above the trailer park, Hellhag Hill rose another hundred feet, its bulk seeming to press the narrow shelf with its frail trailers, far too close to the edge.

"I seldom look up there," Lucinda said. "Usually I sit where I can't see any sign of civilization. From the first time I came here, the hill has put me in mind of the wild, empty hills in the old, old tales that Shamas told me."

She looked shyly at Pedric. "That was what first drew me to him. The stories. I loved his stories, and the caring and passion with which he told them."

She sighed. "This hill gave me back that sense of magic. Gave me back that quality in Shamas that I found so appealing—and that he took away from me."

Pedric gave her an odd look. "This is not the old country, Lucinda. Not the old world, where such tales are a dear part of one's life. In this modern world, magic—if such ever existed—most surely does not happen."

She looked at him quietly. "That is not how you make me feel, when you tell your stories."

He shook his head, looking around him. "The hill is delightfully wild, but it is only a hill, an ordinary California hillside—probably with poison oak growing beneath us, right where we're sitting."

Lucinda laughed. She looked up at the trailers and RVs. "Which of those is yours, Pedric?"

"The green trailer, there at the end."

"Right at the edge," she said softly. "So that, every morning when you wake, and every night before you sleep, you see not the other trailers, but the open hill dropping away below you." She smiled. "Why did you park just there, where the view must be vast and empty? Don't tell me you're not touched by a sense of *otherness* about this place?"

He simply smiled.

After a moment, she said, "And why have all these frightened animals come to the hill so suddenly? The strange, wild cats that I feed, and those two thin, uncared-for puppies that Clyde Damen has taken in? Why did they appear all at once? No one abandons that many animals all at one time." She watched him intently.

"I can tell you where the pups came from," the old man said. "All very ordinary. But yon cats," he said, falling into the old speech, "th' cats be a band of strays that wandered here, that's all." He looked hard at her. "You are not imagining th' cats are anything other than common, stray beasties? Why, th' world be full of such, Lucinda."

She laughed at him, and touched his hand.

"Not imagining th' hill be full of burrows?" Pedric persisted. "Not imagining th' bright eyes looking out?" He smiled and raised a shaggy eyebrow.

Pedric's gentle teasing made such a notion seem silly even to Dulcie; though she was certain the hill was not ordinary.

And when Dulcie looked up, the little kit was hunched not a yard away from her, crouched deep in the bushes, peering out, her yellow eyes round and amazed, her fluffy tail twitching with curiosity.

"Maybe I *am* picturing that old tale of the cats beneath the hillside," Lucinda said to Pedric. "Who is to say what is possible?" She fixed an intense look on the old man. "There *is* something strange about Hellhag Hill. You will not admit it, but I think you see it. And I am not the only one who has noticed."

"So," Pedric asked softly. "And what about th' yon cat watching us? Th' yon beastie half-hidden in the grass? Is there something strange about that little cat?" Looking into the tangles, he watched Dulcie with interest. He did not see the kit. "Wo'd that little beastie, who is spying on us, rise up and speak to thee as do th' cats in the old tales? Wo'd this cat maybe bid thee good morning?"

He can't see the kit, Dulcie thought. *He means me. Why is he staring at me?*

Lucinda looked to where Dulcie sat beneath the bushes, and came to kneel there, pulling away the heavy growth.

"What a sweet little cat, curled up in a bed of leaves." She looked up at Pedric. "I believe this is Wilma's cat— my good friend, Wilma. Same dark stripes and peach-colored ears and nose. Yes, the same green eyes. Oh, Wilma would not want her roaming way out here. What brought her out to this wild place? Do you suppose she has followed us?" She reached to pick Dulcie up.

When Dulcie moved away, Lucinda drew back. "This little cat," she said diffidently, "comes to sit on the back fence behind my house. I think she hunts for birds among the maple branches. Sometimes she seems to be looking right into my parlor." She laughed. "Maybe she watches reflections in the glass, the movement of clouds and birds.

"Won't you come out, kitty?" Lucinda asked softly. "It *is* Wilma's kitty. We won't hurt you. Whatever are you doing up here? Come on out, puss. Puss? Puss?"

Dulcie came out reluctantly. She hated to be called puss. She leaped atop the boulder before Lucinda could pick her up. Stretching, she curled down on the smooth granite, out of Lucinda's reach, and slitted her eyes as if to nap again.

"Come away, Lucinda. The little cat doesn't want to be taken home. Well, there's nothing here to hurt her. You can tell Wilma where you saw her." And he began to ask Lucinda questions about Shamas and their years together.

Lucinda's answers made Dulcie sad. Pedric asked about the sale of the house, but made no comment as to whether he thought Lucinda should sell the old family home. As the two sat talking, watching the sea brighten, the tortoiseshell kit drew closer again to Dulcie, listening to every word. What a nosy little creature she was. What did she make of this conversation? What a bold, inquisitive, *interesting* scrap of cat fur.

And as both cats eavesdropped on the two humans, up the hill where the trailers and RVs cast their shadows long beneath the rising sun, another watcher sat, looking down, observing Pedric and Lucinda, frowning and tapping his closed fist against his lean, tensed thigh.

13

"**I** DON'T want a dog," Charlie told the pup. Hestig looked up at her sadly, pressing against her leg, as she stood at her apartment window sipping her first cup of coffee. Beyond the window, the village rooftops, the library and shops, and the eucalyptus trees that shaded Ocean's wide median, all were muted by the fog, as indistinct as an oriental watercolor. Putting her cup on the table beside her sweet roll, she sat down to her quick breakfast, petting Hestig when he pushed close to her chair and laid his head on her shoulder.

"You know I can't keep you," she said softly. "Or do you just want my breakfast?" She laughed at his sad expression. "The housing arrangement's temporary, my dear. Three or four days, maybe a week, and back you go to Clyde." Already the apartment looked as though Hestig had moved in for good, his folded blanket in the far corner comfortably matted with dog hairs, his water and food bowls taking up most of the floor in the small kitchenette; a huge chewbone occupied the center of the rag rug beside Charlie's cot, his leash and choker lay on the table beside her coffee cup.

She had to admit, his manners were improved without his brother to distract him; he minded her most of the time, was turning into a solemn and loving companion. He was beginning to put on weight, too, his ribs resembling far less an ancient washboard.

But when she imagined keeping him, she shook her head. "Look around you. I'm living in one room, here. No yard, no deck, not even a balcony."

Hestig whined.

"And in case you hadn't noticed, I'm a working girl." She scratched under his chin. "I can't take you on the job. What, tie you to the bumper all day? I can't take you into the houses that I clean and repair." She looked deep into Hestig's brown eyes. "Clyde will find a nice home for you, just you wait and see."

The pup sighed, his eyes sad enough to melt concrete, his black ears drooping. Gently, she touched the thick black scar that ran jagged across the top of his head. "How did that happen? What—or who—struck you so hard as to leave a scar like that?" She stroked the ropy wound. "You must have been very small; you're not very old now, and it takes a while for such a thing to heal."

Hestig's tail whipped so hard it nearly toppled a dinette chair.

"Who would hit a little puppy like that? I'm surprised the blow didn't kill you."

Hestig smiled and wagged and snuggled closer, leaning into her shoulder with all his fifty pounds. She tried to imagine taking him to work with her. Surely, when he grew older and had more training, he would behave with impeccable manners.

But common sense prevailed. "I really can't. I can't keep you."

He nuzzled her hand, finding no joy in such solemn pronouncements.

She pushed back her kinking red hair. The fog made it curl so tight. "I have a business to tend to, it takes all my time. You've been around on the jobs with me." She took his long canine face in her hands. "Did you like being shut in the van all day with the ladders and mops and tools?"

Hestig's sigh said that he'd loved it because he was near her.

"I don't have time for a big, active dog, not and clean for people, do their household repairs and their yard work, and build up a really nice service." She stroked his long black ears. "You should be on a ranch somewhere, like up with Max's horses." She sipped her coffee. "Maybe I can talk Harper into giving you a try. How would you like that?"

Hestig gazed at her sadly.

"Look at it this way. Burying bones and digging them up is top priority for you. Charlie's Fix-It, Clean-It is top priority for me."

He laid his head on the table, sniffing at the last bite of sweet roll. She tapped his nose gently, and he drew back. The time was six A.M., time for their walk. In half a week, Hestig had the routine down to perfection.

Picking up his leash, she triggered an explosion of ungainly leaps and pirouettes. She stood waiting for him to calm so they could leash up, then made him stay by her heel going down the steps to the little front foyer, between the antique shop and the jewelry store, and on out to the sidewalk. Stepping out into the wet, chill fog and turning south toward the sea five blocks away, she expected Hestig to dance and try to pull ahead; usually he could hardly contain himself until he reached the sand, where he could run free.

This morning he didn't dance.

He didn't pull the lead but moved slowly and warily ahead, pressing against her thigh. She could see nothing in the fog. He lunged suddenly into the mist, his bark a bold challenge, *wooo, wooo, wooo*. She had to turn sideways and pull the leash taut across her upper legs to hold him; he was so strong and lunging so hard that if he'd jerked her straight on, he'd have pulled her over. She could see no one, no gray shadow waiting in the fog, nothing to alarm him, only a few parked cars along the curb, barely visible. But the pup saw something, and was barking and straining.

Again she pulled him back to her and ran her hand down his shoulder, trying to calm him—and trying to see through the mist, listening for any scrap of sound over his barking. He lunged again, and she heard a car start—saw a dark smear move away from the curb, its tires hushing on the wet pavement. At the same moment, she saw Lucinda Greenlaw just a few feet from her, walking along the median toward the shore, her tall thin figure wavery and insubstantial—a mysterious early-morning wanderer. Later in the day Lucinda would appear perfectly ordinary, doing her errands among the village shops as sedately as any elderly lady— but now she seemed ghostlike and exotic.

Hestig had quieted; Lucinda passed them, not glancing in their direction, seeming totally lost in her own thoughts, perhaps aware only of a dog walker out in the foggy morning. Charlie knelt and hugged the pup, feeling the tension of his thin body. He was still shivering.

Who had frightened him like that? Who had been there and driven away? Rising, she tightened his lead and hurried toward the shore. Already, Lucinda had disappeared.

Hestig was quiet and obedient again, until she passed the contemporary wooden building that held the public rest rooms, an attractive redwood-and-stone structure, appealing on the outside but dank and cold within, as were most such seaside facilities, its wet concrete floor strewn with wadded paper towels and damp sand. The building stood at the edge of a small seashore park of sand dunes and cypress trees and was flanked by a variety of handsome native bushes. Hestig shied at these and backed away, staring at a pair of legs stretched out behind a bush, a newspaper over them as if for warmth—one of Molena Point's few homeless, she supposed, sheltered within the dense foliage. Or maybe some late-night drunk sleeping it off. Like Hestig, she quickly moved away. As she turned toward the rolling breakers, she saw that Lucinda had reached the other side of the park, a thin vague shadow walking swiftly.

Heading across the soft, dry sand to where the shore was wet and hard, and turning south, Charlie let Hestig off his leash. He looked behind them once, then trotted ahead, sniffing at the sand but not straying far from her. Even when they reached the southerly beach, where the waves crashed among dark, rising boulders, and half a dozen dogs were running the shore or playing ball with their owners, Hestig remained near her. She sat on a rock watching him. She was so happy to be living in that quiet village, away from the bustle and heavy traffic of San Francisco where she'd gone to art school.

She'd not have thought to come to Molena Point if her Aunt Wilma hadn't retired there. She had to smile, when she remembered how she had come crawling, totally defeated after two years of failing at various commercial art jobs for which she wasn't really prepared, or talented enough.

Well, she was glad she was there. She loved the smallness of the village, loved that she could walk from the sea up into the sun-baked hills in just minutes. And, she thought, watching Hestig, one of the hundred things she liked best was that people walking their dogs could stop at any sidewalk restaurant, have a light meal while their canine companions napped beneath the table. She would see leashed dogs in the bank, in the shops—places where, in any other town, dogs would not be allowed. And the little open-air restaurants, their courtyard tables surrounded by flowers and sheltered by the old, twisted oaks, never ceased to enchant her. "When I die," she'd told Clyde once, "this is exactly how it will be. Charming villages all crowded among the flowers, all of them beside the sea, with the smell of the sea, the crash of breakers."

She'd met Clyde soon after she arrived; he'd been Wilma's friend since he was eight, when Wilma was his next-door neighbor: blond, twentysomething, and beautiful; Clyde said he'd had a terrible crush on her.

Charlie's first date with Clyde was a trip to the wrecking yard to find parts for her old van, then to a small Mexican restaurant, where no one noticed their grease-stained clothes. They'd been dating ever since, their relationship swinging from casual and easy to sometimes very warm and loving. Once in a while she thought about marrying Clyde; more often she liked the arrangement just as it was.

Around her, the fog had thinned, the dawn brightening. She called Hestig, and as they started back she heard, over the thunder of the breakers, sirens begin to scream up in the village, their ululations growing louder as they headed for the shore. She thought of someone drowning, and her frightened gaze turned quickly toward the sea.

She saw no disturbance, no one in the water—not even one surfer, and it was far too cold for swimmers. Only when she neared the little park again did she see the ambulance and police cars, their red whirling lights staining the fog like smeared blood. She thought of Lucinda, wondered if the older woman might have fallen or maybe become ill. Hurrying up to the gathering crowd, she found Lieutenants Brennan and Wendell stringing yellow police tape around the rest-room building and its adjacent bushes, out into the street and around a large portion of the sandy park.

The homeless man still lay beneath the bushes. His newspaper was gone, revealing shoes that were nearly new and looked expensive. Two paramedics knelt over him. She couldn't see what they were doing. Three early walkers, two with dogs, stood to one side talking to an officer, answering his questions. She didn't see Lucinda.

14

THEIR BELLIES full of rabbit, the cats were headed home through the mist, the village empty and quiet around them, its scents of flowers and bacon and coffee homey and comforting. Licking blood off their whiskers, ignoring the sting of various wounds inflicted by the enraged rabbit, a deep sense of well-being filled the cats. They had hunted, they had fed. All was proper and right with their world. Their territory—Molena Point village and far beyond—was suitably at peace. Except for various human affairs, which were not cat business, but which neither cat would leave alone.

"He's cozying up to Lucinda for some reason," Joe said of Pedric. "What's he after?"

"He's not cozying up at all; he's the only one of that family who's her friend—well, Newlon, of course."

"And why Newlon? How does she know him so much better. I thought—"

"Wilma says he often came out to sail with Shamas;

Lucinda's known him a long time."

"Well, I don't trust him, or Pedric."

She cut him an annoyed look. "I don't know about Newlon. But Pedric's good for her. She needs a friend just now."

"He's a Greenlaw."

"You're so suspicious."

"Hasn't it crossed your mind that Pedric is deliberately gaining her confidence? That while the rest of the family quarrels over her money and makes her mad, that old man with his sweetness and shared confidences is setting her up to rip her off big-time?"

Her ears flattened, her green eyes flashed. "Don't be such a cynic. Can't you see that he's different from the others, that he truly likes Lucinda?" She looked at him narrow-eyed. "Don't you believe in anything anymore?"

"Pedric is a Greenlaw. Don't you know the police are watching the whole family? All week those Greenlaw women and kids have been a problem in the village shops—stealing, Dulcie. Shoplifting."

He gave her a hard yellow stare. "They're too quick for the store owners to catch. But after they leave, merchandise comes up missing—a lot of expensive merchandise. Such a shabby, greedy little crime."

"Has anyone seen *Pedric* stealing?" Her eyes had gone black with anger; her tail switched and lashed.

"Why would Pedric be any different? Face it, Dulcie. The Greenlaws are a family of thieves."

"That doesn't make sense. What kind of family— Not a whole family, stealing—"

"You think that doesn't happen? Of course there are families of thieves—what about the Mafia. The

Greenlaws are small pickings compared to that, but—"

Dulcie lowered her gaze, looked up at him quietly. Of course there were such families, she had read about them, the children were raised from babies to live outside the law.

"But," she said softly, "even if it's true, even if the rest of them steal, that doesn't mean Pedric does. He *could* be different, Joe. If you'd watch him—in the evenings when he comes for supper, how polite he is, not just barging in like the rest, ignoring Lucinda. How pleased Lucinda is to get him settled in the softest chair, see that he's comfortable."

"So he's a smooth operator. You know better than to trust how people act."

"Lucinda wouldn't take him walking with her if she didn't trust him, and if they didn't truly enjoy each other. She wouldn't share Hellhag Hill with him, that's her private place. They have exactly the same interests. I don't see him using her."

Joe laid back his ears, his yellow eyes narrow. "You're seeing what you want to see. I've never known you to be so gullible. You follow them, listen to Pedric sympathizing with her, and you go all sentimental."

She hissed, lowering her own ears, switched her tail in his face, and hurried on down the grassy median— then stopped, crouching, looking fearfully around her as sirens screamed from the direction of the fire and police stations.

A rescue unit thundered past, shaking the earth, prompting the cats to cower beneath the bushes. It was followed by three black-and-whites. Joe and Dulcie, their hearing numbed by the blast, watched the heavy vehicles heading fast for the shore.

Following, galloping down the median toward the crowd gathered beside the sandy park, their first thoughts were the same as Charlie's had been, that someone had drowned, on this chill, foggy morning, some poor soul alone out in the dark sea. Then they saw a man lying on the ground, the paramedics bent over him—maybe a homeless man? They often slept in the park, near the rest rooms.

But as the medics lifted the victim up onto a stretcher, the cats recognized a Molena Point resident, a man they knew only by sight. White hair, baby-soft face that was usually very red, whether from sunburn, excessive scrubbing, or excessive booze, they had no idea. Now he was as pale as a bedsheet.

Trotting in among the crowd between jogging shoes, sweatpants, and bare, hairy legs, the cats stayed away from the uniforms—no need to upset Max Harper, no need to endure his puzzled glances. A confusion of comments assaulted them:

". . . stabbed. He was stabbed. I saw . . ."

". . . is he dead?"

"Still alive, can't you see . . ."

". . . was lying there when that lady found him, I'd have fainted . . . some transient . . ."

"No—he lives here, he comes in my shop."

". . . George Chambers. You know, the guy who . . ."

The cats did a double take. George Chambers? Swerving out of the crowd, they skinned up a cypress tree beside the rescue vehicle, for a better look.

George Chambers, a member of the sailing party when Shamas Greenlaw died. The man who, with his wife, had slept through the attempted rescue, had not awakened until the next morning, when the *Green Lady* put in at Seattle.

From among the thickly massed cypress trunks that rose around them like dark, reaching arms, the two cats got a good look at Chambers. He kept moving his hand, trying to press at the stab wound in his chest that the medics had bound with gauze and tape, the clean bandages already soaked with blood. One of the medics was covering him, with a pair of thick brown blankets.

So this was George Chambers. The passenger Harper had talked with twice about Shamas's accident, the mild-mannered fellow who had given Harper no indication that either he or his wife had, that stormy night, been awake to observe anything questionable about Shamas's death.

So why had he been stabbed?

They watched Captain Harper drop a rusty, blood-smeared butcher knife into an evidence bag. As the paramedics lifted Chambers's stretcher into the rescue vehicle, the cats clawed higher among the arms of the cypress, up into its dark foliage, out of sight of the police. Below them, Lucinda was talking with Officer Davis, a private conversation away from the crowd. The cats could catch no word; there were too many idle onlookers expressing their opinions.

The two cats remained within the branches through several hours of photographing and examination of the crime scene. Among the areas of interest to forensics was a patch of sand where someone had been digging. They watched a kneeling officer brush sand away with a little paintbrush and sift sand tediously through a strainer. Four officers went over the cordoned-off area thoroughly, inch by inch. They bagged some bits of paper, a few loose threads caught on bushes, items that might link to the attacker, or might have been exposed in the damp and rain for months or years. When the cats left the beach they dropped down to the roof of the public rest rooms and to the far side of the building, out of sight of Max Harper. They came away from the Chambers stabbing knowing very little about what had happened. It was not until that evening that they were able to fill in some blanks.

Joe woke from a nap in late afternoon hungry despite his feast of rabbit early that morning; somehow eating wild game always made him want human food to top it off. Half an hour before Clyde was due home, he called Jolly's Deli and ordered takeout, telling them to charge it and leave the food at the door. He had told Clyde he wouldn't do this anymore, but he hadn't exactly promised.

Listening to the delivery truck pull away, he hauled the white paper bag in through his cat door and enjoyed, on the living-room rug, a nice selection of smoked herring, sliced Tilsit, and cracked crab. It was these little added luxuries that made his peculiar talents well worth the trouble they caused him. When he had finished eating, he pawed the containers back into the bag, licked up all telltale crumbs from the carpet, and carried the bag through the kitchen, out the dog door, and over the back fence.

Glancing at the next-door neighbor's windows and seeing no one looking out, he stuffed the evidence into their trash. Clyde wouldn't know a thing until he got his deli bill—then he'd pitch a royal fit.

Clyde didn't know a thing about the stabbing, either, when he got home from work. Only what he saw in the evening *Gazette*. After reading the front page he glanced at Joe, but made no offer to call Harper and glean a few additional facts. Joe wasn't about to ask him for that kind of favor. He'd be back on cheap, cardboard-flavored kitty kibble that hadn't passed his whiskers since his kitten days in San Francisco.

As it turned out, it was Wilma who got the particulars about the Chambers stabbing, and told Dulcie. Joe found Dulcie on the back fence in her usual perch. "You might as well move your bed and supper bowl up here," he said, settling down beside her.

She hissed gently and lifted a soft paw as if to belt him. "Something's going on. Dirken and Newlon are all worked up, really hassling Lucinda. You can't hear a thing, even with the windows open, with all those women in the kitchen. Can't they wash the dishes without so much jabber?"

Dirken and Newlon stood before the hearth looking down at Lucinda where she sat in her favorite chair, sipping her after-dinner coffee. She looked drawn into herself, tense, glaring up at them. Both men were talking at once. The cats couldn't make out their words, but they were apparently interrogating her.

"Chambers is more or less out of danger," Dulcie told Joe. "That rusty knife had sand from the park on it; forensics is pretty sure that's what was buried—it might have lain there for years, maybe a dog dug it up, or a transient making his camp, and the attacker found it."

"Harper's not assuming that Chambers was stabbed by a transient?"

"Of course he isn't. You know Harper better than

that. Chambers was on the boat that night. Don't you suppose Harper's digging, don't you suppose he's got his teeth into this!"

"How did you . . . ?"

"Wilma happened to drop into the Iron Horse, earlier this evening. A special favor, for yours truly." Harper often ate at the Iron Horse when he was working late.

"That's all she found out," Dulcie said. "It's all the police know, so far. Wilma said Harper had that tight, preoccupied look he gets when he's caught up in a tangle of evidence, when he's digging for the missing pieces."

She returned her attention to the parlor window. "Dirken and Newlon tried all through dinner to get Lucinda to talk about the stabbing, to tell them what she saw this morning.

"It was Lucinda who called 911. She told them she'd been out walking, saw the man lying there when she came across the park to use that awful rest room, that she thought he was asleep. Then she saw the blood. She ran to the phone, there between the men's and women's, but it was out of order. She hurried back to the village and called the station. She told Dirken that the rest is public knowledge—they could read it in the *Gazette*."

Joe grinned. "So why all the fuss? They think she saw something more?"

"Evidently. They're pretty wrought up."

"You think *they* stabbed Chambers? That they're afraid Lucinda saw them?"

"Maybe. Or maybe they want the goods on whoever did. Well, they've finished with the dishes," she said, glaring in at the Greenlaw women as they trooped toward the parlor.

Dirken and Newlon had pulled up chairs facing Lucinda; they sat forward, pressing their questions at her. The kitchen crew wandered in silently and found places to sit—an eager audience, all watching Lucinda.

"But you must have seen something else," Dirken was saying. "And why *were* you in the park at that hour? Just to say you went walking, Aunt Lucinda, doesn't make any sense. Who else was there?"

"Enough!" Lucinda snapped. She stood up, scowling down at them. "That is enough. Stop it, both of you. I have had quite my fill of this."

The cats watched with amazement. All the family was quiet, shocked that Lucinda was no longer a bystander in her own home, that she had made herself the center. Standing so fiercely, glaring at them, her very frailty seemed to increase her sudden surprising power. The cats thought she was going to say something about the stabbing; but instead, folding her hands before her in the traditional stance, Lucinda prepared to tell a tale—as if putting the subject of the stabbing behind her, letting the Greenlaws know that the matter was closed.

Whether the old lady was becoming stronger in dealing with Shamas's family, or whether this was a move of extreme desperation, to gain a little peace, was uncertain. Standing in the place of storyteller, so skillfully did Lucinda lay out her tale that soon she had drawn them all in. The stabbing seemed forgotten—and they were carried into a story that surprised Dulcie, that made her fur prickle with excitement, made the tip of her tail twitch, and made Joe Grey fidget uncomfortably.

"It is an American Indian tale," Lucinda said, "one I

have read in three sources, as told by three different tribes. I don't believe the story springs from any Celtic telling; I don't believe there is any connection. But yet it is the same tale that comes from the Celtic lands.

"It is peopled with the same enchanted beings, it tells of the same lost world. The Iroquois call it 'The Tale of the First People.'

"In the beginning," Lucinda said softly, "in the beginning of the world all living things, all beasts, all men, all reptiles and insects and birds dwelt in the netherworld that lies below our plains and mountains. All was darkness in that place save for a thin green light that glowed down from the granite sky.

"In those days the animals could speak, and many of them were shapeshifters. Human hunters would turn themselves into ponies. Great eagles flying beneath the granite skies could transmute into warriors. There were women and men who could slip from hearth to hearth in the form of cats but soon were gone again, unwilling to warm for long any hearth but their own.

"The cat folk had their own cities among the hidden mountains, their netherworld caves fashioned into soft-cushioned bowers rich with carven furnishings, their walls set with pictures made from turquoise and jade.

"One day when a princess of that people was digging at the roof of her cave, carving a new sleeping bower, she dug though into vast space. Her paw thrust out, into the upper world.

"Shining through the paw-sized hole was a blaze of light that made the cat maiden cry out in fear. All the clan came running. The bravest crouched, squinting through the hole up into a gleaming and endless sky.

"And the boldest among the cat folk dug the hole larger and slipped through, up onto the face of the earth, with only emptiness above them.

"Soon other netherworld folk gathered, creatures from the hell-pit, the bird folk and serpent folk and then the giants, all peeping out into the upper world.

"Many turned away again, too afraid to step out beneath that bright sky, but not the cat folk. They went up into that world digging and clawing their way, and not until evening came and the ball of fire rode through the sky toward the mountains, were the cats afraid.

"They watched the sun sink down behind the peaks. They saw the sky grow dark, and they thought that by entering this land they had made the gods angry. They slept close together that night, crowded beneath a rocky ledge, sure that their spirits were doomed.

"But the next morning, the sun returned. The cat people came out to preen in its warmth, and they knew that they were blessed, that this bright world welcomed them.

"They wandered away over the land in every direction, and soon made this world their own. So the folk-of-the-cat came to our world," Lucinda told. "And so they have come and gone ever since, returning to the netherworld when they choose, living in both worlds and in both forms, sometimes cat, sometimes human.

"And if there are cat folk in the upper world who can no longer change their form, it is because they have strayed too far from their beginnings, because they have forgotten the ancient ways."

Lucinda turned from the hearth. The Greenlaws nodded and sighed with satisfaction. As Lucinda moved away from the storyteller's place, Pedric reached to take her hand, in a tender and personal gesture.

Dirken watched the two old people with a cold scowl. Newlon turned away, his look uncomfortable.

And on the fence beneath the maple branches, tears rolled down Dulcie's whiskers, their wet streaks marking her dark fur. The tale filled her with excitement and it scared her; it made her feel *more* than herself. The emotions it stirred turned her giddy.

But Joe Grey leaped from the fence up into the maple's highest branches, his ears back, his scowl deep.

He didn't like tales of a netherworld. Didn't like anything to do with his and Dulcie's mysterious history. Being himself, being Joe Grey, was quite enough. He didn't hold with some amazing and frightening past. He needed only himself and his loving lady.

Dulcie was still purring extravagantly when Dirken and Newlon came out the back door and sat down on the steps. Newlon produced a pack of Camels, and they lit up.

Newlon said, "You think she saw something more, on the beach this morning?"

Dirken shrugged. "More to the point, you think she heard anything?"

Newlon turned to look at him. "Did you do him, Dirken?"

Dirken stared at Newlon, drawing on his cigarette. "Hell, no. Didn't you?"

"I swear."

But Dirken kept looking. "You did him. Stands to reason."

Newlon turned to glance behind them through the screen as two large, aproned women began moving about in the kitchen, filling the coffeepot and cutting pieces of pie. Scowling, Newlon and Dirken shuffled a little more, then tossed away their cigarettes and went back inside.

The cats, highly irritated at the vague and unfinished conversation, galloped away along the fence and headed up into the hills to hunt, Joe Grey so frustrated by the lack of solid facts that he felt like attacking the biggest granddaddy wharf rat he could find, launching into a raking, screaming battle.

 15

WILMA LEFT her desk at the automotive agency just before noon, hurriedly smoothing her gray hair and snatching up her purse, frantic to get out of the tiny salesman's cubicle before she started throwing heavy objects through its glass walls. Working in a transparent box made her feel like a lab specimen.

Well, the job was only temporary. She'd be glad to get back to work at the library. She hadn't planned to use her month's vacation working a second job, even if it was proving more interesting than she'd anticipated.

She had spent the morning running a credit check on the out-of-town purchaser of a white-and-cream Jaguar XJR. What she'd found had her most interested. With her mind on the buyer's skillfully forged IDs, she glanced across the automotive showroom, past the drive-through that separated it from Clyde's repair shop, and she had to laugh.

Clyde had brought one of the pups to work, had left him tied just inside the glass door of the automotive-repair wing of the building, the pup all groomed and polished and sitting on a new plaid dog bed. All Clyde needed was a hand-lettered sign advertising the pup's many virtues.

Who knew, maybe Clyde *would* find Selig a home among his customers; most of them were well-to-do; surely it would take someone with money to feed that big fellow and care for him.

Hurrying down Ocean, enjoying the sun and the cool breeze skimming in off the Pacific, Wilma puzzled over her last three loan applicants.

The first credit scams she'd investigated when she started work for Sheril Beckwhite, had occurred over a two-month period. From these, she had passed to Max Harper enough information to launch seven police investigations.

But then this past week the action had heated up. She'd had five new applicants with impeccable credit ratings; her phone calls to their home numbers had been answered by a wife or by household staff. Their social security numbers, driver's licenses, all records corresponded to information filed in the issuing departments across the country. All were excellent credit risks. Each buyer had made a minimum down payment with a personal check, taking out the maximum loan; two had said they needed the tax write-off.

She'd turned them all down. It was after requesting hard-copy records from the archives of the various agencies, asking them not to use their computer information, but to go back to the originals, that she came up with the discrepancies. Every one was a scam.

Entering Birtd's Grocery through the back door near the deli, she was mulling over the legality, under today's criminal-friendly courts, of fingerprinting all loan applicants and running them through NCIC before approving their loans. The idea made her smile—too bad it would never fly.

She thought about her early days in Probation and Parole, when information was so much harder to gather—long before computers, before the statistics available through National Crime Information Center—back in the horse-and-buggy days, she thought, grinning.

Heading for the deli, she heard angry voices from the front of the store, and spotted gentle-natured Lewis Birtd near the bread display. He was arguing with an irate tourist, a dark-haired, meaty woman dressed in a sloppy Hawaiian shirt and baggy shorts, pushing a baby in its stroller and hauling a two-year-old by the arm.

Birtd's Grocery, located among the village motels, catered heavily to the more affluent tourists. Mr. Birtd carried a fine selection of the nicer party and snack foods and good wines, specializing in the two local wineries, and a complete line of imported beers and ales. He stocked only carefully selected fruits and vegetables and the finest meats. His deli was not as extensive as George Jolly's, but what he did provide was delicious and nicely presented. Local residents stopped by Birtd's for dinner-party items and for sudden whims. Though for everyday purchases—of hamburger, bulk rice, and canned tomatoes, for cat food and paper towels—village folk went up the valley to one of the three grocery chains, all of which offered discounts in a constant competition that kept prices down and the residents of Molena Point coming back.

Waiting at the deli counter for her avocado-and-prosciutto-on-rye and a container of dilled coleslaw, Wilma listened with interest and then concern to the quickly accelerating argument at the front of the store; the woman seemed to be claiming that Mr. Birtd had sold her an open box of cookies and that the cookies had made her children sick. The children didn't look sick. Mr. Birtd didn't seem to know quite what to do with the woman. Her tirade had grown so heated that Wilma wondered if diminutive Lewis Birtd was in physical danger. When a second altercation broke out near the checkout counters, a puzzled unease gripped her. She craned to see.

A woman in a bright dirndl skirt and loose black jacket had backed Frederick Birtd into a corner beside the shelves of pickles, upbraiding him so violently that poor Frederick shuffled with embarrassment.

The Birtds were never rude to customers; the Birtd family was patient, polite, gentle-mannered. The store was run by Mr. and Mrs. Birtd and their two grown sons and, like most Molena Point shopkeepers, they went out of their way to please their clientele. As the woman's shouting increased, Frederick's voice rose in unaccustomed rage. At the same moment, to Wilma's right near the soft drinks, a tall, heavily pregnant woman began to yell and stamp, trying desperately to discipline three wildly screaming children. Business at the three checkout counters had ceased as checkers and customers watched the disruptions. When the three children began hitting their mother, pounding her with their fists, one of the checkers left his register to help her—at the same moment, Wilma realized what was happening.

Her first thought was, *This can't be real! You read about this stuff in the police journals.* Her next thought: *It's not only real, and they're not only pulling it off, I know these people!*

She flew for the front door, fighting her way past Frederick Birtd's assailant and through the checkout lines. Glancing back, she saw the big woman swing her purse, hitting Frederick so hard he staggered backward against a Coke display, the cans and wire racks flying. Everything happened at once; the checkout lines were a battlefield as impatient customers tried to push on through. As she slid through between the registers, a large woman spun from the far register and ran for the street. At the next register, another big boned, dark-haired woman was scooping up handfuls of bills. Wilma tripped her and slammed the drawer on her hand, forcing a scream. The woman dropped a fistful of money and ran; hitting the street, she slid into a waiting car. When Wilma turned to snatch up the phone, she found that its line had been cut.

Hurrying to the motel next door, she stepped behind the empty counter, grabbed the phone, and dialed 911.

The black-and-whites must have been just around the corner. As she returned to the riot-filled store, two squad cars slid to the curb. At the same moment, four civilian cars pulled out of the parking lot fast, skidding to a pause by the front door. Half a dozen big, dark-haired women came boiling out, their loose coats and long skirts flapping. The cops grabbed three. Two jumped into the waiting cars. A third black-and-white coming around the corner gave chase.

Wilma returned to the checkout stands feeling as

though she'd been caught in the middle of a movie shoot, a well-planned script. Except this drama had been real, and devastating. Lewis Birtd stood at the cash registers, pale with shock. One of the three registers lay on the floor upside down, spilling loose change. The drawers of the other two hung open and empty. Lewis looked up helplessly.

"Cleaned out all three," he said to Wilma, and turned to a pair of uniformed officers as his son Frederick approached, holding the arm of the woman who had hit him. Within minutes, seven arrests had been made, the women secured in three black-and-whites and driven away to the station. No man had been involved in the store riot; the only men Wilma had seen had been driving the getaway cars. All of the cars were new and expensive.

Wilma had, as the cars sped away, jotted down three license plate numbers. One of the cars was a blue Thunderbird, and as it wheeled a U-turn picking up its passenger, she got a close look at the driver.

She stared after the car trying to be sure, her anger rising—she hadn't seen Sam Fulman since the day in San Francisco Federal Court, maybe ten years back, when she petitioned the court to revoke his probation.

She'd only had a glimpse of the driver, but she sure didn't forget a man she'd twice tried to revoke before she was successful—a man she had hassled constantly about his lack of permanent residence, lack of a job, and the fact that he refused to pay his restitution. It seemed like only yesterday that she faced Fulman before the bench. She didn't like seeing him in Molena Point. Fulman was totally bad news.

But of course he'd be in Molena Point just then.

What did she expect? With Shamas Greenlaw's funeral pending, every shirttail Greenlaw relative in the country had made a beeline for Molena Point, looking for a share of the leavings.

She'd never told Lucinda that one of Shamas's nephews had been her probationer; what good would it have done to tell her?

Working her way to the back of the market, stepping over fallen cans and paper goods, Wilma slipped and nearly fell on a slick spot left by spilled fruit cocktail. The floor was littered with broken glass, scattered candy and cookies. And now the aisles were crowded with uniforms talking with the remaining customers. All those present during the riot seemed eager to tell the officers their particular version.

Wilma gave Lieutenant Wendell the license plate numbers she'd noted down, then collected her lunch. Leaving Birtd's, hurrying toward Ocean, she was just crossing the broad, tree-shaded median when she saw Clyde coming up the street, probably returning from his own lunch. He walked at an angle, leaning back, pulled along the sidewalk like an unwilling puppet by the young dog—and nearly fell over Selig when the pup stopped suddenly to sniff at the street.

Sniffing along pulling Clyde, the dog bolted away, suddenly jerking the lead from Clyde's fist, charging along the median toward a blue Thunderbird parked at the curb.

Leaping at the car's windows, barking and pawing, scratching the gleaming paint, he spun in circles, his wagging tail beating against the metal—then he cowered away, ducking as if with fear.

There was no one in the T-Bird. Wilma looked

through the windows. In the front seat lay the same plaid jacket that one of the woman rioters had worn. Wilma glanced into the nearby shops and cafés. She didn't see Fulman. She turned to look at Clyde.

"Tell Sheril I'll be a bit late," she said. "Tell her . . . tell her I'm chasing a loan applicant." And she headed away, across Ocean, in the direction of the police station.

The station was mobbed with women, pale-haired women dressed in jeans or shorts, and T-shirts—not the heavily garbed brunettes she had seen in Birtd's—all shouting. They were arguing and weeping, firing questions at the officers in some foreign language, screaming indecipherable accusations. A dozen officers were trying to sort them out. Entering, Wilma was nearly knocked flat by an energetic arrestee swinging her heavy arms and yelling.

Max Harper's station was one large, open squad room. The counter at the front was big enough to accommodate the dispatcher and her radios, a clerk, and, behind her, a row of tall file cabinets set into the wall. Beyond the counter, a dozen officers' desks filled the room, their surfaces invisible beneath stacks of papers and bound reports. Along the far, back wall, a credenza held a coffeemaker and assorted cups. Harper's desk stood near it, with a clear view of the room, of the front door, and of the hall to the back door and alley. Harper, at the moment, was near the front counter in the midst of the melee, five women screaming and crowding at him, waving their arms, demanding answers to questions that seemed to have no meaning—though the women at Birtd's a few minutes before had spoken in clear English. Wilma was backing away from a pair of enraged ladies when Harper saw her and motioned her on back to his desk.

At the credenza, Wilma busied herself making fresh coffee. Harper marched past her escorting two of the women toward the back door, taking them to the jail across the alley. He was followed by a line of officers, each with a female in tow. All blondes or sandy-haired, and one redhead, not a brunette among them.

Harper returned to his desk and poured himself a cup of coffee. Wilma sat down across from him. "How many black wigs did you collect?"

Harper smiled. "Eleven, most of them from the three cars we pulled over. Clothes, too. Big floppy coats and skirts. One of the women was in the midst of changing, Blake caught her with her skirt around her knees. Brennan and West are at Birtd's talking to witnesses." He settled back, sipping his coffee.

"Those are Greenlaw women."

Harper nodded. "I'm afraid so."

"My God, poor Lucinda. I wonder if she has any idea."

"They were booked in with all kinds of aliases. These people have been working up and down the coast for nearly two weeks. Here in the village, they've kept it low-key, until today. In most instances, the store owners thought it was just a couple of annoying customers. They didn't know what was coming down until the troublemakers left, and they found the cash drawer cleaned out."

"One of the drivers," Wilma said, "in the blue T-Bird,

was a probationer of mine. Sam Fulman. Just a few minutes ago his car was parked over on Ocean." She gave him the license plate number that, earlier, she had given to Brennan.

Harper motioned an officer back to the desk and sent him to impound the T-Bird and bring Fulman in for questioning.

"I haven't seen Fulman in ten years."

"And he's a Greenlaw?"

"Shamas's cousin. A real loser. There are a few darker-haired, lighter-boned members of the family."

"We have two witnesses on store diversions up the coast that might be reliable. If we can ID the same women, here, and with your ID of Fulman, we might make something stick."

"*Might?*" She raised an eyebrow.

"Most of these cases walk, Wilma. You get them in court, no witness seems able to make a solid ID. Different hair color, different way of dressing, and the witness isn't that sure. And these people turn the court-room into the same kind of circus, shouting, mouthing off in a language you can't understand."

Harper shrugged. "A judge can charge them with contempt and lock them up, but besides disrupting the whole courtroom, they'll trash the jail cells—those women can tear up a jail worse than a hundred male felons. And most times, the judge gets so tired of the noise and confusion in his courtroom and no solid wit-nesses, that he'll do anything to be rid of them.

"I've never seen you so negative."

"You've never seen me faced with one of these rene-gade families. You heard them up there at the desk, couldn't get anything intelligible out of them. That's the way they are in court. You can lock them up, but if your witnesses are uncertain, you've got nothing to hold them. Then usually, their hotshot attorney shows up and offers full restitution." Harper shook his head.

"All the shopkeeper wants is his money and the value of the goods they stole. Lawyer puts a little pressure on him and offers plenty of cash, and he'll drop charges."

Harper shrugged, and lit a cigarette. "Without charges, they walk."

He set down his coffee cup. "Your Sam Fulman—did he ever tell you anything about the Greenlaw family? Anything more than you know from Lucinda?"

"He said the clan is thick, that most of them come from one small town in North Carolina. Donegal, I think. Three-story brick houses, long, curved drives, swimming pools and private woods, landscaped acreage. He claimed they practically own the town."

Wilma watched the officers settling back to their desks, the room calm now, and quieter. "Fulman told me the families all work together, but he never would say just what kind of work—the construction trades, I remember him saying once, rather vaguely. He said they all intermarry, all adhere to the family rules. Much, I suppose, like a tightly controlled little Mafia.

"Fulman is something of a renegade among them. He didn't knuckle under like the rest, didn't behave as the elders dictated. He moved out when he was young, came out to the coast, set up his own operation. I had him on probation for a chop shop. Later, at the time I got him revoked, he'd gone into business with Shamas."

"What kind of business?"

"Selling machine tools."

"What about Shamas's other business affairs?"

"When Lucinda and Shamas met, she told me, he was a rep for a roofing company in Seattle. Before they left Washington State, he had started the machine-tool company and entered into several related businesses— something about electroplating tools."

Harper swiveled his chair around, reaching for the coffeepot. "When they moved down here, he kept those enterprises?"

"That's what Lucinda told me, but she was pretty vague. Evidently Shamas didn't like to talk to her about business, would never give her any details. Never told her anything about bank balances, just gave her an allowance."

She looked at her watch. "Do you have anything on the Chambers stabbing? How is he?"

"He's doing okay. Doctors got the lung reinflated and repaired—he was lucky. He should be home in a few days. He says he didn't know his assailant, that he got only a glimpse. Said he'd stopped to use the phone, there by the rest rooms, that he was out walking and forgot he had an early appointment. The guy grabbed him from behind, a regular bear hug, and shoved the knife in his chest. Chambers fell and lay still, hoping the guy would think he was dead. His assailant heard someone coming and ran."

"Wouldn't that pretty well clear Lucinda? Grabbing him from behind hard enough to hold him and stab him?" Lucinda had been questioned as a matter of routine because she'd been in the area and had reported the body, but also because Chambers was on board the *Green Lady* when Shamas drowned.

"I'd think it would clear her. Though she's tall,

almost as tall as Chambers; and the miles she walks every day, she has to be in good shape for . . ."

"For an old lady?" Wilma grinned. "But what would be her motive?" She glanced again at her watch. "Didn't know it was so late—Sheril will pitch a fit, want to know if I've been shopping on her time." She rose, picked up her sack lunch from his desk, looked hard at Harper. "She's such a bitch to work for. You don't know, Max, the bad luck I've wished on you."

Harper smiled, and rose, and walked with her to the front. The squad room was silent now, and half deserted, only a few officers at their desks. Wilma wondered, as she pushed out the door, how long the Greenlaw women would stay in jail before someone approached the Birtds with enough cash so they would drop the charges and Harper would be forced to release them. She stopped in a little park to eat her lunch, enjoying ten minutes of solitude, then headed for work. And it was not until the next afternoon that she learned, with amazement, that Clyde, too, had been arrested, that same afternoon. That her good friend had, uncharacteristically, also run afoul of Molena Point law enforcement—that about the time the Greenlaw women were set free, and Sam Fulman was picked up for questioning then released, Clyde, too, was cooling his heels behind bars.

16

THE TIME was past midnight. Rain beat against Wilma's shuttered bedroom windows; a fire burned in the red-enameled woodstove, its light flickering across the flowered quilt and the white-wicker furniture. Wilma sat in bed reading, Dulcie curled up beside her.

She had spent the evening at her desk, poring over a map of the U.S., tracking the locations of auto-loan scams across the country, using an NCIC list that Max Harper had printed out for her from the police computer. The report covered the last six months, but the operations that interested her specifically had occurred within the last few weeks.

Her map bristled with pins, but the work had gone slowly, as she had not only to locate the scams, but then to find routes according to dates, marking each route with different colored pins. Some of the trails were circuitous, moving back and forth among half a dozen cities or to several adjoining metropolitan areas.

But one, a line of red pins, delineated a well-defined series of auto-loan scams over the last three weeks—beginning in Greenville, North Carolina, half a day's drive west of Donegal, the home of the Greenlaw clan, and leading directly across the U.S.—scams that would not have been reported so early on, if not for one fortuitous accident.

When one of the small car dealers, driving a newly purchased BMW home for the weekend, was hit by a delivery truck, the officer who answered the call ran a routine check and came up with the fake registration.

This dealer had bought four cars within a twenty-four hour period; the fake registration made him so uneasy that he asked the police to check on the other three vehicles.

All four cars had come to him with fake paper.

The subsequent investigation spread from one small town to the next; dozens of false registrations were uncovered and reported to NCIC, long before any of the dealers would have been alerted by overdue car payments.

The trail ended at Bakersfield. Police had no record of any suspicious car purchases beyond that point. The perpetrators could have traveled north up the coast or south, or turned back east again.

Wilma's next step was to phone the car agencies that had been ripped off, compare the MOs with those she'd been dealing with at Beckwhite's: all had very professional IDs, excellent credit records that checked out with the credit bureaus. These people had to have, within their sophisticated operation, at least one very skilled hacker.

"Presume," she told Dulcie, laying down her book,

"that the Greenlaws were notified of Shamas's death the morning after the accident, that most of them started out within a few hours, driving across country for Shamas's funeral. They make their first stop at Greenville, to pick up a little cash. They buy two new BMWs, two Cadillacs and a Buick convertible, all listed by NCIC as sold in Greenville within hours of one another, at three separate dealerships, and all purchased with the maximum loans.

"Half a day's drive down the road, then, they sell the cars for cash to small, out-of-the-way dealers, or through quickly placed ads in the local paper, give the buyer a forged registration certificate that wouldn't come to light until they were long gone.

"Maybe thirty thousand apiece," she told Dulcie. "They pick up maybe a hundred and fifty thousand for walking-around money, for their little jaunt out here to the coast."

"Not too bad for a few hours' work," Dulcie said. "Do you think NCIC could link pigeon drops the same way? Store diversions and shoplifting?"

"No," Wilma said. "They couldn't. Only the big stuff is reported, things that might be interstate. Like stolen cars moved from one state to another. The little crimes, if they were reported to anyone beyond a local PD, would go to that state's crime bureau. You'd have to contact each state, see what might have been logged. The Greenlaws could have worked the local stores all across the country, picking up their groceries and a little loose change—now doing the same here while they wait for the last of the relatives to arrive for the funeral."

"Very nice," Dulcie said, "traveling along in their homes on wheels, stealing as they go. Just like Gypsies."

Wilma sat looking at the little cat, taking that in.

"Have you ever heard of Travelers?" Dulcie said. "Irish Travelers?"

Wilma's eyes widened.

"In the library books on Gypsies," Dulcie said, "the Irish Travelers are almost exactly the same. The whole family steals; it's how they make their living."

"But all Gypsies aren't . . ." Wilma began.

"Not all Gypsies steal, just some clans. I was reading about them late last night—the library is so peaceful at night," Dulcie said. "Well, not all Irish are Travelers. But the Travelers' ancestors centuries ago in Ireland—they were tinkers just like the Gypsies. Tinsmiths and peddlers traveling across Ireland in their pony carts, stopping at little farms, trading and doing repairs. According to the books, some of the Travelers would steal anything left lying loose."

"You're not turning into a racist?" Wilma said, raising an eyebrow.

"What? Against the Irish?" Dulcie laid her ears back. "Why would I do that? I'm telling you what I read. It's supposed to be fact. Besides, you're part Irish. So is Clyde."

"And how come," Wilma said, teasing her, "how come you, of all cats, are talking about other folks stealing?"

Dulcie ducked her head. "That was . . . mostly . . . before I knew any better." She looked up at Wilma. "It was never for self-gain. It's just that . . . Such lovely little sweaters and scarves and silky things, so pretty and soft . . ." She looked pleadingly at Wilma, deeply chastened. Wilma grinned at her and stroked her ears, and at last the little cat began to purr.

"But it is a touchy subject," Wilma told her. "Many

people in the East are still bitter about prejudice against the Irish. It started when Irish families came over here during the potato famine—the 1800s—They left Ireland to survive, to make a new start, their whole country was starving, people were starving by the thousands. But when they arrived in this country, there was so much bad feeling about them."

"Maybe that's because of the Travelers," Dulcie said, "because *they* were stealing." She licked her paw and looked up at Wilma, filled with a quick, electric energy. "This Fulman that you had on probation, Shamas's cousin. What were he and Shamas doing in Seattle?"

Wilma's eyes widened. "For one thing, selling supposedly high-quality machine tools that were really junk. I don't remember all the details, but it involved a switch—showing the buyer fine merchandise as a sample, then shipping him shoddy stuff. They were paid up front, of course.

"When I checked out his family, through the probation office in Greenville, the information they gave me was that the family was clean. Not a thing on the Fulmans or the Greenlaws."

"Smooth," Dulcie said. "And how would you know any different? Most people never think about whole families living that way, their entire lives dedicated to stealing and running scams."

"My job was to look for these things. And Greenville had to know."

"Maybe. Maybe not. The books say they're very law-abiding in their own town." Dulcie grinned. "Maybe the probation officer was a shirttail cousin."

Wilma looked at her, torn between laughter and chagrin. "I should have thought about that kind of connection. I've always known there were families in San Francisco running roofing scams, asphalt-paving scams, home-repair swindles. It's their way of life." Wilma shook her head. "I never put that together with Fulman and Shamas—and it was my business to know.

"I hate to think how this would affect Lucinda if she should find out about Shamas. It would break her heart to know that her husband was a thief and a con artist."

Dulcie licked her whiskers. "I think she knows. From the things I've heard her say to Pedric, and to Charlie, too, I think she knows very well what Shamas was."

Wilma looked at her quietly.

Dulcie looked intently back at her. "How could Lucinda live with him all those years and not know there was something wrong?"

"You'd be surprised," Wilma said, "how thoroughly humans can deceive themselves." She settled deeper into the pillows, sipping her cocoa—and straightened up, nearly spilling it, when they heard above the pounding rain, a thud on the back porch, then the back door creak.

The noise brought Dulcie up rigid, too, her every hair standing straight.

Wilma slid out of bed, snatching up the fire tongs, and Dulcie dropped softly to the floor—then they heard Dulcie's cat door slap, banging against its metal frame.

"Anyone home?"

Dulcie relaxed. Her fur went flat, her claws drew back into their sheaths. Wilma sighed, and laughed as Joe Grey came swaggering down the hall, his silver coat soaked dark, dripping on the Persian runner. "I was around back, came down the hill, saw the bedroom light. Are those cookies I smell?"

Wilma trailed to the bathroom, snatched up a towel, and tossed it to the bedroom floor. Joe, giving her a sour look, rolled on the terry cloth until he was relatively dry, then leaped to the bed.

"Why are you out in the rain?" Dulcie said. "You weren't hunting, on a night like this."

"I took a little jaunt by Cara Ray's motel, after you said she wasn't at Lucinda's for supper." He licked a few swipes across his shoulder.

Wilma shoved the cookie plate in his direction. He took one in his teeth, crunching it with pleasure, dropping crumbs. The quilt was due for a washing; this was why Wilma liked washable furnishings, so she and the cats could enjoy, and not fuss.

"So what did you see?" Dulcie said. "Was that Sam person there at her motel?"

"No. Nor Cara Ray, either. I nearly drowned climbing up to the roof, nearly broke my neck on those wet, slick shutters, slipping down to Cara Ray's window. Lucky someone didn't find me smashed on the pavement below, lying in the gutter broken and my poor cat lungs full of water. All I got for my trouble was a cold bath, and a view of Cara Ray's messy motel room.

"I waited for maybe an hour, thinking she might bring him back with her, and the rain pounding against the windows like shotgun blasts. Where would they go on a night like this? So damned wet—couldn't get a claw into anything."

"You haven't been home?" Dulcie said.

"I was home for dinner. Why?"

"Clyde didn't say anything?"

"About what?"

"Clyde was arrested."

Joe stared at her. Stared at Wilma. "You're joking. There's no way Max Harper . . . Arrested for what? Who would arrest him? In what town? For speeding? Oh, that would—"

"Not for speeding," Wilma said. "For creating a public nuisance."

Joe settled down on the quilt, his yellow eyes fixed on Wilma. "What stupid thing has he done now?"

"Selig broke his collar," Wilma said.

"I told Clyde the pups had been chewing on each other's collars," Joe said, "the whole time they were together."

"Clyde was walking the pups down Ocean," Wilma said, "when a big Harley came roaring around the corner. The pups went crazy, hit the end of their leads bellowing, and Selig kept on going, chasing the Harley and baying like a bloodhound—and Clyde chasing him, dragging Hestig through traffic, yelling and swearing."

Joe Grey smiled, his yellow eyes slitted with pleasure.

"A squad car came around the corner," Wilma said, "following the roar of the Harley." In Molena Point, motorcycles were just as strictly forbidden as were unleashed canines.

"Another black-and-white screamed down Ocean, and when they got the Harley cornered, Selig and Hestig and Clyde were right in the middle, Clyde trying to hold Hestig and slip the other leash around Selig's neck."

Wilma smiled. "All of this in front of the Patio Café, and half the village looking on." She and Clyde had been close friends forever—if she had a little laugh at his expense, he'd had plenty of laughs at hers. "My friend Nora was waiting tables and had a ringside view. Those two rookies that Harper just hired—they don't know Clyde."

"They arrested him," Joe Grey said, rumbling with purrs.

Wilma nodded. "Arrested him while the pups had him tangled in the leash."

Dulcie looked from one to the other, half amused, half feeling sorry for Clyde.

"Clyde got himself untangled," Wilma said, "but Selig wouldn't let the rookies near the Harley. The puppy seemed to think that *he* had caught the cycle, and they had no right to it. He stood guarding it, snarling like a timber wolf, and Clyde trying to pull him away.

"One of the rookies stepped into the café and bought a prewrapped beef sandwich. He distracted Selig with that until his partner could lock the Harley driver in a squad car. Ordinarily, a rookie wouldn't be assigned alone to a unit, but there was some kind of changeover at the station."

Wilma settled back against the cushions, and for a long, perfect moment, she and the cats envisioned Clyde Damen in the backseat of a black-and-white, confined behind the wire barrier.

"Nice," Joe Grey said. "Wait until I lay this one on him."

"He didn't mention it?" Dulcie asked.

"Silent as a mummy in the tomb." He looked at Wilma. "So what happened when they got to the station? Did you talk to Harper, get a blow-by-blow?"

"When rookie Jimmie McFarland tried to get the

pups out of the unit, they set their feet and wouldn't come.

"McFarland had saved back a little of the sandwich. He bribed them out with that. But when he got them into the station, Selig took a look at all those nice uniforms and began to bark and leap in the officers' faces, kissing everyone. And Hestig grabbed McFarland's field book, raced around the station with it, dodging anyone who got close.

Wilma smiled. "When the dispatcher called the dog catcher, that's when Clyde began to shout."

Joe Grey rolled on his back, laughing.

"At about that time," Wilma said, "Harper came in the back door, saw McFarland tackle Selig, saw Officer Blake trying to corner Hestig. Harper grabbed Selig by the nape of the neck, shook him, and turned on Clyde as if he'd shake him, too."

Dulcie's purr bubbled into laughter. Joe lay grinning, thinking about what he'd have to say to Clyde.

"Before Harper could get them sorted out, Selig jerked loose from him, snatched a sheaf of reports from Officer Blake's desk, and ran off chewing on them. Three officers caught him but, without a collar, he slipped free of them—snatched Lieutenant Brennan's ham sandwich, then grabbed the photo officer's reflex camera. The officer tackled him, rescued his camera, stood cradling it like a baby. Harper was so mad, he told me, and was laughing so hard, that he could feel tears."

"And I missed it all," Joe said. "The event of the—"

A tremor shook the bed. Joe leaped up. Dulcie rose into a wary crouch. Wilma's cup rattled in its saucer.

But then the room was still again.

They waited, but no second jolt hit. The three

friends looked at each other, and shrugged. A second later, the phone rang.

Wilma picked up, listened, then pressed the speaker button.

Lucinda's voice was weak and unsteady. ". . . he's . . . I'm at the hospital. He's hurt, Wilma. Broken arm, some broken ribs. He was soaking wet and so cold, shivering. I only hope . . . I don't know how long he lay there, in the cold and rain."

Wilma leaned close to the phone's speaker. "Start at the beginning, Lucinda. Tell me what happened. Take it slowly, please."

"The police found him—not our police," Lucinda said. "The highway patrol. They—in the dark. Pedric was lying halfway down Hellhag Hill. Someone . . ." Lucinda's voice shook. "Someone tried . . ."

"How would they find him in the dark and rain? What were they doing . . . Never mind. I'll come. Who's the doctor?"

"Dr. Harliss."

"I'll be there." Wilma slipped out of bed. "I'll be . . ."

"No. Don't come here. I'm . . . I'll stay with him. Go there. Go to Hellhag Hill. Find out . . . Talk to the police. Find out who—what happened."

"But . . ."

"Hurry, while they're still there. Please find out what happened."

"But they won't be . . ."

"They'll still be there. I came away in the ambulance. They were still there, seeing to Newlon."

"Newlon?"

"Newlon's dead. They found him lying on the highway in the rain. Please find out, Wilma." Her voice shook. "Find out who killed Newlon, and tried to kill Pedric."

Wilma hung up the phone and sat looking at the cats. "First, Chambers is stabbed. Now, another man in the hospital, and a man dead. And all of them," she said, "connected to Shamas Greenlaw."

Swinging out of bed, she snatched up some clothes and slipped into the bathroom to wash and dress. Within minutes, she and the cats were headed for Hellhag Hill, Joe and Dulcie staring out through the rain-soaked windows, shivering in the cavernous, cold car.

 17

TWO HIGHWAY patrol units were nosed in along the shoulder, their lights shining across the rain-matted grass at the base of Hellhag Hill. Passing them on the wet black two-lane, Wilma pulled up ahead, behind two Molena Point black-and-whites. Beyond these stood the coroner's gray sedan, its headlights shining on a makeshift tent, a green police tarp erected to keep the rain off Newlon Greenlaw's body. Other illumination was provided by three large butane lanterns. The coroner, John Bern, a thin, button-nosed man wearing a yellow raincoat, knelt beside the body. As Wilma stepped out of the car, she saw Max Harper leave the tent and start up the hill, his torchlight bouncing off curtains of blowing rain. She saw, up the hill just below the trailer park, in the beam of other torches, two more uniforms and a gathering of onlookers.

"Up there," Officer Davis told her, coming up to Wilma, wringing water from her uniform skirt. "That's where Pedric Greenlaw fell, just above those boulders. Ambulance left with him about half an hour ago." Davis was a middle-aged woman, solidly built, short dark hair, dark and expressive Latin eyes.

"What happened?" Wilma said. "I've only talked with Lucinda Greenlaw, and she was pretty upset."

"You knew Newlon Greenlaw?" Davis said, gesturing toward the body.

"I've met him."

"Head cracked open. We've found no weapon. Apparently the two men were fighting, up around the trailers. It's dark as hell up there at night; they've never had good lighting.

"People in the trailers woke up, heard thumps and scuffling, then groans. Grabbed flashlights and ran out. Someone thought there were three men, but they couldn't be sure. We've not found any traces of a third man. Pedric fell maybe twenty feet, into those rocks just above the cave.

"When the people up there called 911, California Highway Patrol was just up the road. They came on down to see if they could render assistance, spotted Newlon's body in their headlights here beside the road.

"We won't know much until it gets light," Davis said. "And maybe not then, with this rain. Sure makes a mess."

Moving to the tent, Wilma watched the coroner examine the dead man's head wound and take the temperature of the liver, a procedure which never failed to make her queasy. She flinched as the needle went into the abdomen.

She had left Joe and Dulcie in the car. She hoped they'd stay there, hoped the heavy rain would keep them confined. Knowing those two, she doubted it. A promise from either of them was subject to all manner of feline guile.

As Harper's light moved up the hill, someone started down toward him with another torch. The rain had slacked off, but the damage to the crime scene would be significant, blood washed away, evidence destroyed. When she glanced down the road toward her car, the torch of one of the CHP officers caught four bright flashes low to the ground racing across the highway, accompanied by a gleam of white.

"Damn cats," she muttered; but already the cats had disappeared. Joe and Dulcie were doing as they pleased, and no one was going to stop them.

The turmoil on the hill, men shouting and striding through the dark grass with lights swinging, had terrified the clowder of wild cats. Already disoriented by the heavy rain, by the jolting of the earth, and by the earlier violence of the men fighting and then the crowd gathering and the scream of the ambulance and not knowing where to escape, they had withdrawn to cower among the rocks in a state of near shock. Even the bellowing mewl of the ragged kit, which they had heard earlier, had seemed terrifying, coming alone out of the night.

Still cowering against the boulders as men moved all over the hillside, they refused to go into the cave; none of them would enter the cave when the earth shook.

Long after the police cars and most of the men had left and the world grew quiet once more, they crouched in the soaking grass, belly to ground, waiting for further disaster—perhaps for the earth to open entirely, for the hill beneath their paws to crumble away.

All but the tattered kit. The ninth and smallest, she was of another mind.

The cave did not frighten her. She sat in its mouth, where the others wouldn't go, had sat there earlier, stoically enduring the earth's trembling. If she died, she died. She wasn't going to run away.

After the earth stopped shaking she had stood up on her hind paws like a little rabbit, looking all around her, delighted at the brilliance of the sky. When the quake ceased, the rain had ceased for the moment, too, and a strange, thin gleam lit the sky. Not the light of dawn, but a silver glow shimmering beneath the rain clouds. Ignoring her soaking fur and the icy chill that reached down into her thin little bones, she had looked around her, thrilled with the beauty of the world.

But at the same time, too, she tasted fear. She could still smell the blood from the man who had lain among the boulders. She had seen him fall. She had seen another man die. These matters deeply distressed her.

It had happened just at midnight. She had been hunting beneath the trailers, where field mice had burrowed away from the driving rain, mice displaced and disoriented and easier to catch than most. Despite her lack of skill she had trapped two and eaten them; and as she padded along beneath the wheeled houses, hoping to find more such foolish morsels, smelling from above her the sour scent of sleeping humans, hearing through the thin trailer floors the rumbling of their ragged, crude snores, she had heard something else. Footsteps thundered overhead, and she heard a door creak open.

She stopped suddenly, spun around, and drew back against a wheel.

A man left the trailer, heading across the sodden yard to a shed where firewood was stacked; she was afraid of him until she saw that it was only the old man who came here with the lady—the lady called him Pedric. The kit was crouched to leap past him when another man came out, shutting his door so softly that only a cat would hear it.

He walked soundlessly in the rain, following Pedric. The smell of him, in the wet air, made her fur bristle. A cruel smell, and when he drew close behind Pedric, she hissed with fear.

Suddenly in the darkness the silhouettes of the two men merged. She heard a loud crack, saw Pedric fall heavily into the splattering mud.

Immediately the man who had hit Pedric grabbed him and dragged him down the steep hill. He bent over him listening, studying him, then he half threw, half pushed him. Pedric fell, rolling limply down and down, until his body lay against the boulders that formed the mouth of the cave.

The thin man climbed again. Before he reached the trailers a third man came out of the shadows, crouching low, a big, heavy human, broad as a rutting bull. The two fought, pounding and grunting, hitting one another until the big one fell and lay still; that surprised her, that the smaller man had been so clever and quick. Then she saw the rock in his hand. He had hit with that. He dragged the big man down the hill past her. She smelled the death smell.

He dragged and threw him, just as he had thrown old Pedric; how strong he was, like a fighting weasel. The big man rolled farther than Pedric had. Rolled and fell. The thin man ran after him, kicked him, threw him again so he slid down and down onto the highway; the heavy soft thuds of his falling body made her think of the mice she had crushed between her young, sharp teeth.

The thin man went away, down below the road. She crept out to look at Pedric.

The old man was alive, twisted among the rocks. Nosing at him, she could feel his breath, faint and ragged. She knew nothing to do but yowl.

For such a little thing, she had a huge, demanding cry. Leaping to the top of a boulder, she faced the trailers and bawled.

She mewed and cried until a light went on, then another light, spilling into the night like a yellow river. A woman shouted at her to shut up. A door burst open, and a man ran out, hefting a shoe. Then another man, swinging a hunk of firewood; he heaved it at her, and she dodged. Yowling twice more, she fled down the hill behind the thin man who had hurt Pedric.

Down swiftly past the dead man. There, the thin man ran across the dark highway and down again, down the steeper cliff. She was close behind him; humans were so slow. At the edge of the cliff he lifted his hand, she saw the rock and smelled the blood, the rock that had killed the big man, watched him heave the rock away into the sea.

Rain came again, beating into her face. Above her, up the hill, car lights were racing among the trailers. A siren screamed, and men shouted.

She followed the thin man up again, across the road and up the hill, and watched him vanish among the trailers. But in a minute he was back, pushing in among the crowd, crying out with surprise, and then with pain and anger, a mourning cry that, to the little kit's ears, was as fake as the kitten-mewl of a seagull.

Galloping up the hill through the dark, she drew as close as she could to the killer and tried to catch his scent, but she could not; too many humans were crowded all together. Before, when she had followed him downhill, she had smelled only the dead man's blood.

Frightened and puzzled at humans, the little cat went down to the dark, empty cave and sat hunched in its yawning mouth, looking out, watching the moving reflections of lights from above, and on the road below. Despite the shouting, she dozed, mewling in her sleep. She woke fearful.

Alone on the hill, she waited. It was her nature to wait, to expect something better to happen. Ragged and starving, bone-thin, outcast by her own kind and without any reason to hope, the small kit was filled with hope.

She thought of the hills her clowder had come from, hills like this one, dripping wet in the rain but, in the sunshine, bright with yellow grass, sweet and rustling above endless, sunstruck sea, and she was filled with hope. She believed that no matter what trouble came, all would be well again if only one waited and watched—and moved swiftly with a fast paw at the right moment.

Closing her round yellow eyes, she dozed. When next she woke, two shadows approached her, padding up through the dark wet grass; two pairs of long, gleaming eyes silvered by the pale sky, two pairs of eyes, watching her.

• • •

Joe and Dulcie studied two round yellow eyes peering out at them from the black and dripping grass. They could see no more than the eyes, disembodied in the blackness—until the shadows re-formed themselves, turning into mottled black-and-brown fur.

The waif stepped delicately forward through the sodden grass. She was so thin that the sea wind should have blown her tumbling across the hill. Her narrow little face was all black-and-brown smudges. Her expression was not the innocent look of a normal kitten, but brighter and more intelligent, more lively and knowing than any ordinary cat. Dulcie lifted her paw, enchanted; this kit was like them. Not for an instant did she doubt the wonder she sensed in this small kitten.

But the kit made Joe uneasy.

The two experiences he'd had with cats of their own kind had badly shaken him. First, Kate Osborne, whose skill at shapeshifting had left him nervous and unsettled: to know a human woman who could become a cat, deeply disturbed him. And then Azrael, that other like themselves, black, lecherous, lording it over them, coming onto Dulcie all testosterone and gleaming claws.

Now here was this ragged kitten. Like them. And frightening in her wide-eyed yearning—but before Joe Grey knew what had happened, he had reached a protecting paw to scoop the little kit close to him. Before he knew what he was doing, he was washing her smudgy face.

She had a little, tilted nose, a dish face. How boldly she rubbed against his leg, purring so hard that the ragged rhythm shook her thin body, and shook him, too.

Dulcie came close and licked her face, purring.

But around them, hidden in the night, Joe could sense the clowder of wild cats creeping close, could sense their anger as stealthily they moved closer through the dark wet grass, the wild beasts watching them—as if they did not want the kitten to be with outsiders. The darkness around them felt brittle with feline rage.

Joe stood up tall in the night, glaring into the darkness, daring the beasts to so much as hiss at them.

He caught a startled gleam, but it was quickly gone. He scowled and leered, then licked the kitten's face.

Dulcie said to the kit, "A man was killed tonight."

The kit's eyes widened, she looked up at Dulcie and twitched her long, wet tail. "How did you know to speak to me?"

Dulcie smiled. "I knew. A man was killed tonight, kit, and another man was hurt. Did you see? Can you show us who did this?"

The kit's yellow eyes grew wide. "I saw," she said softly. "I was hunting mice, and I saw."

"Was it someone from the trailers?" Dulcie glanced up the dark hill. "Someone who came from there?" She looked deeply at the kit, her green eyes kind and without guile. "Can you take us to that man? Can you show us his smell?"

The kit looked at Dulcie a long time. Twice she cut her eyes around at their unseen observers. She hissed at them and glowered as Joe had done.

At last she led Joe and Dulcie uphill, passing through the invisible cats. Passing a low growl, and snarls. Beside her, Joe Grey thundered and rumbled. No cat moved to strike them.

Up through the matted wet grass, their paws sodden, then splashing through the mud under the trailers. All the trailers were dark above them; no human was abroad now. Only the scents lingered, human stinks riding on the damp air. The kit sniffed and prowled, trying to sort them out. But no cat on earth could have sorted those smells.

"Do you *know* his smell?" asked Dulcie. "If one could sort anything, would you know it?"

"No," the kit said. "When I followed him, I could only smell blood."

They stood in the sopping mud between the grease-coated wheels, their wet fur clinging to their shivering bodies. "Which trailer?" Dulcie said. "Where did he come from?"

"He came out from between them. There." She cocked her ears toward the trailers. "I didn't see where exactly. I heard a door shut, then there he was." Again the kit moved away. They followed her.

"Somewhere here," she said, scenting at the wheels and at shoe prints all filled with water. But she could find no certain trail.

"We'll come back," Dulcie told her, "when this tangle of stinks blows away and when the rain is gone. Maybe then . . . ?"

"Maybe," said the kit. "Maybe I will see him again, and I can learn his smell. I will watch. I will follow him, and I will find his scent. If the others . . . if they don't chase me away for being with you, for talking to you."

Joe Grey leaped down to the boulders and looked around him. He could feel the clowder watching.

"If any cat," he growled, "any ragged mangy vermin among you touches this kit, if any moldy creature among you does this kit harm, you will *all* of you wish you had never come to this hill. You will *all* die, slowly and painfully, by the force of my claws."

His eyes blazed into night. "I have your scents. I will track you wherever you go, and I will leave you bleeding and immobile. I will watch the gulls swoop down, to pick meat from your living bones."

The kit pressed close to Dulcie. "If they try to hurt me, I will go deep in the cave. They won't come there; they fear the cave. They long for it, they want to go where it leads, but they fear it." She looked brightly at Dulcie. "I will find the man who hurt Pedric. I will find him, and I will lead you to him."

 18

MAN KILLED, ONE INJURED,
IN FALL DOWN HELLHAG HILL

Newlon Greenlaw, nephew of the late Molena
Point resident Shamas Greenlaw, was found dead
shortly after midnight, his body lying in the rain on
Highway One at the base of Hellhag Hill. A California
Highway Patrol unit spotted the body as they answered
a 911 call to an accident victim higher up the hill,
where just below the Moonwatch Trailer Park elderly
Pedric Greenlaw lay injured in a fall. The two men
may possibly have been victims in a bizarre double
accident.

Relatives had no explanation as to why the men
were out on the hill during the midnight storm.
Newlon and his uncle were staying in their campers at
the trailer park with other members of the extended
Greenlaw family, gathered here for Shamas Greenlaw's
funeral. Shamas died earlier this month in a drowning

accident during a cruise off Seattle. His rosary and funeral will not be scheduled until additional family members arrive.

Pedric Greenlaw is under observation at Molena Point Hospital. His condition, doctors told reporters, is stable. He will be hospitalized for several days.

Pawing open the morning paper and glimpsing the headline, Joe saw that the *Gazette* had been swift and efficient. Last night's death and injury filled the front page above the fold, displacing whatever local news the paper must have already set up. He imagined the last-minute bustle, late into the night, as editors worked to change the front page.

If the paper were printed out of town, as some small papers were, they'd never have made it. Probably the ink was still wet when the truck delivered its stacks of *Gazette*s to the pickup stations.

As for the *Gazette*'s take that Newlon's death had been an accident, Joe didn't believe it for a minute.

He had arrived home in darkness, long before the newspaper hit the porch. Soaking and cold, he had gone directly through the kitchen to the laundry and snuggled down on the lower bunk against old Rube's stomach, absorbing the doggy warmth.

Rube slept alone or with the cats. Selig slept on the back porch in a huge TV shipping carton that Clyde had lined with old flannel shirts and a blanket—a far cry from the cold wind on Hellhag Hill. There was barely enough room for two, though, when Hestig was there and not with Charlie.

Snuggled against Rube, Joe had dozed until just before seven, when he heard the morning paper hit the front porch. Galloping through the living room and out his cat door, he had dragged the *Gazette* through the house and onto the breakfast table; ripping off the plastic, rainproof cover, he'd heard Selig pad across the back porch, whining, to paw at the plywood barrier of the dog door. Of course that woke Clyde. Joe heard him stamp across the bedroom, then heard the shower running. He had barely finished reading the article when Clyde schlepped into the kitchen and began to fill the coffeepot in a sleep-drugged morning ritual. A shower alone was not enough to transform Clyde Damen from sleeping zombie to real-live person.

Soon bacon was sizzling in the pan, and the animals were lined up, eating. Clyde had spoken no word. His one glance at Joe was a deep scowl. Before he broke the eggs into the skillet he moved to the table. Standing behind Joe, loudly sipping his coffee, he read the front page. For some time, he said nothing.

Then he breathed a sigh and turned away. Joe glanced up to see a relieved, and puzzling, smile.

So what's with you? Joe wanted to say; but some errant wisdom kept him silent.

Possibly Clyde, knowing nothing about last night's excitement on Hellhag Hill, had been prepared for a humorous front-page story at his expense, a comic piece about the arrest of the village's best-known auto mechanic and his two pups. Not encountering such an exposé, he seemed far more pleased with the morning. It was not until Clyde noticed the muddy pawprints leading across the kitchen from the living room that he sat down at the table, giving Joe a long, direct look.

"So where were you last night?"

"I was hunting." Joe considered that his trek up

Hellhag Hill and the information he had painstakingly gathered was the most difficult kind of hunt. "Why do you always ask me where I was at night? I don't ask where you've been. I'm not some teenage kid you have to keep track of, afraid I'll wreck your car or get arrested. You have absolutely no cause to—"

"You were on Hellhag Hill last night."

"If you don't turn the bacon, it's going to be charcoal."

Clyde rose and flipped the bacon, then picked up the paper, reading the lead article with more care. Joe waited patiently for Clyde's inevitable and long-winded lecture.

"Do you want to tell me why, Joe, that the minute the paper hit the porch, you were into it?"

Joe looked at him blankly.

"You knew about this accident, that's why. And the only way you could have known, is if you were up there yourself last night. Certainly you were not hunting rabbits in the rain."

"Actually, rain makes for good rabbit hunting. If it floods their holes, the rabbits come right on out. Disorients them. I enjoyed, some time before midnight, an unusually fat young rabbit. If you ever—"

"Can it, Joe. You want to tell me how you just happened to be on Hellhag Hill when Pedric Greenlaw fell and Newlon Greenlaw died? I presume Dulcie was with you. Dare I ask if you were there before the cops arrived?"

"How could we have been?" Joe fixed a shocked yellow gaze on Clyde. "You can't think we had anything to do with the accident? Why in the world would we, two little cats . . ."

"Give it a rest, Joe. What were you doing on

Hellhag Hill in the middle of the night, in the pouring rain? How did you know about the accident?" Clyde was pale with anger. Joe didn't want to be the cause of a coronary. With the way Clyde ate, his arteries were probably lined with gunk thicker than transmission oil.

"If you must know," he said softly, "if it's really any of your concern, Lucinda called Wilma from the hospital. I just happened to be there at Wilma's house, eating cookies, so of course she took Dulcie and me with her. Lucinda asked her to go out to Hellhag Hill and meet with the police, to find out what had happened."

"And Wilma took you with her? Why would . . . Why would she . . . ?"

"She made us promise to stay in her car, out of the way."

"And of course you did that. Stayed in her car, warm and dry and minding your own business. Never touched a paw outside the car, never went near the body and the police."

"You really don't think we would get in the way of the police. The fact that . . ."

"Please, Joe. It's too early."

"Bacon's burning," Joe said helpfully.

Clyde leaped to rescue the charred slices. As he tried to scrape the black off—which worked better with toast than with bacon—Joe pawed through the paper, wondering if the *Gazette* had had a front-page piece on Clyde and the pups, before the accident replaced it. Such a humorous story was exactly the kind of local interest that the *Gazette* loved for page one.

Clawing out Section B, Joe began to smile.

There it was, right on the front, where no one in Molena Point would miss it.

He read the article with quiet satisfaction. Reporter Danny McCoy had been able to get a photograph, too. The shot showed the two rookies impounding the Harley as Clyde tried to coral the pups. The picture was taken at some distance, so it was a bit blurred—but still effective. Joe wanted to roll over laughing. "First-class circus," he said, addressing Clyde's back.

Clyde turned to stare at him. "The death of a man and the injury of a second man is a circus?"

"Not what I meant. That was certainly a tragedy. But this—" He stared pointedly at the page with Clyde's picture. "Tell me, how did they treat you in jail? I expect everyone in town got to enjoy the event— except yours truly. I hate when I miss your really illustrious moments."

"You want eggs and bacon and toast this morning? Or do you want that cut-rate brand of cat food that you said tastes like secondhand snuff mixed with floor wax?"

Joe subsided. He said nothing more until he had finished his burnt bacon and scrambled eggs. Completing his meal, he sat comfortably on the table, washing his paws and whiskers, cutting only an occasional glance in Clyde's direction. Clyde had not offered any gourmet embellishments this morning, no smoked kippers or a little dab of Beluga caviar or even a slice of Tilsit, to create a memorable dining experience.

Clyde finished his eggs without speaking. You wouldn't think that a little friendly ribbing would make him this mad. But maybe he wasn't feeling well. Joe studied him, looking for some sign of illness.

He saw only a deep, dark fury.

Finished eating, Clyde laid down his fork and gave

Joe his full attention. "I really appreciate your alerting Danny McCoy to this choice bit of news." He looked Joe over coldly. "With your thoughtfulness, you have treated the entire population of Molena Point to a long and sadistic laugh at my expense."

"I didn't call Danny McCoy! Hey, I might enjoy the joke, but I wouldn't have given it to a reporter. Don't lay this on me, Clyde. Everyone saw you—and heard you, shouting at those rookies on the street. Shouting at the pups. McCoy heard the story the way he gets all of his information, probably two dozen shopkeepers called the *Gazette*. Why do you always think I have something to do with your self-inflicted misfortunes! That is so tacky. If you—"

"Of course you had something to do with it. Look at the smart-assed grin on your face. You hardly took time to feel sympathy for those poor Greenlaw men. Talk about cold-hearted. You couldn't wait to paw through the rest of the paper, find McCoy's story. You were grinning wide enough to make the Cheshire cat look like a death-row inmate."

"How could you see if I was grinning. You had your back to me. And wouldn't you smile, if *I* got arrested accosting a police officer?"

"I was not accosting Officer McFarland. I was rescuing the pups—your pups, if I might remind you—from a cruel incarceration at the dog pound."

"My pups? *I* was the one who wanted to take those two to the pound. *I* wanted to let the pound feed them and find homes for them. But not you. Mr. Do-Gooder. No, you couldn't bear the thought. 'Look at the poor babies, Joe. Look how they're starving. How could you lock them in cages? Oh, just wook at the oootsy wootsy doggies.' And now look at them; you've already spoiled Selig rotten."

"Well, at least *I* . . . " Clyde stopped, looked again at the paper. Picked it up, jerking it from under Joe's paws. "What's this?"

"What's what?"

"The Letters-to-the-Editor column. You didn't read it?"

"How could I read it? You've been picking at me all morning. When did I have time to read it?" Leaping to Clyde's shoulder, he balanced heavily, scanning the three columns of letters.

SHOPLIFTING LOSSES TRIPLE IN RECENT WEEKS

What is Captain Harper doing to prevent the sudden increase in crime in our village? Molena Point relies heavily on the tourist trade, on its reputation for a slow, people-friendly, low-crime environment. We don't need shoplifters and petty thieves. The sudden outbreak of such crimes seems to have received no response from Police Captain Harper. Local businesses are losing money, our visitors have been approached by confidence artists, and the police are doing nothing to arrest and detain the lawbreakers.

Joe snorted. "Who wrote this? Some guy who doesn't like Harper. Probably some clown who lives on the wrong side of the law himself. Some cop-hater with an ax to grind." He dropped from Clyde's shoulder to the table and ripped his claws down the letters column. "The *Gazette* has no right to print such trash. If I paid for this paper, I'd cancel the damn subscription."

And he left the house, stopping to rake the living-room rug, then shouldering out through his cat door.

But, trotting quickly up the sunny street, he forgot the petty letter-writer, and fixed again on the tragedy of last night, on the dark, rainswept hill, on the swinging lights of the police torches.

Who *else* had been on Hellhag Hill last night, before the cops arrived? Who would want to kill Newlon Greenlaw and hurt Pedric? And Joe Grey wondered, would the little, wild tortoiseshell kit succeed in picking out the attacker?

But even if she did identify the man, still they needed proof. They couldn't drop a killer in Harper's lap without some hard facts, without enough solid physical evidence for Harper to take to the grand jury and for a prosecutor to take to court.

And Joe Grey moved on into the village, turning over in his sly feline mind every possible method he could think of for snaring the murderer.

 19

THE TORTOISESHELL kit stood high up Hellhag Hill, above the cave, atop the pale rocks that flanked it. Joe and Dulcie saw her at once as they came up from the village onto the grassy verge along Highway One. The moment she spied them she lashed her bushy tail as if she had been impatiently waiting. The two cats, watching her, hurried across the empty two-lane highway and started up the hill. After the rain, the tall grass through which they padded was fresh and sweet-scented, alive with insects buzzing and rustling. Over their heads, sparrows and finches zoomed, diving low in the watery sunshine.

"Do you suppose," Dulcie said, slitting her eyes, "do you suppose it was Dirken on the hill last night?"

"Why Dirken?"

"He's the one doing all the digging and tearing the house apart. Whatever he's looking for, did Newlon and Pedric find it? And Dirken went after them? And did he think he'd killed Pedric, did he leave Pedric for dead?"

Pedric was still in the hospital, while Newlon waited in the morgue, duly tagged and examined by forensics. The official word was that he had died from a blow to the head, not from an accidental fall. Fragments of Molena Point's soft, creamy stone, which was used all over the village for fireplaces and garden walls, had been found in Newlon's abraded scalp, deep in the wound. The specific piece of stone that killed him had not been retrieved. The natural outcroppings on Hellhag Hill were granite.

"Interesting, too," Dulcie said, "that Cara Ray buttered up Newlon, then dumped him, and now he's dead."

She paused, glancing at Joe. "Maybe Dirken's looking for a will, to override Shamas's trust and leave the house to him? If he is, he wouldn't want Newlon and Pedric snooping around."

"Not likely there's a will," Joe said, "with the trust. Not in California, not according to Clyde. He says it isn't needed—unless you're disgustingly rich, as Clyde puts it."

"Well, but Shamas could have written one?"

"I suppose. What are you thinking?"

Dulcie flicked her ears. "Could Shamas have been fool enough to write Cara Ray into a will—and stupid enough to tell her?"

Joe smiled. "And to hurry the process along, she slips out on the deck of the *Green Lady* that night and pushes him in the drink."

"Possible," she said. "Would Cara Ray be strong enough to push a man overboard?"

"So someone helps her; she say's she'll cut him in."

"Newlon," Dulcie said. "Or Sam. Take your pick."

She glanced up to where the kit waited. "She *is* impatient." The dark kit was fidgeting from paw to paw, her ears back, her yellow eyes gleaming. The cats broke into a gallop, leaping through the grass; they were nearly to the cave when they crouched suddenly, low to the earth.

They felt the vibration first through their paws, like an electrical charge. At the same instant the insects vanished, and all around them flocks of birds exploded straight up into the sky.

The jolt hit. Shook them hard. As if the world said, *I am the power.* They saw the kit sprawl, clinging to the boulder.

Then the earth was still.

The three cats waited.

Nothing more happened. The insects crept out and began to chirp again. The birds spiraled down and dived into the grass, snatching up bugs. An emboldened house finch sang his off-key cacophony as if he owned earth and sky.

And the cats saw that someone was on the road below them. Down on the black ribbon of asphalt, two small figures were rising—Wilma helping Lucinda up, dusting themselves off.

The two women stood talking, then climbed quickly toward the outcropping where they liked to sit— where the kit had been poised. Where, now, the rocks were empty.

The two cats moved away, intent on finding the kit—they hadn't gone far when the little mite was right before them, stepping out of the grass.

"I found him," she said softly. "A white trailer with a brown door."

"How do you know it's the killer's?" Joe said.

"He left his shoes on the stoop. I can smell the blood. He wiped them with something wet, but I can still smell it. He washed his shirt and hung it on a chair, where the sun shines in through the screen. *It* still smells of blood."

They rose and followed her up the hill, across the trailer park's brick walks, across a narrow, scruffy bed of poppies and beneath half a dozen trailers, trotting between their greasy wheels.

"This one," the kit said, slipping underneath, losing herself among the shadows.

Joe sniffed at the wheels and then at the little set of steps, flehming at the man's scent. "It might be Fulman; I never got a good smell of him. He's always with other people."

"He was alone with Cara Ray," Dulcie said.

"In the middle of a geranium bush, Dulcie, everything smells like geraniums."

"Well, if—" she began, then hushed as footsteps drummed overhead. They heard water running, heard a man cough.

Padding up the narrow steps, Joe peered in through the screen then backed away.

"It's Fulman," he said. "In his undershirt and shorts, eating a salami sandwich." He turned to look at the kit. "You sure it was that man?"

"That man. He hit the old man. He makes my fur bristle."

"Well, we can't toss the trailer with him in it. Have to hope he goes out."

Moving back down the hill, the three cats settled in the grass some way above Wilma and Lucinda. The two women had brought a picnic lunch; the cats could smell crab salad. Licking whiskers, they watched Wilma unwrap a small loaf of French bread and take a bottle of wine from her worn picnic basket.

Softly, Dulcie said, "Tell us why the other cats are so shy—and so angry."

"Angry because they can't go home," the kit said. "Because the shaking earth drove them out. Afraid to go down again."

Joe frowned. "Down again, where?" He looked toward the cave. "You didn't come from—in there?"

"From a place like it. I was little, I hardly remember. The earth shook. The clowder ran and ran—through the dark—up onto hills like these. That way," she said, gazing away south where the coastline led wild and endless along the ragged edge of the continent.

"We were in a city when I was little. Somewhere down the coast. We ran from packs of dogs at the edge of a city. I remember garbage in alleys. I could never keep up. My mother was dead. The big cats didn't care about me, but I didn't want to be alone. I knew we were different from other cats, and I didn't want to be in those alleys alone.

"We went away from the garbage place and through the city to the hills. The others would never wait for me. I ran and ran. I ate grasshoppers and lizards and bugs, and sometimes a butterfly. I never learned to hunt right; no one wanted to show me.

"Then the world shook again, and we ran again. We came here. I was bigger then, I could keep up. Or I'd find them the next morning when they stopped to sleep.

"Hungry," she said. "Always hungry." She glanced down the hill at the picnickers, sniffing the sweet scent of their luxurious meal.

Dulcie licked the kit's ear.

"Well, that was how we came here. Along that cliff and these hills. They told me, home is here, too. They mean the cave. They mean it will lead to the same place the other cave did. They said we could go home again into this hill if the earth would stop shaking. They want to go in, and down to that place, but they are afraid." She placed her black-mottled paw softly over Dulcie's bigger paw. "I do not want to go there; it is all elder there."

"Elder," Dulcie said. "Elder and evil, as in the old stories."

And at that instant, as if the small cat had summoned demons, another quake hit.

First the quick tingling through their paws as the world gathered itself. Then the jolt. It threw Dulcie and the kit against a boulder, knocked Joe sideways. Dulcie kicked at the air and flipped over. The kit crept to her, and she gathered the little one close, licking her.

Below them, Lucinda was sprawled, and Wilma crawling on hands and knees to reach her—and still the earth shook and rocked them, the hardest, longest surge the cats had ever known. Clinging tight to the traitorous earth, they refused to be dislodged; fear held them, as fear freezes a hunted rabbit, turning it mindless and numb.

Then all was still.

The earth was still.

They stood up, watched Wilma rise and lift Lucinda to sit against a boulder. The only movement in all the world, then, seemed the pounding of the sea beating through their paws.

And the tortoiseshell kit, who, before this day, had

hidden each time Lucinda brought food, who had never shown herself to any human, padded down the hill.

She stood looking at Lucinda, her round yellow eyes fixed fiercely on Lucinda's frightened face.

Lucinda's eyes widened.

Wilma remained very still. Joe and Dulcie were still.

Lucinda asked, "Are you all right, kitten?"

The waif purred, her thin sides vibrating. She stepped closer.

Lucinda put out her hand. "The quake didn't hurt you? Poor, poor kitten."

The kit tilted her little face in a question. She moved closer still, her long bushy tail and thick pantaloons comical on that thin little body. Lucinda said later that her black-and-brown-mottled coat was as beautiful as hand-dyed silk. The kit went to Lucinda and rubbed against her hand.

And Dulcie, watching, felt a sharp jealousy stab through her. *Oh*, she thought, *I don't want you to go to Lucinda. I want you to come to me.*

But what a selfish thought. What's the matter with me?

The kitten had turned, was staring at Dulcie. The expression on her little streaked face changed suddenly, from joy to alarm. And she fled. She was gone, flying down the hill, vanishing in the long grass.

"Oh," Lucinda said. "Why did she run? What did I do to frighten her?"

But behind Lucinda, Wilma looked accusingly at Dulcie. And Dulcie hung her head: something in her expression or in her body language had told the kit her thoughts, as surely as if she had spoken.

Lucinda looked after the kit with longing. "Such a tiny little mite. And all alone. So thin and frail."

Wilma helped Lucinda to stand up and brush off, and supported her until she was steady on her feet. She picked up the picnic things, and as they started down the hill again, Wilma looked up sternly at Joe and Dulcie.

"Come on, you two."

Chastened, Dulcie followed her. Joe, watching them, fell into line. Lucinda seemed too shaken by the quake and by her encounter with the little wild cat to wonder at Joe and Dulcie's willingness to trot obediently home beside Wilma.

Reaching the village, they found shopkeepers and customers standing in the streets among broken glass, broken shingles, shattered roof tiles. The cats could see no fallen walls, no buildings that looked badly damaged—only one small section of broken wall where a bay window jutted over the street. Bricks had fallen out, but the window glass itself was still in place.

Everyone on the street was talking at once, giving each other advice, recounting what life-threatening objects had fallen narrowly missing them. Wilma, glancing down at the cats, led her little entourage quickly across Ocean's grassy median, away from the crowd and debris. Lucinda remained quiet. Not until they were half a block from her house did she make any sound.

Stopping suddenly and staring ahead, she let out a startled gasp.

Lucinda's Victorian home stood solidly enough. But her entire parlor seemed to have been removed, by the quake, onto the front lawn. Delicate settees and little tables stood about in little groups. A circle of needle-point dining chairs accommodated eight Greenlaw women chatting and taking their ease.

As they approached, Dirken and his cousin Joey emerged from the house carrying the dining table. Behind them, three of the bigger Greenlaw children appeared, hauling out cans of food, stacks of plates, and a potful of silverware—whether to prepare an emergency meal or to cart away Lucinda's possessions wasn't clear. Beside the drive, a mattress lay tilted against a tree, and at the edge of the lawn, a pile of bedding and pillows beckoned to the tired and weary.

Lucinda approached stiffly—and suddenly she flew at Dirken. He dropped the table as her fists pounded his chest.

"What have you done, Dirken? What is this about! What are you doing!"

"There was an earthquake, Aunt Lucinda." Dirken put his arm around her. "A terrible jolt. I'm so glad you're all right."

Lucinda slapped his arm away. "All of this, because of an *earthquake*?"

"Yes, Aunt Lucinda. One has to . . ."

"Take it back. All of it. Every piece. Do it now, Dirken. *Take it back inside*."

"But you can't stay in the house when there's been . . ."

Her faded eyes flashed. "Wipe the grass off the feet of the furniture before you put it on the carpet. And place it properly, just as I had it. What on earth did you think you were doing?"

Dirken didn't move. "You don't understand about

these things, Aunt Lucinda. It's dangerous to stay inside during a quake. You have to move outdoors. The house could fall on you."

She fixed Dirken with a gaze that would petrify jungle beasts. "*You* are outside, Dirken. I am outside. My furniture does not need to be outside. If my possessions are crushed by a quake, that is none of your concern. Take it back. You are not camping on my lawn like a pack of ragtag . . ." She paused for a long, awkward moment. "Like ragtag hoboes," she shouted, her eyes blazing at him.

Dulcie twitched her whiskers, her ears up, her eyes bright. She liked Lucinda better when she took command, when she wasn't playing doormat. "But what is that?" she whispered to Joe, looking past the furniture to where Clyde's two pups lay, behind the Victorian settee, chewing on something white and limp.

The cats trotted over.

The pups smiled, delighted to see them, then growled to warn them off their treasure. It was strange, Dulcie thought, that the only cat they feared was that tiny waif up on Hellhag Hill.

Dodging Selig, she swiped out with a swift paw and hauled the rectangular piece of canvas away from them. It was as heavy as a buck rabbit, and wet from their chewing: a big canvas bag with a drawstring top.

It smelled most interesting. The cats sniffed at it, and smiled.

They could see, behind the pups, broken concrete scattered from a wide crack in the foundation, where the bag must have lain, just beneath the fireplace.

Driving the pups out of the way with hisses and slaps, Joe pawed the canvas bag open. Dulcie stuck her head in.

The bag was empty, but the cloth smelled of old, musty money.

So the Greenlaw men *had* been searching for money. How very prosaic. No one buried money anymore.

Except, perhaps, someone who didn't like the IRS, she thought, smiling. The cats were still sniffing the bag when Joe nudged Dulcie, and she looked up at a crowd of trousered legs surrounding them, and a ring of broad Irish faces, all intent on the empty bag.

All seven Greenlaw men swung down, snatching at the bag. Dirken was quickest, jerking it away.

He pulled open the bag and peered in, then looked around the lawn as if expecting to see scattered greenbacks blowing across the grass like summer leaves.

The men were all staring at the empty bag and shuffling their feet when Lucinda pushed between them, put out her hand, and took it from Dirken.

"Were you expecting something more, Dirken? Were you expecting the bag to contain something you've been looking for?"

She didn't wait for his answer. She turned and walked away, folding the bag neatly into a square, as if she were folding freshly washed linen. A huge silence lay behind her.

Only slowly did the Greenlaw men disperse, moving away, bewildered. Even the pups were subdued, trotting from one solemn figure to another, then away again when no one paid attention to them.

But when Sam Fulman appeared, coming out of the house, Selig raced to him leaping and whining—then backed away snarling, as if uncertain whether to kiss Fulman or bite him.

Hestig dropped to his belly and ran—straight to

Clyde, who came hurrying around the corner toward the crowd, evidently summoned by the loud barking. Grabbing Hestig's collar, Clyde knelt to put a leash on.

Selig was still leaping at Fulman, alternately growling and licking. Fulman, tired of the furor, gave the puppy a hard whack across the face. When Selig yelped, Fulman hit him again on his soft ear. Selig screamed and spun around, plowing into Clyde, pressing against Clyde. The cats, close to Fulman, got a good whiff of him, over the scent of dog.

They would not forget that sour smell. Glancing at each other, they ran for Joe's place. They'd had enough—too many people, too many dogs, too much to sort out. They needed space, time to think. They needed a square meal.

Pushing in through the dog door, they pawed open the refrigerator.

Wilma's larder boasted far superior offerings. She kept a shelf for Dulcie stocked with Brie, imported kippers, rare steak, and custards. In Joe's house, they simply had to make do; there was no time to call Jolly's Deli, with Clyde sure to barge in. The half-empty box offered cold spaghetti and a slice of overripe ham. This, with a bag of kitty kibble hastily clawed from the cupboard, completed their meal. Crouched on the kitchen floor lapping up spaghetti, they wondered how long Lucinda had had the money, how she came to find the bag, and where the money was now.

"Maybe in a safe-deposit box?" Dulcie said, pawing at an escaped strand of spaghetti. "One thing's sure, that poor old house might survive, now, with Dirken done tearing it up."

Finishing their dull repast, they left the spaghetti-stained dish in the middle of the kitchen floor, like the receptacle of some bloody sacrifice, and curled up on Clyde's bed for a nap. They slept long and deeply. But as dusk fell, dimming the bedroom, they trotted out to sit on the back fence.

They wanted to be sure Fulman was there for dinner, to be sure the coast was clear.

They had no idea what they would find in Fulman's trailer, what additional piece of the puzzle. Hopefully, something that would tie Fulman to Raul Torres and maybe to Chambers's stabbing. As for last night's double "accident," they already had a witness. Though she could never testify. What they wanted now was hard evidence.

They waited until the clan had gathered at the table for a heavy meal of roast beef and potatoes, but Fulman didn't show. Nor was Lucinda present. Though often, when there was a heavy meal, Lucinda would appear toward the end, for a salad and dessert.

"Surprised Cara Ray isn't there," Joe said. "She's there often enough."

Dulcie narrowed her eyes. "Maybe she and Fulman are at the motel having a little party."

"You have a low mind. But I hope you're right. I don't relish being trapped in a trailer with Sam Fulman; he looks as if he'd as soon squash a cat as swat a fly." Joe thought for an instant about waiting to toss Fulman's trailer until they knew he was absent. But what the heck. They were only cats. Who would suspect them? He dropped down from the fence, beside Dulcie, and they headed for Hellhag Hill.

20

THE EVENING was dark in human terms. But to
Joe and Dulcie the cliffs and the sea and the house
trailers that rose above them were as indistinct and
faded as an old, worn movie projected with a failing
bulb.

Beneath the looming trailers, wind soughed
between the greasy wheels.

They saw no light in any trailer except far down at
the end, where a lone square of yellow spilled onto the
asphalt; thin voices came from that direction.

They had not found the tortoiseshell kit.

Approaching Sam Fulman's trailer, they studied its
black panes and tightly closed door. The wind shook
and rocked the big, wheeled home, snapping its white
metal sides. Above the sporadic rattling, they listened
for some sound from within.

Only the wind.

Leaping at the doorknob, grabbing it between raking claws, Joe swung, twisting it. Kicking the door open, he dropped inside.

Crouched on the dirty linoleum, they listened again. The dark, chill interior had a hollow, empty feel. Joe sniffed at a shirt that hung over a chair, its wide, red and green stripes resembling a circus tent—a shirt they had seen Fulman wear. And now they knew his smell, from their encounter in Lucinda's yard.

"Ease the door closed," Dulcie whispered. "Someone's out there; I can hear him walking."

Joe pushed the door—he didn't mean to latch it. But the wind took it, and the sudden slam sounded like thunder. Leaping away, the cats looked for a place to hide.

There was no space under the couch or under the bed, both were built atop drawers. Every inch of the trailer was filled with cupboards and drawers made of dark, wood-grained plywood, with here and there a dead panel. The footsteps approached, stopped just outside.

No use trying to conceal themselves in the shower; the curtain was transparent. They fought the closet door, but couldn't open it. As the visitor came up the steps, they dived behind the bed's bolsters. Crouched among the dusty upholstery, they were gently rocked as the trailer, itself, was rocked precariously in the twisting wind—they felt as if they were adrift at sea.

They heard the door open and peered out from behind the bolster as Dirken stuck his head in.

"Sam? Sam, you there?"

When no one answered, Dirken entered. "Fulman? You here?"

Receiving no reply, Dirken walked the length of the

trailer, looking into the bathroom, the bedroom, and the closet; he moved warily, as if he had heard the front door close.

At last, deciding he was alone, he began to snoop. There was no other word for his stealthy prodding, as he opened the closet and rummaged among Fulman's clothes; turning away, he left the door ajar. Returning to the kitchen, he pulled out drawers and opened the cupboards, examining the contents of each; every few minutes he stepped to the window to look out. He seemed to find nothing of interest in the kitchen except some small cellophane packets. Tearing off the wrapping, he stood munching; the cats could smell peanut butter. He picked up a magazine from the table and leafed through it, grinning—then from somewhere down the row of trailers, a door slammed.

Dirken left the trailer quickly, shutting the door without a sound.

"What was he looking for?" Dulcie said. "Not the money; he knows Lucinda has that." She sneezed from the dust in the bolster.

Joe turned to look at her. "What if Fulman and Lucinda made off with the money together—to keep it from the rest of the family? Or to hide it from the IRS? Maybe Dirken thinks they stashed the money here?"

Dulcie looked back at him, her eyes gleaming like black moons. "But what about Cara Ray? Did they cut her out?"

"Why not?" Joe shrugged. "What if Cara Ray's not what we think? What if she came here to get the goods on Fulman? Maybe from the start was working with Torres on his investigation?"

"But the way she talked—as if she—" Dulcie sighed.

"This stuff makes my head ache. Come on, Joe, let's toss this place and see what we can find."

Fighting the ornate latches that had been designed to keep the cupboards and drawers closed when the vehicle was in motion—and apparently designed to keep out nosy cats—they pawed into every inch of the trailer, looking for money, for bloodstained clothes, possibly for the crude weapon that had killed Newlon. The gold-and-black linoleum beneath their paws, the gold alligator couch and thick maroon carpet and cloth-of-gold drapes amused Dulcie. "I wonder—did he plan the decor himself?"

Springing to the kitchen counter, she pawed through the dish cupboard, through canned goods and a small stack of clean shirts and underwear. She found nothing to interest the police.

Joe, investigating the clothes hanging in Fulman's closet, leaped to the high shelf, where the laundry was wadded. Flehming at the sour, musty stink, he gave a ragged *mrrrowr* of discovery.

Dulcie sprang up beside him. Pawing through Fulman's dirty clothes, they smelled human blood.

"Here," Joe said, fishing out a plaid flannel shirt.

The front and sleeve smelled of blood and, hardly visible in the red-and-brown squares, were tiny splashes of dried blood.

With a clever paw, Dulcie began to fold the shirt into a packet small enough to carry in her mouth. "Better leave it," Joe said. "For Harper to find, where the killer left it." He leaped down, among a tangle of shoes.

"What if Fulman comes back? What if he has second thoughts, decides to get rid of it?"

"Leave it for the moment, Dulcie. Look at this."

She dropped down beside him.

At the side of the closet, a bottom panel was loose, the screw holes in the plywood enlarged so they were bigger than the screws; the panel appeared secure until you looked closely.

Sliding and lifting the plywood between them, the cats pulled it off, easing it down onto the carpet.

Its dusty surface recorded pawprints as Joe slipped into the dark recess.

There was a long silence. Soon he peered out at Dulcie, flicking his whiskers in a broad grin.

He backed out dragging a cardboard folder, one of those rust-colored accordion numbers meant for the organization, by the neatniks of the world, of their paid bills and canceled checks. Behind Joe, in the gloom, loomed four white shoe boxes.

The cats dragged the boxes out into the little hall where faint starglow seeped down through the trailer windows. They opened the folder to find bank receipts that were, at the moment, of little interest to them. The first box they clawed open held letters that did not seem pertinent. But under these lay a small black ledger, each page headed by a proper name, above columns of dates and numbers—Fulman had kept careful financial records. But of what?

"Records of his scams?" Dulcie said. Pawing through the box, they were aware of increasing sounds beyond the trailer, of women's voices. Clawing open the last bundle of letters, their eyes widened.

The return addresses were all the same: Shamas Greenlaw, at a Seattle Post Office box. The letters were addressed to Sam Fulman, and had been written over a period of approximately ten years.

Sharing out the envelopes between them, they read each letter, looking for clandestine financial deals or for any hint of a scam—leaving, unavoidably, a few innocent tooth and claw marks.

The missives contained nothing more exciting than discussions of family affairs—though it did seem out of character for Shamas to be so concerned about the health and welfare of his great-aunt Sarah. In each communication to Fulman he had apparently enclosed a sizable check, each letter mentioning the amount of the check that was to be deposited to his aunt's account at her nursing home. At the bottom of each letter Fulman had noted the amount received and the date deposited.

All very efficient.

All displaying a degree of unselfishness that did not seem natural to Shamas Greenlaw.

"And," Dulcie said, "if he was supporting his aunt, why didn't he send the money directly to the nursing home?"

The cats looked at each other, and smiled.

"Nice," Joe said. "Very nice."

"It's only conjecture," she said.

"Yes," he said, pawing through another box. "And here are the receipts. Valencia Home for the Elderly. Greenville, North Carolina." He compared the first few receipts with the letters, and with the ledger. The dates and amounts matched. He looked at Dulcie, his yellow eyes as keenly predatory as if the two cats had a giant rat cornered. "Any bets that no such home exists?"

Dulcie grinned; then stiffened as they heard a car pull away and a trailer door slam.

Then silence.

In the next box was a stack of purchase orders from

Bernside Tool and Die Works in Spokane, Washington, to a variety of customers. Payments to this company had been made directly by the purchasers. No name appeared more than once. These payments, too, were entered in Fulman's ledger. Each date coincided, within a few days, with the gifts to Aunt Sarah.

"So," Joe said, "it was Shamas's company, and he was donating his income to Aunt Sarah."

"Sure. Right." Dulcie fished a letter from the stack, a statement and the matching purchase order. Setting these aside, they pawed the rest of the papers back into their boxes. The cats were inside the closet, maneuvering a shoe box back into the cubbyhole, when the trailer was jolted as if someone had burst through the front door. Glancing around the door as a second jolt hit, they saw the dining chairs flying on their casters, banging into the walls. The closet door slammed closed. Something crashed against it. They heard dishes fall and breaking glass.

When the earth was still again, they felt as if all air had been expelled from the trailer, leaving a gigantic vacuum. As Joe fought the doorknob, they heard, from the far end of the park, scattered cries of distress and amazement.

They worked at the door until they were hissing at each other, but couldn't open it. When they heard the front door bang open, they thought it was another quake—then wished it had been a quake.

"Fine," Fulman snarled, stomping in. "Go on back to your suppers. A little jolt never hurt nothing." The door slammed and a light flared through the crack beneath the closet door—and Fulman's papers lay scattered, in plain view, up and down the hall.

21

"WHAT THE hell!" Fulman shouted. The cats heard him heaving broken glass or china, as if into a metal container. "Damned quake! Damn California quakes. I'll take a North Carolina tornado any day."

Cara Ray giggled, a high, brittle laugh.

Crouched on the closet shelf beneath Fulman's dirty clothes, Joe and Dulcie listened to his heavy step coming down the hall.

"And what the hell's that!"

He stood just outside; they imagined him looking down at the scattered letters and invoices, then they heard him snatching up papers. He stopped once, perhaps reading some particular letter. "Damn it to hell. The quake didn't do this. Someone's been in here."

"Who, lover? What is it? What's happened?"

He was quiet again, shuffling papers. Outside among the trailers the excited voices had quieted, as if those residents alarmed at the quake had taken Fulman's advice and returned to their suppers.

"Don't look like they took nothing," Fulman said. "Maybe the quake scared 'em off. Check the windows, Cara Ray. See if one's open or unlocked. Get a move on." He jerked the closet door open; light from the kitchen blazed in through the rumpled shirts and shorts, beneath which the two cats crouched, as still as two frozen cadavers.

From beneath a fold of laundry, they could see Fulman kneeling below them, pushing papers and boxes back into the hole, his brown hair rumpled, his thin shoulders stringy beneath a thin white T-shirt. Sliding the plywood panel onto its screws, he turned away from the closet but did not close the door. They heard, from the kitchen, a drawer open, and in a moment he returned, carrying a hammer, his thin lips pursed around a mouthful of nails.

Kneeling again, he nailed the panel in place tighter than the surrounding wallboard had ever been secured.

When he had gone, the cats burst forth, panting for fresh air, and peered out where he'd left the door cracked open.

A sickly yellow light burned over the kitchen sink. They could see one of the shoe boxes and the small black ledger on the kitchen table; they watched as he fished a white-plastic grocery bag from a kitchen drawer and shoved the ledger and papers inside.

Dropping the bag on the table beside the empty box, Fulman fetched a bottle of vodka from the cupboard, with two glasses and a can of orange juice.

The cats remained in the closet for the better part of an hour. If the great cat god had been smiling down on them tonight, he'd have provided them with a tape recorder—or an electronic bug hooked directly into

Molena Point PD. If ever a murder confession was thrown in their furry faces, this was the moment.

As Fulman mixed the drinks, Cara Ray prowled the trailer. Instead of her little pink skirt, she was wearing form-fitting tights printed with Mickey Mouse, an item she had apparently picked up in some children's department, maybe as a lark, little-girl clothes that looked far more fetching on Cara Ray than on any child they were made for. Above Mickey Mouse, she was snuggled in a huge chenille sweater the color of raspberry ice cream. Her long blond hair hung loose. Her face was scrubbed clean of makeup, making the tiny blonde look vulnerable and innocent. If she were to appear in court like that, she'd snow any jury.

Sipping her drink, wandering down the narrow hall, she moved into the bedroom, trailing her fingers along the walls and molding, prompting Dulcie to wonder if she had already tossed the cupboards and drawers at some earlier time, and was now pressing for less obvious hiding places. She opened the closet door, her head inches below the cats, stood looking down at the wall where Fulman had nailed up the plywood.

But what was she looking for? Certainly she'd heard from Fulman about the empty canvas bag. But maybe she didn't believe that Lucinda had the money.

Sitting down at the table, Cara Ray's glance scanned the ceiling, as if imagining the dead spaces above the thin plywood.

Fulman's expression was dryly amused. "You won't find any money in here, Cara Ray."

She did not look embarrassed, only startled. She looked back at him evenly.

"What I want to know, Cara Ray, is how did she get

into that concrete wall? When that wall cracked, in the quake, well, hell, you saw it. That whole wall—as thick as the wall of a federal pen."

"So how come it cracked?"

"Someone cracked it before the quake." He looked at her intently. "That old woman had to have help."

"Whatever. She has the money now." She paused. "Doesn't she, Sam?" Beneath the table, Cara Ray's fist tightened. "Or maybe it was Torres; maybe he got here before he said."

Fulman shook his head. "I searched his car that morning. He didn't have nothing. And why would the old woman act like she had the money if she didn't?"

"I don't know, Sam. Could Torres've come up from L.A. earlier than I thought? Used a second fake name—been in another motel? Could've been here all along while I was down seeing my 'sister' like I told him? Snooped around that old house, found the money—maybe knew right where to look? Could've gone up into that wall from under the house?"

Cara Ray pushed back her long, pale hair. "So when I called him that morning, said that I had car trouble coming back from my sister's, he'd already got the cash?

"He could have hid it right there in his motel room, the one at the Oak Breeze, even, and I never thought to look. Damn it to hell. I should have tossed his room, before . . . Before, you know. So where is it now? You think maybe the maid got it, some little bitch sneaking into the dresser drawers and feeling under the mattress? Or maybe," she said hopefully, "maybe Torres put it in a safe-deposit box."

Fulman snorted. "Torres wasn't that fond of banks.

And you can't get a safe-deposit box, Cara Ray, without having a bank account, not in California."

"So he had a bank account. He *traveled* up and down this coast! If you'd done some phoning to the banks, you could've found out. You had plenty of time, Sam."

"Don't snap at *me*, Cara Ray. I didn't know the old woman had gotten the money. You're the one who didn't toss his room. You're the one who said the money was in the house wall. Said it was the last thing Shamas told you. If you'd found out exactly *where* in the damn wall . . ."

He gulped down a shot of vodka. "Dirken thought it was there. All those repairs. Who knew that old woman could be so sneaky? And then those two damn dogs find the empty bag!"

She held out her glass. "You never even suspected the old woman."

He slopped vodka into her glass. "Why would I? Her acting like she was about out of it, like she didn't know nothing about what Shamas did."

He sat down at the table. "Maybe she didn't know—until that old fool Pedric told her."

"That why you tried to do him, Sam?"

"I never thought he'd tell her about the money."

"So why did you—"

"The Seattle stuff, Cara Ray. He knows about that, from Shamas. I don't need her prying into that."

"And now, the old man can still tell her. Thanks to your messing up." She sucked at her drink. "And probably he will."

"Well, he doesn't know about the other."

"Unless Newlon told—"

"Newlon can't testify now. And what did he know?

Newlon was the one who searched for Shamas, who went down in the sea for him. Newlon was the one who found him, hanging there with his foot tangled in the line—Newlon didn't have a clue."

Cara Ray's face colored with a blush of guilt.

"What the hell? What did you tell him, Cara Ray?"

"I didn't tell him. He knew there was something, all that scuffling before you shouted that Shamas was overboard. Newlon looked right at me, said, 'No one would trip over them dogs, Cara Ray. Not Shamas. Shamas was sure on his feet.'"

Fulman shrugged. "Well, he can't say nothing now."

Cara Ray's heart-shaped face fell into a pouting scowl. "I still don't see why you made all that fuss, hustling those dogs off the boat before you called Harbor Patrol. Seems to me—"

"Because, Cara Ray, they were driving me crazy. I didn't think I could stand the damn dogs another minute, jumping all over me—cops all over the place, and them dogs underfoot every time you turned around."

"All the more reason for the cops to believe Shamas fell over them. I still don't see why you changed your story at the last minute, why you were in such a hurry suddenly to get the dogs out of there."

"Because, Cara Ray, the cops might think we were all drunk or crazy on drugs, letting those dogs run on deck at a time like that. Who knows, cops might try to slap a manslaughter charge or something on us, for carelessness."

"That's a crock, Sam. You don't believe that."

But then her eyes widened. She fixed a cold look on him. "Did Shamas have a stash with him? Big money, hidden on the boat somewhere? Is that why you left before the cops got aboard? Is that why you took the dogs off—used them for an excuse? So you could get into Seattle and hide the money before we called the cops?"

She stared hard at him. "Is that it, Sam? The dogs covered for you, while you took the money off?"

Dulcie cut a look at Joe, mirroring his disgust. These people were beyond sick. No matter how big a womanizer Shamas Greenlaw had been, he hadn't deserved being pushed overboard by these scum.

"Here it is," Joe whispered, "the whole scene laid out for us, and what are we going to do with it?" He sat up tall on the closet shelf, his yellow eyes burning with frustration.

"Shamas was stupid anyway," Cara Ray said. "Dogs don't belong on shipboard. I told him . . ."

"Well, Cara Ray, they—"

"Filthy beasts, doing their mess all over. I told Shamas I wasn't cleaning it up." She widened her eyes at Fulman. "You cleaned up plenty of dog crap. Cleaned it up all the way from Seattle back to San Francisco."

She looked puzzled. "You get all the way back here with those mutts, then you turn 'em loose. Why did you do that, Sam?"

"Getting too big to handle. Got loose the morning I—the morning Torres wrecked his car. They were wild, jumped out of my car, ran down the road. I figured to hell with 'em, let 'em go. They'd make their way, someone down in the village 'ud feed 'em—and someone did," he said. "Anyway, I decided I didn't want to be hauling them around, right in Newlon's face. Keep reminding him, keep him all shook up. Not too swift, was Newlon."

"And that old couple, Sam. That George Chambers. You botched that one, too. Don't you think the cops—"

"Someone was coming, Cara Ray. Right up the street headed right for me. I thought—Chambers didn't move. Went limp as a rag. I *thought* he was dead, Cara Ray."

"Trouble with you, you try to do someone, and you panic. Decide they're dead when they're not. Why do you do that, Sam? We could've just skipped. Now you've got two men dead and two wounded, and don't you think the cops—?"

"You do one man, Cara Ray, you might as well go for it. The ones after that don't count. Besides, the Fulmans and Greenlaws never get caught. Well, caught maybe once in a while, but we always walk. Worst that can happen, the family goes bail and we skip, lose the bail money."

Fulman smiled. "It's in the family, Cara Ray. Luck. Plain Irish luck."

Cara Ray watched him nervously. Her scrubbed face was not glowing now; she looked pale, as if she was having doubts about Fulman, as if she was losing her nerve.

But then her eyes narrowed. "I want my share of the money, Sam. I don't need all this grief for nothing." Her gaze widened. "Are you sure there ever was any money in that bag? Or was the old woman making an ass of you?"

"Shamas always buried money, Cara Ray. Everywhere he lived. The other women never knew— you're the first he told."

"Maybe he was getting senile," she said, laughing. "I would have sworn Lucinda never knew."

Cara Ray rose, poured herself another drink, found a box of sugar, and stirred two heaping teaspoons into the vodka-laced orange juice. "You never make it sweet enough."

She turned on him suddenly. "Maybe Shamas took it *all* with him on shipboard. Maybe you have it all, Sam." Leaning over the table, she pushed her face close to his. "How much money did you get, Sam? How much of Shamas's tax-free stash, as he called it?"

"Don't be stupid, Cara Ray, you know I wouldn't cut you out."

She sat down again, ran her hand down her leg, smoothing her Mickey Mouse tights. "Far as that goes, maybe Pedric and the old woman and their sweet little early-morning walks, maybe they carried the money away then, a little at a time."

"And hid it where, Cara Ray? In Pedric's trailer? He's not that stupid."

She shrugged. "Maybe buried it, maybe down the hill somewhere, under those rocks."

She lifted an eyebrow. "And why not his trailer? Brought it right on up here and hid it somewhere in there that even you wouldn't think to look—maybe inside a wheel? In the water tank or something."

"I don't know, Cara Ray, that's—"

"And now with the old man in the hospital, and his trailer empty, I'd think you'd—"

Fulman rose. "He wouldn't hide it there, Cara Ray. He'd know we'd all look there. Me, Dirken, Newlon . . ."

He stood watching her. "But I guess it wouldn't hurt to smoke it over—now, while he's out of the way."

Snatching his jacket from the chair, he headed out the door. Cara Ray gulped her drink and followed him.

And Joe and Dulcie abandoned the closet, intent on their own hurried agenda.

22

Fulman had left the kitchen light burning; it cast a greasy yellow glow across the gold-and-black decor and the fake mahogany paneling. The plastic bag was no longer on the table; only wet rings remained where Fulman and Cara Ray had set their glasses. Sniffing at the glasses, Dulcie lifted her lip in disgust. "Take the paint off a fire truck."

"It's here," Joe said from beneath the table. He backed out, pulling the bag. Peering inside to be sure the papers were still there, he left it in the middle of the floor and galloped to the bedroom, where he had seen a cell phone on a shelf beside the bed.

"Joe, Cara Ray left her purse, they'll be coming back."

Joe paid no attention. Pawing open the phone, listening for the dial tone, he punched in the number. The phone's small buttons made it hard for a cat to hit the right digit. These manufacturers that called their products user-friendly didn't have a clue.

Lieutenant Brennan answered, evidently relieving

the dispatcher. Brennan didn't want to put the call through; he said Harper could not be reached.

"This is really urgent. There's no time—"

"He's on a missing person call—possibly a drowning. That is extremely urgent," Brennan said coldly, and he again refused to contact Harper.

Well, he needn't be so surly. But maybe he'd had a bad night. Maybe he had stomach gas, with all the fried food he ate. Hanging up, Joe dialed Harper's cell phone. He hadn't memorized Harper's several phone numbers for nothing; though sometimes the connection on the cell phone wasn't too good.

Harper answered; he sounded gruffer than usual, short-tempered and preoccupied. Joe described the papers and ledger they had found that linked Fulman to Shamas Greenlaw's scams and maybe to his death. "Most of the papers are in a hole behind his closet, you have to pull the wallboard off. But the ledger and the most important letters, Fulman put in a plastic bag— meaning to take them with him. He'll be back here any minute, to get them."

"What do you mean, linked to Shamas Greenlaw's death?"

"Fulman and Cara Ray Crisp pushed Shamas overboard; I heard them talking about it. And with Cara Ray's help, Fulman killed Raul Torres—caused the accident that killed him."

"You'll have to give me some facts," Harper snapped. Joe could picture the captain in his squad car, scowling at the phone as he drove. Joe would not, at one time, have made so bold as to expect the police captain to act on his word alone, without proof. But since the first murder that the cats had been involved with, all the information they had passed to Harper had resulted in arrests and convictions. Every phone call Joe had made had helped the department; he and Dulcie had furnished Harper with information from conversations that the police would not be in a position to hear, discussions the police had no reason to listen to, and for which they would have had no legal right to employ sophisticated electronic equipment—yet conversations that held the key to solving the crimes in question.

"I can't give you any proof, Captain. From what I overheard tonight, Shamas Greenlaw didn't pitch over the boat's rail unassisted. Fulman and Cara Ray did the job; then, because Raul Torres grew suspicious, Fulman set Torres up to die. Fulman stabbed George Chambers and left him for dead. He killed Newlon Greenlaw—hit Newlon with a rock, and he injured Pedric Greenlaw, went away thinking he'd killed Pedric."

"That's a long list. Who is this? I can't run an investigation on anonymous tips like this," Harper said irritably.

"My tips have been useful in the past, Captain."

"Will you give me your name, give me a number where I can reach you?"

"You know I can't do that. Never have, never will. But I just witnessed, in Sam Fulman's trailer, a direct confession that incriminates both Fulman and Cara Ray Crisp. You'll have to take my word.

"However," Joe said, loving to play Harper along slowly, "there is a bit of proof. Fulman's shirt, a red-and-brown plaid flannel, that is wadded up in his laundry on the closet shelf, is spotted with tiny flecks of dried blood. I'm willing to bet it'll turn out to be Newlon Greenlaw's blood.

"Right now, Fulman and Cara Ray are searching Pedric's trailer, looking for hidden money that they think was lifted from under the Greenlaw house. Two dogs—those dogs that Clyde Damen keeps—dug out an empty bag this afternoon, evidently found it just after the quake, in the cracked foundation.

"Fulman is convinced that it had contained money buried by Shamas. He told Cara Ray that Shamas always buried money, that Shamas called it his tax-free account."

Harper was silent for so long that Joe thought he'd lost the connection. But then, in a dry, tight voice, "I'm on my way up there. Why don't you hang around?"

"I'm taking the grocery bag with me, Captain, before Fulman comes back. But the laundry is in the closet, the plaid shirt and, under it, one sample letter and one receipt.

"The bag I'm taking contains ten year's worth just like them. I'll leave it in the cave, say, twenty feet back from the entrance, in whatever crevice is handy. White-plastic grocery bag. Should be easy to spot."

Joe hung up before Harper could accuse him of tampering with the evidence. He stiffened as a ripping noise exploded in the bathroom.

"They're coming," Dulcie hissed. "We can't use the front door. Come on—I ripped the screen off."

He started to drag the bag toward the bathroom, then leaped back to the bed, took the phone clumsily in his mouth, nearly unhinging his jaws, and shoved it in with the letters. Hauling the heavy bag toward the bathroom, he left it in the hall long enough to slip into the closet and rub his shoulder back and forth across the dusty plywood panel where their pawprints were incised. It was possible

Harper would send forensics up here to get fingerprints, depending on what came down. If the officers picked up pawprints, so be it—but he hoped they didn't. That had been a professional hazard as long as he and Dulcie had been at this clandestine business.

Dragging the bag into the bathroom, he saw that Dulcie had gotten the glass open. It was a tiny little window. Pulling the plastic bag between them, up onto the sink, they barely got it through. As they squeezed through after it, Dulcie caught her breath.

"Look," she breathed, staring away down the hill.

Down on the highway, two black-and-whites were parked along the shoulder. The cats could see officers moving along the lower cliff. "What are they doing?" Dulcie said softly. "They can't be here already to answer your call. What's happening?"

But Joe's mind was on the package. On the ground below them, its stark white plastic reflected light where there was no light. If Fulman came around behind the trailer, he couldn't help but see it.

They heard, behind them, the trailer door open. They flew out the window as Cara Ray's soft tread came down the hall. Landing hard in the darkness, grabbing the bag, they hauled it underneath the trailer, against a rear wheel.

They were crouched beside the wheel, trying to punch in the number for North Carolina information, when Joe saw, standing between two trailers, a dark figure nearly hidden: a tall, slim man, his dark jacket and pants fitting neat and trim—a uniform. A cop. And the man's lean, easy stance was unmistakable.

Every hair down Joe's spine stood at attention. Harper couldn't be here so soon—he had barely hung up the phone from talking to Harper. "Dulcie, Harper's out there—"

But Dulcie was busy speaking to an operator three thousand miles away. He listened to her make several calls, then she looked up at him, her green eyes wide and dark. "I got a disconnect for Bernside Tool and Die. No such number."

"Shh. Keep your voice down. Dulcie . . ."

"The special operator couldn't tell me how long it might have been since that was a good number, if ever." She licked her paw. "Those Bernside Tool and Die invoices were dated just a few months ago."

"Dulcie, Harper's here." Joe crouched, watching Harper's feet coming toward them, up the brick walk, the police captain moving swiftly and silently in the shadows. But Dulcie was dialing again, speaking in a whisper, asking information for the number of Valencia Home for the Elderly.

"I can't speak any louder. Please listen." She asked the operator several questions, then looked up at Joe.

"No listing. Not in Greenville, North Carolina."

Before he could stop her, she had dialed again, and asked for a special operator, and was laying out a long list of questions. She hung up at last, dropped the phone into the plastic bag. "There is no Valencia Home for the Elderly," she whispered. "Not in Greenville, South Carolina, either. Not in any nearby city."

"Dulcie, Harper's standing just on the other side of this wheel, at the bottom of the steps."

She paid attention at last, creeping out to look. Above them, they could hear Fulman and Cara Ray arguing—the floor must be thin as paper.

"Harper's going to knock on that door," Joe said, "and we—"

"We, what?" she hissed. "No one knows we're under here. And if they did . . . ? We're cats, Joe. *Cats.*" She dialed again, and asked for the number of the Greenville, North Carolina, PD.

She asked several questions, and hung up, grinning.

"They never heard of Valencia Home for the Elderly. They suggested I try Greenville, South Carolina. I told them I'd already done that, that it was the same story." She began to purr. "Fake nursing home, fake machine-tool business. I can't wait for Harper to find these letters."

"He isn't going to find them if we don't hike them out of here and stash them. I don't . . ."

There was a knock at Fulman's door, then soft, sliding footsteps above their heads, as if Fulman had slipped off his shoes, approaching the door quietly. They heard Cara Ray mumble.

"Don't be stupid," Fulman hissed. "Why would a cop—?"

"They know something, Sam. Oh my God—"

They heard rummaging from the area of the dinette. "Where is it? Where the hell is it, Cara Ray? What'd you do with the papers?"

"Forget the papers. I don't have them. I want out of here."

"Where did you put them? What the hell—?"

"I didn't touch the damned papers!"

"Keep your voice down. What the hell! Has that damn cop been inside? He can't do that. What about my rights!"

"I want out, Sam. I don't—"

"And how would you suggest we do that without walking right into him? Go out through the roof?"

"A window—the bathroom window's open."

"It's the only window on that side, Cara Ray. Except the kitchen window. They're both dinky. You might squeeze through, but I can't. Go on if that's what you want."

From between the wheels, the cats could see, on the little porch, Max Harper's size eleven police-issue black oxfords. They heard Cara Ray in the bathroom, fiddling with the window. But suddenly right above them came a sharp, metallic click. The kind of businesslike double click of heavy metal, as when someone slips a loaded clip into an automatic. *Thunk, click.*

Joe leaped at the phone and slapped in Harper's number, praying he'd answer.

He got the little recording that informed him the phone was not in use at this time. Harper had turned it off, to avoid it ringing as he stood watching outside Fulman's door.

But maybe Harper had heard the click, too. He had moved off the porch fast, backing against the wall. The door was flung open.

Stepping out onto the porch, Fulman looked down at Harper. The cats didn't see a gun. Fulman's hands hung loose.

"You remember me, Fulman. Captain Harper, Molena Point Police. I'd like to talk with you."

Fulman stepped back into the trailer. Harper moved in behind him. The door closed.

No sound came from within. The cats strained to hear. Joe made one more hasty call, whispering, then they fled down the hill, dragging the grocery bag, the plastic shining stark white in the darkness—it would look, to a casual observer, as if it was hurrying down under its own power; the cats would be only shadows. Backing down the hill, hauling it along together like a pair of bulldogs, their teeth piercing the plastic, the thin plastic tearing on rocks and bushes, they got it down at last between the boulders and into the mouth of the cave.

In the wind they heard no sound from up the hill, not Harper's voice or Fulman's. Whether the silence portended good, or signaled that Harper was in trouble, they had no way to know. Hauling the bag into the cave, they tried to gauge twenty feet, then to find, in the blackness, a crevice or niche in which to stash the evidence. Joe didn't like being so far beneath the earth. As they moved deeper still, all sounds from without faded to silence.

 23

JOE GREY'S paws began to sweat. He'd rather fight a dozen hounds than creep down into the earth's dark belly. He might be a civilized tomcat, might be well informed on many matters, but he was not without his superstitions, not without some deep feline fears. And he did not like anything about Hellhag Cave.

Behind the cats, wind swirled into the cave, snatching at their backsides like a predatory beast, making the fur along Joe's back stand straight up; his every muscle felt as taut as wire cable.

"This deep enough?" he growled around a mouthful of plastic.

"Not yet," Dulcie said, dragging at the bag, and she pushed deeper, into darkness so profound that even their night vision couldn't penetrate; they had only their whiskers to guide them, and their sensitive pads to feel the way, to keep them from pitching over a ledge into empty space. He said not another word until at last she stopped, dropping her corner of the bag.

"Here. In this crevice. Help me lift the bag. Push it here."

"You seem to know the cave very well."

"I've been down here once or twice," she said casually. "There's a narrow slit here. I'm going to crawl in, push it farther back.

"Wait, Dulcie."

"I'll only be a minute. I know this little niche. When the sun's out, in the afternoons, you can see it well enough."

"You don't know what it's like since the last earthquake."

She paused, was so still he could hear her breathing.

"Oh my God," she said softly. "I could have lost the whole package in there."

"I could have lost you in there. Did you think of that?"

She backed out, pushed close to him, and licked his nose. Turning back, they found a ledge partly concealed behind a rough outcropping, and dragged the package up onto it among scattered rocky debris. Harper should find it there, should see its curve of white between the stones.

Their errand completed, Joe raced for the cave's mouth, unashamed, leaving Dulcie to take her time. His paws were sweating; his fur felt prickly all over. He was soon sucking fresh air again beneath the open sky, reveling in the sky's vast and endless space. Dulcie came out laughing at him and gave him a whisker kiss.

Above them, up the hill, there was no sound from Fulman's trailer. They could see no movement, no shadow within the yellow square of the kitchen window. Had Harper arrested Fulman? Arrested him without any sound of battle reaching them in the night?

"Look," Joe said, rearing up. Beyond Fulman's trailer, a large, dark shape was slipping along between the wheeled houses; soon the cats could make out the pale markings of a squad car: the backup that Joe had called. It stopped behind Fulman's trailer. Two officers emerged, silent and quick.

Down the hill, the first two police units were still parked at the edge of the cliff.

"Brennan mentioned a missing person," Joe said. "Maybe those units are part of the search."

"Wonder who's missing," Dulcie said softly. "I hope not a little child." Beyond the patrol cars, to the south, they could see two officers searching below the road along the lower cliff, appearing and disappearing, their flashlight beams swinging through the shrubs; and where a tiny steep road led down toward the sea, the cats caught the gleam of another car, parked among the scrub oak, and saw a flash of light and hints of other dark figures moving. Dulcie started down the hill, wanting to see more—then she stopped suddenly, staring away where the grass whipped tall and concealing.

Something small and dark lay among the blowing stems. It lay very still, no sign of movement, something blackish brown and limp. Dulcie plunged to reach the still little form, letting out a frightened mewl.

She reached in a tender paw to touch the unmoving lump.

She went limp, too, as if all the starch had gone out of her. Joe sped toward her.

Moving to press against her, he saw that it was not a

cat at all, not the little stray that Dulcie had surely imagined; it was only a purse, a woman's purse. An ordinary leather purse with an open top, lying in the tall grass.

"Cara Ray's purse?" Joe said, wondering how it had gotten down here.

"No, not Cara Ray's. It's Lucinda's. I thought—"

"I know what you thought," he said, rubbing his cheek against hers. "It's not the little waif. But, Lucinda's purse?" He stood up on his hind paws, looking around them, searching the windy, empty night for a sign of the thin old lady. "She doesn't come up here at night, Dulcie."

Dulcie stretched tall, scanning the grassy verge. "Well, she wasn't at dinner. But even if she was here somewhere, why would she leave her purse?"

"Are you sure it's hers?"

"Oh yes, it's hers. I recognize it, and that's Lucinda's scent—but there's another smell, too." Puzzled, she pushed deep into the handbag, her rear sticking out, her tail lashing, her voice muffled.

"Musty smell. Like mildew." She nosed around, pawed at something—and backed out with a thin packet of hundred-dollar bills clutched in her teeth. Dropping the musty bundle, she held it down with her paw.

"It was tucked into the side pocket. Smells just like the canvas bag." A reflection of starlight gleamed in her dark eyes. "Is this part of the buried money? Is it Lucinda who's missing? Has she run away, taking the money? Or did someone—?"

"Dulcie, Lucinda's not some baby to run away or be lost."

"Then what is her purse doing here?" She looked at him intently—then glanced up toward the cave, her eyes widening, searching the shadows at the cave's mouth.

"There was no one in there, Dulcie. We'd have caught her scent."

"Would we? Over the reek of damp earth?" She looked down the hill at the searching officers, their lights sweeping and flashing, and at the car parked below the road. "Is that Lucinda's car?" She leaped away, was yards down the hill, making for the half-hidden vehicle, when shouting erupted from the trailer above them; she stopped to look back. They heard thudding, as if men were fighting—and the crack of a shot. Dulcie dropped, belly to ground.

"Come on," Joe hissed. She crept to him. They slid behind a boulder as, above them, Fulman burst around the end of the trailer, running, swerving downhill straight at them, dodging between the dark bushes.

They didn't see Harper or the other officers. Fulman fled for the rocks where they were crouched and on past them. He careened into the cave as if he knew exactly where to run. Joe sprang to follow him—if Fulman went deep enough, and if he had a light, even if he only lit a cigarette lighter to find his way, he was sure to see the gleam of white plastic.

But Fulman stopped just inside the cave. Hunkered down, he watched the road below, watching the four officers race up the hill, heading for their cars, summoned by that single shot.

As the two black-and-whites spun U-turns and headed around the hill for the road that led up to the trailer park, Fulman slipped an automatic from his hip pocket.

The cats, crouched six feet from him, had turned to creep away, when Dulcie whispered, "Look."

Down on the road, another car came around the bend from the village, Clyde's yellow convertible, the top up but the rumble seat open, where the pups rode wagging and panting. Before Clyde had stopped, Selig leaped out, tumbled tail over nose, then danced around the car, barking. Clyde parked on the narrow verge above the sea; immediately Hestig jumped out, sniffing at the air, his tail whipping.

"What the hell is Clyde doing?" Joe hissed. "Why would he bring the pups, with all this confusion?"

The passenger door opened, and Wilma stepped out.

"They're looking for Lucinda," Dulcie whispered. "When she wasn't at dinner, I thought she just . . . Oh my. What's happened to her?"

Clyde was trying uselessly to corral the two dogs, as they ran circles around him. He gave up at last and moved along the verge, looking down the cliff, dangling the empty leashes. But Wilma headed straight up Hellhag Hill, hurrying for the cave where Lucinda liked to sit—straight toward Sam Fulman, crouched in the blackness, cradling his automatic. The cats flew to meet her.

Dulcie leaped into Wilma's arms, nearly choking as she tried to get out the words. "Go back. Fulman's in there. He has a pistol. He shot—he shot at Harper."

Wilma dropped behind the nearest bush and slid downhill, rolled twice, and fetched up behind a boulder out of the line of fire—her reactions as sharp as when she had worked parole cases; Dulcie supposed the body didn't forget; like snatching a fast mouse, the habit was with you forever.

The cats crowded close to Wilma. Shielded by the rocks, they could barely see the cave; but they could see, high above it, Fulman's trailer, where Harper and an officer were easing Cara Ray into the backseat of a squad car, Cara Ray fighting and swearing.

"What happened?" Dulcie whispered to Wilma. "Where's Lucinda?"

"She hasn't been home since just after the quake, when the Greenlaws hauled her furniture out of the house."

"Mightn't she have gone out to eat by herself, because she was angry? Why did they call the police?"

"She and I had an appointment with the priest—she was upset about Dirken's plans for the funeral. When she was an hour late, I went by the house."

Above them, Harper and two officers moved down the hill on foot, keeping low, were soon lost among the dark bushes.

"With all that's happened," Wilma whispered, "with the Greenlaws knowing that Lucinda had found the money, Harper thought it best to look for her. Probably she just got in her car and left for a while, left them to their haggling."

The three officers crouched above the cave among the granite boulders; they would not be able to see into the cave, as Wilma and the cats could. Fulman had moved deeper in, hidden among the inky shadows.

"Fulman," Harper said, "you're trapped. You'd do best to come on out."

Fulman appeared suddenly at the mouth of the cave, his pistol drawn, facing uphill in a shooter's stance.

"Look out," Wilma yelled.

The officers dropped. Fulman fired. Three shots flashed in the darkness. The officers rose and circled fast, down either side of the cave, returning fire. Fulman had disappeared. Wilma and the cats lay flattened, Joe wondering if this was the last night in his and Dulcie's lives—and if they had any lives left, for future use. Watching Lieutenant Wendell slip down beside the cave, Joe's eyes widened at the metal canister in Wendell's hand.

"Come out, Fulman," Harper shouted. "Hands on your head. You have ten seconds, or that cave's so full of tear gas, you'll sell your soul for air."

"My god," Dulcie said, staring at the canister.

"It could save a life," Wilma snapped at her. "Run—get down the hill. If the wind picks up a whiff of that stuff . . ."

But before Wendell could throw the canister they heard a scuffle in the cave, heard a woman scream and Fulman swearing. Another scream, and Fulman loomed in the entrance, pushing Lucinda before him.

"See what I have, Harper. Go on, throw your little bomb."

The officers drew back. Fulman dragged Lucinda out of the cave, staying behind the thin old woman, moving down the hill using her as a shield. Lucinda was limp and obedient.

"She was in the cave all along," Dulcie whispered. "She was there when we went in. Why did she let him see her?"

Fulman had backed a third of the way down toward the highway, dragging Lucinda, when the pups raced up at them, barking, half in play, half with confused anger. Fulman spun, kicking at them, the old lady stumbling. Selig and Hestig leaped and snapped at him. He kicked them again, and forced Lucinda across the road to the edge of the cliff, where it sheared away to the breakers. Lucinda made no effort to fight him; caught between the sea crashing below and the gun he held against her, she was very still.

Clutching her arm, he faced the ring of officers that had followed them. "Get the hell away, Harper. Get your men away—the whole mess of you. Or you'll be picking her out of the ocean."

The officers drew back. But at the rage in Fulman's voice, the pups went wild. They charged him, Hestig low and snarling, grabbing his ankle as Selig leaped at his chest, hitting him hard; at the same instant Lucinda came alive. Clutched against Fulman, she twisted violently, biting his arm. He hit her in the face. She kneed him where it had to hurt, and when Fulman doubled over, she clawed his face and jerked free. Maybe all the anger she had stored, unspent for so many years, went into that desperate bid for freedom. Certainly the violence enraged the pups. They tore at Fulman. Fighting the dogs and fighting Lucinda, Fulman lost his balance. He fell, dragging Lucinda. They were over the cliff, the pups falling with them clawing at Fulman—humans and pups falling . . .

Officers surged to the edge, and began to ease themselves down. Fulman was sprawled on a ledge some ten feet below, lying across Lucinda, tangled with the pups. Lucinda had his gun. As Fulman lunged for it, she twisted away. He hit Lucinda hard, snatched the gun, took aim at the officers crowding down the cliff. "I told—"

Joe Grey leaped.

He didn't think about getting shot or about falling a hundred feet into the sea or about how Max Harper would view his unnatural response or about Dulcie following him, he was just claw-raking, snarling mad: he didn't like Fulman harming Lucinda; he didn't like Fulman's gun pointed up at all of them. Only as he clung to Fulman's face, digging in, did he realize that Dulcie was beside him, raking Fulman's throat.

Their weight and the shock of their attack sent Fulman sprawling on the crumbling edge. They felt Lucinda struggle free, saw her grab a rock. Crouching, she swung, her face filled with rage. She hit Fulman in the stomach, pounding him, pounding.

Only then did Joe Grey face the fact that he and Dulcie might have been blown to shreds by one shot from Fulman, exploded into little bits of cat meat. He watched Officer Wendell swing down onto the ledge, his weapon drawn, covering Fulman—the sight of Wendell's automatic was mighty welcome.

Fulman drew back against the cliff. Lucinda huddled at the edge, staring down at the heaving sea.

As Wendell cuffed Fulman, the cats scrambled up the cliff, past him. From above, they watched Wendell put a leg chain on Fulman, then tie a rope around Lucinda, making a harness, preparing for the officers above to hoist her to the road.

Clyde and two officers lifted her to safety. Her face was very white, her pale hair clinging in damp curls. She said no word. She kept her eyes closed until she was again on solid ground.

The next moments, as the paramedics took over, examining Lucinda and Fulman, Joe and Dulcie fled into the tall, concealing grass.

Pity, Joe thought, *that Fulman didn't crash on the rocks and die. Pity Lucinda didn't shoot him, he deserved shooting;*

she would have saved the state of California a good deal of trouble, to say nothing of the money they'd spend prosecuting this scum.

"What is it with humans?" he asked Dulcie, watching Clyde clip leashes on the chastened pups—chastened not from any scolding Clyde had given them. How could he scold them for their wild behavior, when they had helped to capture Fulman? But chastened from the fall; the two dogs were very quiet, the whites around their eyes showing. It was an amazement to Joe that no one, in that ten-foot slide and fall down the cliff, had any broken bones.

What Max Harper would have to say about his and Dulcie's part in Fulman's capture did not bear considering. Joe guessed he'd better come up with a good story—coach Clyde on it, and fill Wilma in. Set up a scenario about how these two cats got along so well with the pups, that when the pups got excited, the silly cats got excited, too, went kind of crazy—feline hysteria.

Sitting hidden in the grass, out of the way of the police, Joe and Dulcie watched the first rescue unit pull away, transporting Sam Fulman to the hospital. Two police guards rode with him.

"Look at the damage Fulman's done," Joe said. "Shot Harper in the arm, and Lucinda's lucky she isn't dead. Three men *are* dead at Fulman's hands—and for what? To line his greedy pockets. But the paramedics took care of him just like he was worth saving."

"Civilized," Dulcie said. "The result of thousands of years of civilization."

"I don't call that civilized, I call it silly. And if humans are so civilized, how come all the crime—the rise in murder statistics? Rape statistics, robbery, you name it." He looked at Dulcie intently. "If you think there's been progress, then how come the jails are so full?"

But Dulcie only shrugged; she was too tired to express an opinion on matters as complicated and diverse as human ambiguities.

Sitting close together, the cats watched Wilma hurry to retrieve Lucinda's car, preparing to follow the second ambulance, which was taking Lucinda to Emergency. Suddenly Dulcie crouched to race down the hill, to go with her.

But she stopped, turned to look at Joe. "Come on— don't you want to be with Lucinda?"

Joe licked her ear. "You go. I want to be sure Harper finds the bag—see you in Jolly's alley." And he was away after Harper, racing up through the grass as Harper climbed toward Hellhag Cave. Joe paused only once to look back, as Wilma pulled away behind the rescue unit; when he and Dulcie had faced danger together, he never liked to be parted from her.

But what could happen? He watched Clyde's yellow roadster spin a U-turn, following Wilma. The pups rode as sedately, now, as a pair of middle-aged sightseers; he wondered how long that subdued frame of mind would last. Only Harper's squad car remained, beside the highway, where one of the officers had put it after retrieving it from the trailer park. It looked lonely there, strangely vulnerable. Quickly, Joe followed Harper on up the hill.

As the captain stepped into the darkness of Hellhag

Cave, Joe glimpsed a movement among the rocks.

Maybe it was only a shadow cast by the light from Harper's swinging torch, as the captain disappeared inside. Joe didn't wait to see. Swallowing back his fear of the place, he followed Harper.

24

JOE WATCHED the light of Max Harper's torch move quickly into Hellhag Cave, its bright arc slicing through the darkness. Joe took a step in, and another. Swallowing his distaste, he followed Harper, slipping along close to the wall, his whiskers brushing cold stone.

Harper moved slowly, studying each crevice until, ahead, a flash shone out between the stones as icy white as snow gleaming in the torchlight.

Before Harper touched the bag, he slipped on a pair of thin gloves. Carefully lifting out a letter, he held it by a corner, bright in the beam.

In a moment, as he read, that lopsided grin lit Harper's dour face, that smug, predatory smile that made Joe Grey smile, too.

Glancing around the cave, Harper bundled the bag inside his jacket. Instead of leaving, he moved deeper in, swinging his torch so the cave floor was washed in moving rivers of light. Joe could hear loose stones crunching under the captain's shoes. He remained still until Harper turned back, his beam seeking the mouth of the cave again.

Harper stopped before a narrow shelf. Joe heard him suck in his breath.

"Well, I'll be damned," Harper said softly.

Sliding closer, Joe reared up to look, cursing the great cat god who had given him white markings. If Harper flashed the torch in his direction, his white parts would shine like neon.

And even when he stood on his hind paws, he couldn't see what Harper had found; Harper's broad-shouldered, uniformed back blocked Joe's view. Slipping close behind Harper's heels, he peered around the captain's trouser legs.

Harper, bending over the stone shelf, was studying two small, dark objects. Barely touching them, he lifted one, placing it in a paper evidence bag. The billfold was thick and bulging, made of dark, greasy leather.

The black plastic tubing smelled like ether-laced pancake syrup. As Harper bagged it, and his light swung around, Joe slid into blackness, lowering his face over his paws and chest.

He didn't move until the light swung away, leaving a pool of night behind it. He looked out covertly at Harper.

Harper was grinning as if he'd just won the lottery. Folding the tops of the evidence bags and tucking them into his jacket beside the bulge of Fulman's letters, he was still smiling as he headed back for the entrance. Joe hurried out behind him, as pleased as Harper—but deeply puzzled.

There had been nothing on that shelf when he and Dulcie dragged the plastic bag into the cave. He remembered pausing there. The shelf had been empty. And certainly they couldn't have passed the stink of brake fluid without smelling it.

Stopping in the shadows of the cave's entrance, Joe watched Harper descend Hellhag Hill to his police unit.

Had Fulman hidden those objects in the cave, maybe been afraid to throw them in the ocean, afraid they'd wash up on the shore again, or someone would fish them out? Maybe Fulman didn't want to take time to bury them, and was wary of dumping them in some trash can—you read about that stuff, some homeless guy finding the evidence in a trash can.

So Fulman had stashed the brake line and the bill-fold in the cave?

But not in plain sight, not on that shelf.

Frowning, Joe stood up on his hind paws studying the dark, grassy hillside around him. Turning, he stared back at the mouth of the cave.

He trotted in again, listening and scenting out, studying the velvet dark. When nothing stirred, he hurried deeper in, forgetting his fear, sniffing along the cave walls, sniffing at the ledge where Harper had found the evidence.

Nosing at the stone shelf, he smelled not only Harper's familiar tobacco and gun-oil scent, and the sharp whiff of brake fluid, but, besides these, a yeasty, sweet kitten smell.

Looking deep into the cave, Joe Grey called to her.

There was no answering mew, no small voice coming out of the dark.

He was greatly amused and impressed that the kit had found those items. But where did she find them? And how did she know they were important?

What fascinating worlds of thought, Joe wondered, ran in that small, wild mind?

Again he called to her. Why was she so shy? When a third time he called and nothing stirred, when the blackness of the cave lay around him empty and still, he pressed back toward the cave's mouth, hungering for open space.

And there she was.

A small silhouette, black as soot, against the starry sky. A tiny being stretching as tall as she could against the sky's jeweled glow.

"Hello, Kit."

The kit purred.

He sat down beside her, at the cave's mouth. "What did you do back there, Kit?"

The kit's eyes widened, she cringed away from him.

"It's all right," Joe said. "You did just fine. Are you hungry?"

"Always hungry," said the kit.

He wanted to know where she had found the evidence and why she had put it on the ledge. He guessed his questions would wait. "Come on, I'll show you something to please you."

The kit followed him slowly at first, slinking along behind. Joe felt protective of her; he wanted to pat and wash her—and was deeply embarrassed at such maternal thoughts. Joe Grey, macho tomcat, wanting to mother some scruffy little hank of cat fur.

"Come on, Kit. Don't dawdle." He turned to wait for her. The kit was so small and thin, but so bright-eyed and alive. Her gaze at him was as brilliant as stars exploding. She galloped up and trotted happily beside him, her head high, her long, bushy tail waving.

Down into the village they wandered. Joe Grey couldn't hurry her. She had to stop at every new scent, had to look into every shop window, examine every tiny patch of garden.

"I was here before," she said. "When I rode that dog. I jumped off and ran. This is not like big-city streets. Not like the alleys where I was before."

She stood up to peer in through the glass at a display of brightly painted pottery, yearning toward it, lifting a paw as if to touch it, much as Dulcie would do. She stopped to sniff a hundred smells, and to pat a hundred shadows.

Down the oak-shaded, flower-decked streets she and Joe Grey walked, dawdling, creating endless delays, until they arrived at last at the small, brick-paved alley behind George Jolly's Deli.

Despite the late hour, a light burned in the deli kitchen, and Joe could hear cooking sounds, a spoon scraping a bowl; George Jolly was working late preparing his delicious salads and marinades and sandwich spreads.

Jolly must have just set out fresh plates for the village cats; the nicely presented feast had not yet been sampled. No other cat was present.

The kit said, "This is not for cats to eat."

"This *is* for cats to eat."

The kit smelled each individual serving—salmon, caviar, an assortment of cheeses.

"Go on, Kit. You're not hungry?"

The kit gave him a questioning look, then set to

gulping and smacking, sucking up the feast with a fine, robust greed.

She came up for air with cheese on her nose and chopped egg in her whiskers.

And now, her first hunger sated, she looked around her at the little shops that faced the alley, admiring their mullioned doors and stained-glass windows. Her round eyes widened at a bright red-and-blue rocking horse, at the little potted trees beside the shop doors, at the decorative wrought-iron lamps that lit either end of the cozy alley, at the tall jasmine vine heavy with yellow blossoms. She smiled. Then she ate again, rumbling and shaking with purrs.

Dulcie found them there, Joe Grey washing his whiskers and guarding the sleeping kit. The kit lay sprawled on the bricks, softly snoring, her little stomach distended, her face smeared with chopped egg, one paw twitching now and then as if, in dream, she still pawed at the delectable morsels of salmon and sliced Brie.

"Guess what she did," Joe said, as proud as a parent.

"Made a pig of herself."

"Besides that. Something—incredible. She found the brake line and the billfold. Harper has them."

"She didn't!" Dulcie began to wash the kit's face. "Oh, she is clever."

The kit woke, yawning.

"Did you really find those things, Kit? How did you know . . . ?"

"In a crevice," the kit said. "They smelled of that man that came running, the man that hurt Pedric. He was there before. A long time ago he hid those things. Then he hurt the old man, and I didn't like him.

"Then today you hid that white bag. It smelled of him." The kit looked up at them with round yellow eyes. "When he came running into the cave, I thought he would see the bag. But the woman was there. He saw her instead. He hurt her; he hurt that kind woman."

"She's all right," Dulcie told her. "She'll be all right."

"I saw her go in that big car."

"Ambulance. That's an ambulance. The paramedics took good care of her. But why . . . ?"

"After the loud noises and blood and he dragged her over the cliff and everyone was shouting and those dogs barking, I went to the cave. Then the man came and"— she looked at Joe—"you were behind him. He was happy to find the bag. And you looked happy. So I quick brought those things out of the crevice and put them for him to find."

"You were in the cave the whole time," Joe said.

The kit purred.

"You have done more than you can guess," Joe told her. "But what was Lucinda doing in there?"

"She likes the cave. She is peaceful there. She likes to be quiet there."

The kit swished her long, bushy tail. "I never knew a human. The others say humans are bad. Out on the hill, where the others could see, I stayed away from her. But in the cave, when she came today, I went close to look at her. She petted me."

"Did you—talk to her?" Dulcie asked.

"Oh *no*." The kit looked shocked, her yellow eyes widening. Neither Dulcie nor Joe had ever seen a cat with eyes so round; the kit's little thin face was vibrant with life, with the deep, shifting lights of amusement and intelligence.

"Why do the others haze you?" Dulcie said.

"I don't know. I don't care; they will go away soon. They don't like the quakes. They will go where the earth doesn't shake."

"And where would that be?" Joe said.

"They don't know. They mean to search until they find such a place."

"And will you go with them?" Dulcie asked softly.

The kit was silent.

"Will you stay here alone, then? On Hellhag Hill?" She didn't speak.

Dulcie was very still. A terrible longing filled her. "Would you go home with me?" she whispered.

But still the little, mottled kit did not reply.

"Oh," Dulcie said. "You will go to Lucinda?"

"I will go—with the one who needs me," said the kit. "With the lonely one who needs me."

Dulcie turned away and began to wash, trying not to show her disappointment.

The kit patted at Dulcie's paw. "I can't be with humans the whole time. Humans can't climb and hunt." She snuggled close to Dulcie. "I have no one to teach me to hunt."

Dulcie brightened. She sat up straighter, lashing her tail with pleasure.

Joe Grey was embarrassed to hear himself rumbling with purrs.

"And when will you go there, to Lucinda?" Dulcie said.

"When the other humans are gone. Those people that, she says, fill up her house. And when that old man comes back from the hos—hospital, and they are together."

"Together? What do you mean, together?"

"Of course, together." The kit glanced up the hill to the Moonwatch Trailer Park. "Maybe together there in that little house with wheels."

Dulcie stared at her, puzzled.

"They are friends," said the kit. "They need one another. The time is now for them to be together. To start new," she said, "just like me.

"The time is now for me to go away from the clowder. I have been with them long enough. The time is now for me to start another new way to live."

"Then you had best come home with me," Dulcie said in a businesslike manner, "until it's time for you to go to Lucinda."

The kit rubbed against Dulcie's shoulder, extravagantly purring.

And so the nameless kit joined the great and diverse community of Molena Point cats who had fallen, in this one of their nine lives, into an earthly heaven; so the tattered kit was brought home to Molena Point's bright and nurturing village; now she had only to find herself a name, and find her true calling in the world.

 25

T HE FUNERAL was finished. Shamas Greenlaw lay,
at last, in his grave. Whether he rested at peace, no one
on this earth could say. His cousin Newlon lay next to
him, and the family had made a great event of the double funeral. They had ordered matching headstones
carved with angels strumming harps, their wings lifted,
their eyes cast toward heaven—whether smiling up at
the two departing souls, or conveying their regrets as
the deceased were cast out in the opposite direction,
was equally uncertain.

The funeral had not, as Lucinda feared, been an
embarrassing display of bad taste.

She had told Wilma she was afraid Dirken would
take over the rosary arrangements, would create a loud,
drunken Irish dirge, with loud weeping and louder
music, to bid farewell to Shamas. That was why she had
planned to meet with Wilma and Father Radcliff the
night that she disappeared.

On her way out of the house that evening, to keep the appointment, she heard Dirken calling to her to get a move-on, that it was time for the two of them to leave.

She'd had no intention of taking Dirken. Quickly, she'd slipped out the kitchen door, got in her car, and took off in the opposite direction from the church. She didn't have time to call Wilma or call the rectory. "I just wanted to be away—from Dirken, from the whole family."

After Lucinda was released from the emergency room of Molena Point Hospital, the two women had sat at Wilma's kitchen table late that night. Dulcie, curled up on the rug, had tried to imagine the kind of colorful Irish wake that worried Lucinda, and that the Greenlaws seemed to want, tried to envision the long-winded and drunken eulogies, as Lucinda described to Wilma.

"All I want is to get the funeral over," Lucinda said. "A traditional, solemn rosary and mass and burial, and then to be done with it. As cold as it sounds, Wilma, all I want is to be done with Shamas.

"Funerals aren't for the dead anyway," Lucinda said. "They're for those left behind. And I don't need it.

"For that matter, what good will a mass and a rosary do Shamas? Shamas made his bed with the Lord. Nothing in Heaven or earth is going to change that."

Dulcie had been both shocked and amused.

"The empty money bag," Wilma had said, gently changing the subject, "the bag the pups dug out. I'm surely curious about that."

Lucinda laughed. "Oh, I knew about that money, long before Dirken came snooping.

"It started several years ago, when Shamas repaired

the foundation. Shamas never did a lick of work around the house. His sudden, unexpected project so puzzled me that I snooped into the garden shed.

"I found the sledge he used to break the concrete, the bucket and trowel with which he'd repaired it; and after that day I watched him more closely, paid attention to the musty-smelling money that Shamas brought back from the bank a time or two. To the way, when he returned from Seattle after a business trip, he always had some excuse, early in the morning, to putter in the yard. And I'd get home from my walk, find he had done a load of laundry. Washed the clothes that, I suppose, he'd worn to crawl under the house. He'd say he had brought so much laundry home from his trip, he didn't like to burden me with such a lot of work."

Lucinda smiled. "He must have thought little of my reasoning skills. Must have thought I would never crawl under the house myself, but I did. The next time he left for Seattle I put on some old clothes and took a flashlight and went under there.

"I found a patched place about two feet wide, and a little square in the middle of it, maybe six inches across, where fresher concrete had been troweled in. He must have made the big hole the first time, and then just the smaller one, after that—enough to stick his hand in. I got the sledge from the garage and gave it a whack.

"I was surprised it took so little effort, five or six blows, and the smaller patch of concrete fell right out. When I shined my light in, there was a big canvas bag.

"I didn't understand why he hadn't put some kind of screw-plug in the foundation, maybe that looked like a cleanout for ashes, something he didn't need to cement over each time. I suppose he thought a workman might believe it was a cleanout and try to use it, or that someone else might find it and be curious.

"Well, I didn't like reaching into that dark place, but I could feel the drawstring. I got it open, and I could feel money, that greasy feel of money and the right size. The bag was filled with packets of money. My heart was pounding, I didn't know if it was from excitement or if I was scared stiff.

"When I pulled out a packet, I had a whole fistful of hundred-dollar bills! Counting those bills made me feel a little faint. I kept twenty of them and stuffed the packet back into the bag. I was afraid to take more.

"He'd left the box of patching cement in the garage." Lucinda laughed. "It had directions printed on it just like a box of biscuit mix.

"Well, from that time on, when I wanted extra money, that's where I got it. When Shamas never caught on, I grew bolder, took enough to set up a new bank account in my name, in a bank Shamas didn't use, as far as I knew. I had the statements sent to a post office box—I guess I did learn something from Shamas.

"I always knew when he put cash in the bag. I could hear him down there tapping—he would leave the radio or TV on in the living room to mask the sound. And he would either have just arrived home from a trip, or have come directly from the post office or from UPS.

"Well, then Shamas died and Dirken was here poking around. I took all the money out of the bag, put some in my account, but most of it in a pillow slip. Left the empty bag in there for Dirken to find—my little private joke."

Lucinda smiled. "With Dirken sneaking around telling me those silly stories about how the house had dry rot, I found his backbreaking work with the pick and hammer most entertaining."

Dulcie, too, was highly entertained. She wanted to cheer for Lucinda. Well, she thought, the funeral had come off all right. The Greenlaw clan hadn't turned the mass into a loud and abandoned display, or turned the rosary into a dirge of unseemly weeping. Nor was there any unchurchly music at the gravesite, such as the marching band Dirken had favored tramping through the cemetery tootling on horns and beating drums; the mass and burial ceremonies had been restrained and tasteful.

If a number of ushers of severe countenance stood in strategic locations about the church and cemetery, scowling at any show of wildly unleashed emotions, that fact may or may not have contributed to the solemnity that prevailed among the worshipers. If those ushers looked like cops in civilian attire, that, too, may have added to the sober atmosphere, as did Captain Max Harper's presence, where he sat at the back of the church. The Greenlaws, every one, moved through the ceremony as quietly as a gathering of nuns, their bowed heads and clasped hands a solemn credit to Shamas and Newlon Greenlaw.

The Church of the Mission of Exaltation of Molena Piños, with its lovely eighteenth-century Spanish architecture—its heavy beams and antique stained-glass windows, its hand-decorated adobe walls and whitewashed plank ceilings painted with garlands of age-faded red roses, its thick clay floors—and its ancient traditions, embraced the Greenlaws in their parting ceremony as generously as it had embraced, over the centuries, any number of murderers, confidence men, and horse thieves, whenever such deaths occurred among the general populace.

Cara Ray Crisp did not attend Shamas's funeral; nor did Sam Fulman. One could only imagine Cara Ray there among the mourners, dressed in the form-fitting little black dress that she had bought for the occasion, her eyes cast down with maidenly grief.

In point of fact, Cara Ray, like Sam himself, spent the hours of Shamas's leave-taking sitting on a hard steel bench behind the bars of Molena Point City Jail, Cara Ray attired in a gray wraparound dress two sizes too big for her, and prison-made tennis shoes without stockings, and Sam sporting a regulation prison jumpsuit dyed bright orange.

And while the funeral and wake might have been circumspect, the party that followed was another matter. Held in the dining room of the Seaside Hotel, just up the coast, flowing with rich food, Irish whiskey, and loud with Irish music, and paid for with moneys contributed unknowingly by shopkeepers and car dealers across the U.S., the party would have made Shamas proud.

Though Shamas's ghost, if he had attended this parting event, would have been chagrined at the triumph apparent in the eyes of his grieving widow, would have been shocked at Lucinda's high color and contented smile. Shamas's ghost would have boiled like swirling smoke at the sight of Lucinda and Pedric Greenlaw standing close together, their eyes meeting warmly, their hands lightly touching.

Nor would Shamas have liked the ceremony that occurred three weeks later, on the crest of Hellhag Hill.

Not that Lucinda cared what Shamas would think,

any more than she cared if the whole village gossiped about her for making such a commitment so soon after her husband's death, and so very late in her life.

This was her and Pedric's private moment. People could say what they liked. This was a union that carried no load of past expectations, and none of the face-saving that she had tried to maintain while Shamas was alive. The slate, in short, was wiped clean. Lucinda didn't give a damn.

Max Harper, avoiding the wake, did attend with pleasure the gathering atop Hellhag Hill—as did Wilma Getz, Clyde Damen, Charlie Getz, and the three cats.

Only the pups were not invited. They had been confined in a box stall in Max Harper's stable, where they couldn't tear up anything but the stable walls.

The wedding was held on a bright Saturday afternoon three weeks after Shamas's funeral. Now was the time for the Dixieland band and champagne and laughter. The party delectables were catered by George Jolly. The ceremony was performed by a local justice of the peace, a jovial man fond of unorthodox weddings, Dixieland music, and cats; the site of the ceremony was the small, grassy plateau just below Hellhag Cave. The nuptials were simple, and brief. The moment Pedric kissed the bride, the band burst out with a marching number that accompanied the guests as they climbed the steep hill to the reception, held on what had been the site of the Moonwatch Trailer Park.

The trailers were gone; the ledge was empty save for one green vehicle of some age, standing at the edge, with a view down Hellhag Hill to the sea.

On the abandoned concrete trailer pads between the

brick walkways, small tables and umbrellas had been set up, surrounding George Jolly's sumptuous buffet table and the bar. The bride and groom sat at a table with Wilma and Clyde, and Charlie and Max Harper. On the table next to them, the three cats took their ease, Joe and Dulcie nibbling from their own party plates, the darkly mottled kit sitting up straight and wide-eyed, watching every amazing activity, hearing every astounding word, looking this way and that, her ears flicking in a dozen directions, trying to take it all in.

From George Jolly's alley, the kit had gone home with Dulcie. She liked living in a house. She liked life within warm rooms where one was allowed to sleep on soft furniture. She liked the wonderful smells and the surprising, whisker-licking food. She liked this new, loving relationship with humans.

Everything was new and wonderful and amazing to the small, ragged kit. There were no cold winds to bite her. No snarling, cold-hearted cats to haze and snipe at her, to slap her and drive her away from some small nest she had tried to make her own.

She had new friends. She would soon have a new home. Far more adaptable than a human, perhaps, she had launched herself into this new life with all claws grabbing.

But now suddenly she was all tired out. Too much ceremony. Too much talk. Too many new things happening. Surfeited with amazements, the kit curled up on the table and fell immediately and deeply asleep. She slept stretched out with great and trusting abandon, her long bushy tail hanging down over the side of the table, her whole being relaxed into a mass of ragged fur. She looked, with her black-and-brown fur sticking out every which way, more like a moth-eaten fur scarf lying across the table than anything alive.

Lucinda reached quietly to pet her. To Lucinda, the kit was a wonder, a sweet charmer who soon would be their own, hers and Pedric's. Stroking the kit, and looking around her at the shelf of land that would hold their new home, Lucinda felt deeply content.

The hillside setting would accommodate very nicely a small, rambling structure designed to fit their needs, just herself and Pedric and the kit and the feral cats they hoped they might care for.

Lucinda did not know that the tattered kit's clowder had moved on; it didn't matter, there would be other cats.

The house would be designed so the kit would have her own aeries and tall perches among the rough-hewn beams, and of course she would have soft couches to nap on.

Lucinda had not needed the cash soon to come from the sale of her house to Brock, Lavell & Hicks to buy this land; she had used other money for that. Money, she told most people, that she had saved, over many years, from her household allowance. And who was there to say different?

Max Harper listened with some interest to the couple's plans for their new home; but he was quiet. He seemed, to Joe Grey, particularly withdrawn. Ever since the capture of Sam Fulman—except for that grin of discovery and triumph that Joe had seen when Harper found the evidence in Hellhag Cave—Harper had seemed unusually edgy and stern.

Is that my fault? Joe wondered. *Mine and Dulcie's? Have we pushed Harper too far? Did we come close to the limit with Harper, leaping in Fulman's face the way we did? Have we gone beyond what Harper can accept?*

Harper had once told Clyde that when a cop stumbled across facts that added up to the impossible, such a thing might put him right around the bend. That if a cop started believing some of this far-out stuff, he could be headed for the funny farm.

Harper's late wife, Millie, a detective on the force when she was alive, had handled the nutcases, the saucer sightings and souls returned from the dead. Harper said that when Millie got a case that she couldn't explain away rationally, it gave them both the creeps.

Clyde and Wilma had passed off the cats' attacking Sam Fulman as animal hysteria, triggered by the wild leaping and barking of the two pups: the frantic pups had gotten the cats so keyed up that their adrenaline went right through the roof. The two cats went kind of crazy.

Harper might believe them. And he might not. Harper knew animals, he knew that the overexcitement of one creature could infect the animals around him.

He had appeared to buy the story.

But with Harper, one never knew.

The cats watched the bride and groom depart in a flurry of confetti and rice, with tin cans tied to the bumper of Lucinda's New Yorker, setting out for a few weeks traveling up the California and Oregon coasts.

George Jolly served another round of champagne to a handful of lingering guests. Max Harper settled back, watching Clyde and Wilma and Charlie. The three were filled with questions.

"Long before Shamas drowned," Harper said,

"Torres had gotten friendly with Cara Ray, as a source of information in his investigation of Shamas's swindling operations. Of course he was investigating Fulman, too, on the same cases.

"Somewhere along the line Torres, checking on Shamas's bank accounts in half a dozen names, must have realized that Shamas was taking in far more money than he was depositing or laundering, stashing it somewhere. Very likely he knew about Shamas's reputation among the Greenlaw family for burying money.

"Torres got pretty tight with Cara Ray, picking up bits of information from her. When he heard, from Seattle PD, that Shamas had drowned, he called her.

"Maybe he thought she knew about the money, knew where it was, maybe thought they could join up. That's the way we read it. If so, that was the moment he stepped over the line from investigation to the other side, thinking how to get his hands on Shamas's stash. What Torres didn't know was that Cara Ray was also seeing Sam Fulman."

Harper paused to light a cigarette. "Assume Cara Ray knew about the money and played Torres along. There's some indication that she thought Torres was tight with Seattle police, that he might suspect she and Fulman killed Shamas. Say she gets scared. Couple that with the fact that Fulman knew Torres was investigating him along with Shamas, and you have two people wanting Torres out of the way.

"When Torres takes off for L.A., on an investigation and to pick up the antique Corvette he'd bought from a dealer down there, they figure he'll make a little detour into Molena Point to look for the money. They decide to do him.

"Cara Ray honeys Torres up and makes plans to meet him in Molena Point on his way back from his L.A. investigation, have a few romantic days together.

"That early morning, the motel took a phone call to Cara Ray's room. Operator heard a man answer. The call was from a woman, at about four A.M. There's no record of the caller's number; it was local. We have a witness who saw Torres leave the motel at four-thirty, in the Corvette.

"None of the maids had seen Cara Ray for maybe twenty-four hours. We found a note in her room: 'Honey, my sister's sick. Going to run down to Half Moon Bay. Back late tomorrow night.'

"She has a sister there, but she hadn't been sick, hadn't seen Cara Ray for several months. She lied at first to cover for Cara Ray, but then decided she didn't want her own neck in a noose."

Harper smiled. "So much for family loyalty.

"Very likely Cara Ray went up to Fulman's trailer, called Torres from there, said she had car trouble, wanted him to come get her.

"Say Fulman is down on the highway in the fog, waiting for Torres's Corvette. He's sitting there ready to hit a blast on the horn, or maybe parks his car across the road—something to make Torres put on the brakes hard at that curve, squeezing out the brake fluid.

"There were skid marks on the road, but not enough other markings to make much of a picture. However," Harper said, "we have the cut brake line, with Fulman's prints on it. We have Torres's billfold, which was removed from the Corvette along with the brake line, before my men got there that morning.

"The lab found, along the broken edge of glass from

the car window, particles of leather from the wallet. Besides Torres's own prints on the leather and plastic, we have a good partial print for Fulman."

Joe and Dulcie couldn't help smiling—and could hardly help laughing at the expression on Clyde's face. They didn't have to whisper, *We told you so*. Clyde looked suitably ashamed.

"We have a pair of Fulman's shoes from the trailer," Harper said, "and casts of the same shoes at the scene. Enough," the captain said, easing back in his folding chair, "to prosecute Fulman for Torres's murder. And maybe enough to prosecute for Newlon Greenlaw's death. And enough hard evidence, as well, to take Fulman to court on several counts of fraud. Both Washington State and the Feds want him for the machine-tool scams he and Shamas were working."

"But what about George Chambers," Clyde said. "Was it Fulman who stabbed Chambers?"

"No prints on the knife," Harper said. "And Chambers didn't see his attacker. There may not be enough there to make anything." Harper didn't seem to want to talk about Chambers.

Joe and Dulcie glanced at each other, wondering if Chambers had seen Fulman and Cara Ray kill Shamas? If he had not been asleep in his cabin, after all? If Harper might be protecting Chambers as the only remaining witness to the murder of Shamas Greenlaw?

"But then," Charlie asked, "did Fulman try to kill Pedric because he knew about the bag of money?"

"I'd guess the whole family knew there was stash hidden somewhere. That they just kept out of Dirken's way, that it was Dirken's call, and that they knew they'd get their cut. No, I'm guessing he tried to kill Pedric because Pedric was getting too friendly with Lucinda.

"Fulman might have been afraid Pedric would clue Lucinda in on the scams they were running, and that she would come to us, turn him in.

"When Fulman attacked Pedric, he most likely thought he'd killed him."

Joe and Dulcie looked at each other and turned away smiling. Harper would never know that the one witness to that attack and Newlon's murder slept on the table only a few feet from him—a witness who would never face a jury in a court of law.

Joe, licking his shoulder, caught a glance from Clyde, a pitifully chastened look that made Joe want to roll over laughing. Clyde's misjudgment and embarrassment provided a frame of mind that, if Joe played his cards right, should be good for several weeks' worth of gourmet dinners from Jolly's, to say nothing of an improved breakfast menu.

Wilma, on the other hand, had the same smug, I-told-you-so look as the cats. She and Harper had nailed nine members of the Greenlaw clan, including Dirken, on fraud charges across the country from Molena Point to North Carolina. The fact that her old, unreformed probationer was behind bars, as well, and likely to stay there, didn't hurt her mood, either.

Wilma had terminated her investigative position at Beckwhite's, laying all future problems back in the lap of Sheril Beckwhite, and had returned to the library, along with Dulcie. Joe had to say, the moods of both were improved. Dulcie, in fact, was wildly cheerful. Whatever problem she'd had, to make her so moody, seemed to have vanished when the little tattered kit came to stay with her and Wilma—though even the pups had driven away some of Dulcie's scowls and tail-lashings.

It might be, Joe thought, that the pups had found a permanent home. At least maybe Selig had. Selig's silliness seemed a challenge to Max Harper. The pup got along very well with Harper's three horses, too, running and playing with them in the pasture.

Charlie seemed reluctant to part with Hestig. She'd said twice, that week, that she might look for a house with a yard.

Joe knew he had been staring at Charlie. She rose, reaching to stroke Dulcie. "Come on, cats. Come and walk with me."

The three cats dropped down from the table and galloped after her, racing past her as she climbed the steep hillside.

Sitting high atop Hellhag Hill like any four friends out for a walk, Charlie and the cats looked down at the little tables and umbrellas below them, where the last wedding guests lingered, all so small they looked like dolls arranged from a child's toy set. Beyond the umbrellas, out upon the sea, a billion suns winked and danced across the whitecaps.

To the north shone the rooftops of the village, muted red and pale, drawn together by the dark oaks, then the green hills rolled away toward the low mountains, their emerald curves punctuated with tree-sheltered houses, with little gardens and pale stone walls.

Among the hills, the cats could see Harper's acreage, his white house and barn and the roof of the hay shed, the fence lines as thin as threads. Three dark shapes moved slowly across the green field where Harper's gelding and two mares grazed. Two smaller, pale shapes were busy beyond them—deer foraging among the horses.

They could see, down in the village, Joe's own street, Clyde's dark roof that always needed shingles, and, across Ocean past the courthouse tower, Wilma's pale new shake roof and a glimpse of her stone chimney. They could see the red tile roofs of Beckwhite's Automotive Agency and Clyde's repair shop, marking the spot where the cats had tracked their first killer— and where they'd had to dodge bullets. They'd been mighty glad to be alive when that party ended. A lot had happened since they saw Samuel Beckwhite struck down in the alley behind Jolly's Deli.

Below Harper's home lay the old Spanish mansion with its little cemetery, and farther to the north the old folks' home. Beyond these, nearer the village, they could see where painter Janet Jeannot had died, where her studio had burned, and had been rebuilt long after Janet's killer was prosecuted.

Swift movement pulled them back to Harper's pasture. The two deer were running full out, as if something had startled them.

But they moved strangely, for deer. Too low to the ground, and no leaping.

"The pups," Charlie said. "They've broken out of their stall."

The cats pictured solid wood walls shredded, perhaps a door latch broken. Running, the pups vanished in a valley. It was only a moment until they came flying up over the rise below Hellhag Hill. Perhaps they were drawn by the music and by the human voices and laughter.

Racing up the hill, they made straight for the reception, crashing in among the tables, overturning empty champagne bottles, snatching food from the buffet. Clyde and Harper moved fast to corral them.

"What a mess they are," Charlie said, looking at Dulcie and Joe. "What made them attack Fulman like that? Confusion? Selig was terribly confused by that man—he wanted to be friends, then he growled and barked at him."

Charlie smiled. "Hestig just growled and barked. But they're good pups. They'll settle down. They'll grow up to be good dogs."

As good as a dog can be, Joe Grey thought, cutting Dulcie a glance.

"Well," Charlie said, "the pups helped save the day for Lucinda." She grinned at Joe Grey. "You cats did fine work. All those letters from Fulman's trailer. The letters, the ledger, and the shirt. And, with the pups, I know you saved Lucinda's life."

The cats did not reply. They were still shy with Charlie. No need to tell Charlie that it was the kit who had found the two crucial pieces of evidence, or that it was the kit who had identified Fulman as Newlon's killer.

Charlie might learn, one day, the talents of the tortoiseshell kit; Charlie was so open-minded for a human, so eager to understand. But she didn't need to know right away.

And the kit? Dulcie had the feeling that this bright-eyed, ragtag, bushy-tailed kitten might have huge wonders to show them all. To show her and Joe, and show those humans like Charlie—show the innocent and uncorrupted of the world, who had the courage and heart to believe.

If You Enjoyed *Cat to the Dogs*,

Then Read the Following Selection from

CAT SPITTING MAD,

the new Joe Grey Mystery

Available in hardcover January 2001

From HarperCollins Publishers

IT WAS the tortoiseshell kit who found the bodies, blundering onto the murder scene as she barged into every disaster, all four paws reaching for trouble. She was prowling high up the hills in the pine forest when she heard the screams and came running, frightened and curious—and was nearly trampled by the killer's horse as the rider raced away. Churning hooves sent rocks flying. The kit ran from him, tumbling and dodging.

But when the rider had vanished into the gray foggy woods, the curious kit returned to the path, grimacing at the smell of blood.

Two women lay sprawled across the bridle trail. Both were blond, both wore pants and boots. Neither moved. Their throats had been slashed, their blood soaking into the earth. Backing away, the kit looked and looked, her terror filling her right up.

Then she spun and ran again, a small black-and-brown streak bursting away alone through the darkening evening, scared nearly out of her fur.

This was late Saturday afternoon. The kit had vanished from Dulcie's house on the previous Wednesday, her fluffy tortoiseshell pantaloons waggling as she slid under the plastic flap of Dulcie's cat door and trotted away through the garden beneath a light rain, escaping for what the two older cats thought would be a little ramble of a few hours before supper. Dulcie and Joe, curled up by the fire, hadn't bothered to follow her—they were tired of chasing after the kit.

"She'll have to take care of herself," Dulcie said, rolling over to gaze into the fire. But as the sky darkened not only with evening but with rain, Dulcie glanced worriedly toward the kitchen and her cat door.

Wilma, Dulcie's human housemate, passing through the room, looked down at the cats, frowning, her silver hair bright in the lamplight. "She'll be all right. It isn't raining hard."

"Not yet, it isn't," Dulcie said dourly. "It's going to pour. I can smell it." A human could never sort out such subtleties as a change in the scent of the rain. She loved Wilma, but one had to make allowances.

"She won't go up into the hills tonight," Wilma said. "Not with a roast in the oven. Not that little glutton."

"Growing kitten," Joe Grey said, rolling onto his back. "Torn between insatiable wanderlust and insatiable appetite." But he, too, glanced toward the cat door.

In the firelight, Joe's sleek gray coat gleamed like polished pewter. His white nose and chest and paws shone brighter than the porcelain coffee cup Wilma was carrying to the kitchen. His yellow eyes remained fixed on the cat door.

Wilma sat down on the couch beside them, stroking Dulcie. "You two never want to admit that you worry about her. I could look for her—circle a few blocks before dinner."

Dulcie shrugged. "You want to crawl under bushes and run the rooftops?"

"Not really." Wilma tucked a strand of her long white hair into her coral barrette. "She'll be back any minute," she said doubtfully.

"Too bad if she misses supper," Dulcie said crossly. "The roast lamb smells lovely."

Wilma stroked Dulcie's tabby ears, the two exchanging a look of perfect understanding.

Ever since Joe and Dulcie discovered they could speak the human language, could read the morning paper and converse with their respective housemates, Dulcie and Wilma had had a far easier relationship than did Joe Grey and his bachelor human. Joe and Clyde were always at odds. Two stubborn males in one household. All that testosterone, Dulcie thought, translated into hard-headed opinions and hot tempers.

The advent of the two cats's sudden metamorphosis from ordinary cats (well almost—they had after all always been unusually good looking and bright, she thought smugly) into speaking, sentient felines, had turned all their lives, cats and humans, upside down. Joe's relationship with Clyde, which had already been filled with good-humored conflict, had become maddening and stressful for Clyde. Their arguments were so fierce they made her laugh—a rolling over, helpless cat laugh. Were all bachelors the world over so stubborn?

And speak of the devil, here came Clyde barging in

through the back door dripping wet, no umbrella, wiping his feet on the throw rug then pulling off his shoes. His cropped brown hair was dripping, his windbreaker soaking. Dropping his jacket in the laundry, he came on through to the fire, turning to warm his backside. He had a hole in his left sock. Violent red socks, Dulcie saw, smiling. Clyde was never one for subtleties. Wilma went to get him a drink. Clyde sprawled in the easy chair, scowling.

"What's with you?" Joe gave him a penetrating yellow-eyed gaze. "You look like you could chew fenders."

Clyde snorted. "The rumor mongers. Having a field day."

"About Max Harper?"

Clyde nodded. The gossip about his good friend, Molena Point's Chief of Police, had left Clyde decidedly bad-tempered. The talk, in fact seemed to affect Clyde more than it did Harper. To imply, as some villagers were doing, that Harper was having an affair with one of the three women he rode with—or maybe with all three—was beyond ridiculous. Twenty-five year-old Ruthie Marner was a looker all right, as was Ruthie's mother. And Chrystal Ryder was not only a looker but definitely on the make.

But Harper rode with them for reasons that had nothing to do with lust or romance. The cats couldn't remember the villager's, most of whom loved and respected Harper, even before spreading or even tolerating such gossip.

Clyde accepted his glass from Wilma, swallowing half the whiskey-and-water in an angry gulp. "A bunch of damned troublemakers."

"Agreed," Wilma said, sitting down on the end of the velvet couch nearest the fire. "But the gossip has to die. Nothing to keep it going."

Clyde glanced around the room, "Where's the kit?"

"Out," Dulcie said, worrying.

"That little stray's twenty times worse than you two."

"She's not a stray anymore," Dulcie said. "She's just young."

"And wild," Clyde said.

Dulcie leaped off the couch to roam the house staring up at the dark windows. Rain pounded against the glass. That kit was off on another scatterbrained adventure, was likely up in the hills despite the fact that now, more than ever before, the hills were not safe for the little tortoiseshell.

Returning unhappily to the living room, she got no sympathy. "Cool it," Clyde said. "That kit's been on her own nearly since she was weaned. She'll take care of herself. If Wilma and I fussed about you and Joe every time *you* went off . . . "

"You do fuss every time we go off," Dulcie snapped, her green eyes filled with distress. "You fuss all the time. You and Wilma both. Particularly now, since . . ."

"Since the cougar," Clyde said.

"Since the cougar," Dulcie muttered.

Wilma grabbed her raincoat from the hall closet. "Dinner won't be ready for a while. I'll just take a look."

But as she knelt to pull on rubber boots, Dulcie reared up to pat her cheek. "In the dark and rain, you won't find her." And she headed for her cat door, pushing out into the wet, cold night.

SHIRLEY ROUSSEAU MURPHY
—————— Mysteries ——————

Featuring Joe Grey, a cat who not only solves crimes, but also talks!

CAT ON THE EDGE
0-06-105600-6 • $5.99 US/$7.99 Can

Joe Grey could handle having the ability to talk and understand humans. What worried him was finding himself in the alley behind Jolly's Deli the night Beckwhite was murdered.

CAT UNDER FIRE
0-06-105601-4 • $5.99 US/$7.99 Can

Joe Grey knows he's in trouble when his "girlfriend" Dulcie is determined to clear a man in jail for killing a famous artist by finding the real murderer—even if she has to get him killed doing it!

CAT RAISE THE DEAD
0-06-105602-2 • $5.99 US/$7.99 Can

Dulcie and Joe Grey must prove that an old folks' home is hiding more than just lonely seniors: a mysterious doll kidnapper, a severed finger, and a very, very busy open grave!

CAT IN THE DARK
0-06-105947-1 • $5.99 US/$7.99 Can

There's a new cat in town, Azrael, and he's masterminding a crime spree extrodinaire. Dulcie and Joe Grey must find a way to expose Azrael without revealing their secret.